Christmas PEGASUS

Christmas PEGASUS

MARIE CARDNO
WRITING AS
ZOE CHANT

I

JACKSON

LAST CHRISTMAS

He held her close, but delicately, as though she might break. She'd laugh if he told her that was what he was thinking, because he was the one who felt broken. Broken to pieces and put together again. Every rough gasp and longing cry as his and Olly's bodies moved together felt as though it was healing a wound deep inside him.

He was Olive Lockey's mate.

Jackson wasn't a shifter. He knew how the mate bond was meant to work—knew as well as any human could—but he didn't have a shifter's instincts for recognizing their fated mate. All he knew was that he'd loved Olly from the first time he saw her. And Olly—

Olly took her time to be certain of anything. He wasn't sure if that was all her owl's doing, or her human side, or them both combined. She'd waited—watched—until she was sure of what she felt for him. That the spark of attraction between them was the first flicker of a mate bond that would be cemented when they slept together for the first time.

And now she lay soft and warm beneath him, her eyes closed, the lashes fluttering as she shuddered with aftershocks of pleasure. Her pale hair was splayed out across the pillow, her lips red and just slightly parted. Jackson's cock twitched as he looked at her, and her breath hitched again.

"I wish we could stay like this forever," he muttered. It felt juvenile, wishing for something like this—hadn't his whole life taught him there was no point wishing for anything?—but right here, right now, he felt safe letting out a little piece of his heart. "Just us, together. Forget the rest of the world."

He lowered his head to kiss her, and her eyes fluttered open.

For a moment, she looked confused. Then her expression went completely still. She might as well have been wearing a mask.

Jackson's heart stopped. He knew that look.

"Olly," he began, and at the sound of his voice something slammed shut behind her eyes. "What's wrong?" Each word made the wall behind her eyes more impenetrable.

He tripped over his own tongue. The old wound inside him tore open again, inch by inch.

If he was a shifter, he wouldn't have to rely on his clumsy tongue. If he was a shifter he could have spoken mind to mind with her.

If he was a shifter he would know already what he thought she'd been certain of, and was now... reconsidering.

That was what Olly's still mask meant. Some new information had come to light and until she knew what to make of it, she wouldn't let anyone see what she was thinking.

And there could only be one new piece of information that would turn her thoughts so far inwards.

"Oh," she whispered. "No, I... I was so *sure*..."

He was already half out of bed. Cold air swirled over his bare skin. A rose-petal crushed under his foot—oh, God, Olly had been so *sure* he was her mate that she'd planned every ridiculous romantic cliché for their first night together.

She sat up. The walls behind her eyes came down, but the emotion that replaced them made ice grip his heart. "Jackson, I'm sorry, I—"

"I'm not your mate." The words grated in his throat.

Olly pulled the blanket up over herself and whatever it was Jackson had thought was healed inside him tore open again.

"I was so sure," she said again. He wasn't sure whether she was talking to him, or herself, or her owl. "I thought this was how it was meant to work. That once we slept together, the mate bond would…"

She took a deep breath. "I don't feel anything. Do you—"

The hope in her voice was too much. Jackson shook his head.

He didn't feel any different. Even humans could feel the bond that connected them to their shifter mate, once it had formed—but there was nothing inside him except despair.

Olly's face went pale. "I never should have done this," she whispered.

Jackson didn't wait to hear any more. He had all the pieces of information that she did; all the evidence to come to the only conclusion possible.

She'd made a mistake.

He was a mistake.

Present day

4 days before Christmas

Jackson Gilles pulled over to the side of the road and wondered what the hell he was doing.

Ahead, the mountains rose up to touch the darkening sky. He'd been winding through the foothills for the last hour or so, gaining altitude and watching the landscape around him change from rolling snow-swept hills to jagged black cliffs and pines. Even the thick snow couldn't soften the landscape's sharp edges.

The only trace of warmth in all the world was a gentle glow peeking through the trees in the distance. The golden glimmer of streetlights held the promise of civilization and a hot meal to take the edge of the winter off… and a warning.

Pine Valley. The tiny mountain town where Jackson had spent the best months and the worst moment of his life.

He groaned and rested his head on the wheel.

This time last Christmas, he'd thought he was in love. And that she loved him, too. Olive Lockey, small and fierce and wonderful, had been everything he never dreamed possible.

And of course it hadn't been possible. He'd given her his heart, and she'd smashed it into pieces.

Pain shot through his forehead. He groaned and rubbed his brow, then swore as his fingers grazed over the fresh knot of scar tissue over his left eye and sent more daggers into his skull.

Olly had thrown him off because he wasn't her mate. She was a shifter and like all shifters, somewhere out there in the wide world was a person who was perfect for her in every way. The other half of her soul. Her goddamned fated mate.

Not him.

He'd been gone a year. God, if she'd found her mate in that time—

His chest felt tight. He forced himself to breathe through what felt like sudden, desperate panic—which made no sense. The time to panic would have been last year, when Olly had realized that sleeping with him was the worst mistake she ever made and had left him with a deposit on a home he'd never live in, in a town where every street corner and tree branch reminded him of her.

He hadn't panicked. He'd been sensible. Done everything right. He'd packed up, and left, and taken a transfer to the deputy's office in another town. He hadn't hated Olly for not tying her fate to his when her soul knew she didn't belong to him. He understood.

Understanding didn't make it hurt any less.

And now he was going back to Pine Valley. He needed to be sensible, again. Jasper Heartwell, the dragon shifter he'd bought the house off, had told him to stop kicking dirt. He had two options: come back to sign on the dotted line, mortgaging himself to the hilt for a house in a town where everything reminded him of his broken heart, or come back and sign it back to the dragon shifter clan.

The one non-negotiable thing was he had to be in Pine Valley to do it. Something to do with the place being part of the Heartwells' hoard.

If he saw Olly while he was there—

He frowned and leaned on the gas.

If he saw Olly…

He couldn't see Olly. It was as simple as that. He would see Jasper, sign whatever blasted forms the dragon shifter needed, fill up his truck at the gas station, and be out of town again before the sun rose.

His truck's engine growled as he wound his way up the mountain towards the warmly lit town. He knew it already: coming here was a mistake.

Just like everything else about me.

The town of Pine Valley was small, and quiet, but even last Christmas he'd never seen it this deserted. Unease prickled along the back of his neck.

"Where the hell is everybody?" Jackson muttered to himself. The streets were empty. Not just of people, but of everything he associated with Pine Valley at Christmas.

There were no strings of glittering lights. No fully bedecked Christmas trees at every street corner. No warble of carols filtering from the town square.

The hairs on the back of Jackson's neck stood on end as he drove into the town square.

Every other Christmas he'd been here, the square had been the heart of Christmas festivities in the town. The quaint old shops that faced onto it always went all-out with decorations on their roofs and in their windows, and the square itself was transformed into a magical North Pole grotto with Christmas trees, special food trucks, and whatever cold-weather-friendly activities that popped into Jasper Heartwell's head. Even the year before, when most of the town's tourists had been driven off by a rogue pack of hellhounds, the square had blazed with Christmas cheer.

This year, there wasn't a single spray of holly anywhere in sight. The shop fronts were still decorated, but without the fairground atmosphere of the square, they looked small and dark.

Something's wrong.

Jackson hauled on the wheel. He was halfway to Olly's house before he realized what he was doing.

Cursing, he turned into the street that would take him not to Olly's small one-bedroom apartment on the edge of town but further up the valley to the Heartwells' castle-like lodge. That was why he was here, after all. To sign away the last bit of what he'd once hoped would be his future.

And if anyone could tell him what the hell was going on here, it was the dragons.

"Not that it's any of your business," he muttered to himself as he left the lights of the town behind. "Not deputy here anymore. It's all some other idiot's problem now."

He rubbed his forehead absently. The thick knot of new scar above his eyebrow twinged. He had enough problems without adding whatever was happening in Pine Valley to them.

When he got to the Heartwells' lodge, it was locked up tight. All the windows were dark.

Jackson stared up at the looming building as though if he just looked hard enough, the place would suddenly be lit up and full of life.

No such luck.

"Where the hell is everybody?"

His voice was barely a whisper against the majesty of the mountains at night. He was small, insignificant.

His shoulders slumped.

The universe had the same idea about him as the woman he loved. It didn't want anything to do with him.

He turned back to his truck and cursed.

The Heartwells' land overlooked the rest of the valley. The whole town was spread out below. From this distance, it didn't look so abandoned. It was like a children's diorama: tiny snow-topped houses, glittering streetlights, the occasional car crawling ant-like along the roads. He could just imagine hundreds of happy families tucking in for the night, counting down the days until Christmas. Even without the Heartwells' public decorations, each private house would be a festive sanctuary of warmth and cheer.

Or not. From this distance, Jackson could see where the Heartwell party had moved to.

Past the town, the skate rink at the edge of town shone like a mirror, and beyond that…

He cursed again. *There you go, deputy,* he told himself, his jaw tightening. *You wanted to know where everyone is.*

Huddled at the edge of the valley, where the forest was thick and the snow thicker, the Puppy Express headquarters were lit up like the sun.

Jackson had probably spent more time at the Puppy Express than any other business in town. The idea of the place was simple: the owner, Bob Lockey, had a couple teams of sled dogs that he hired out to tourists to explore some of the trails around the valley. That was the "Puppy" bit because no matter how old those dogs got, they still acted like they had all the good sense of a three-month-old fluffball. The "Express" bit harked back to the old Pony Express—visitors could post letters or cards at specific spots along the trails and Bob or one of his employees would deliver them by dogsled.

Jackson's heart sank. He'd told Jasper Heartwell he'd be in town a few days before Christmas to sign the paperwork, but hadn't given him a specific date. Any normal Christmas, there would have been a dozen Christmassy places Jackson would expect to find the Christmas-loving dragon shifter if he wasn't at home. But now, with the town square dark and grim…

Jasper must be at the Puppy Express. Hell, from here, it looked like the whole town was there. Including the one person he wanted to see most and least of all, and who definitely didn't want to see him.

Olly.

2

OLLY

Olly Lockey was not in love with Jackson Gilles. She wasn't in love with him and she hadn't been in love with him for the last year. She'd gotten on with her life, not in love with him. Right now she was putting the finishing touches on some sugar mice for the Puppy Express Christmas party, not in love with Jackson Gilles.

She hesitated. *That's right, isn't it?*

It made her stomach churn, constantly checking in with her owl like this. But not checking in was worse. What had happened last Christmas was a lump of gristly uncertainty lodged under her ribs.

She'd already *liked* Jackson. He wasn't a shifter, but his mother was, so he'd had no problem fitting in at Pine Valley. The first time she'd ever seen him, her owl had been… intrigued. Like he was a puzzle it wanted to solve. And the longer it spent on that puzzle the closer they'd become, and she'd let herself believe that that *like* could be something more, and that her owl's fascination with him meant…

She should have been more careful. She would have been, if it wasn't for the hellhounds.

A pack of them had attacked the town. No one knew what they were, then: men who could shift into creatures that poured terror from their burning eyes, who could walk through solid walls. How could she have any sort of certainty about the world, facing creatures like that?

They'd targeted the Puppy Express. Looking back, she saw that night from two sides of the same coin: on the one, the pack of hellhounds barely out of their teens, forced into causing havoc by their cruel alpha. On the other, her, not knowing they weren't there of their own free will, not knowing they were all doing their best to do as little harm as they could within the chains of their alpha's command. All she'd known was that when she looked into their eyes she was more terrified than she'd ever been in her life.

Everything had been going wrong. The certainty about the world she'd built up around herself was crumbling. Nothing felt safe—except for Jackson.

She'd been so *sure*.

And then after they slept together, when she was still breathless and shaking, she'd looked up at him and—

No, no. She squeezed her eyes shut and clenched her fists. *Don't think about it.*

It was too late. Her owl saw her revisit the memory, and its reaction was the same as ever:

Blech.

It blinked at her, as though it was waiting for her approval. She sighed.

No, not blech, but… She forced a smile. *He's… it's not important.*

Sleeping with Jackson hadn't been *blech.* It had been glorious. Right up until…

She shook her head. It didn't matter, did it? Everything had been going wrong, and she'd made the wrong decision, and that had gone wrong, too. She knew that. But the gristle behind her ribs was still there.

Jackson hadn't wasted any time. He'd left straight after Christmas, less than forty-eight hours after Olly made the biggest mistake of her life. And she'd stayed here in Pine Valley, not in love with him and not able to stop poking at the memory that made her heart ache.

In a few days, it would be a full year since she ruined everything. And the closer the anniversary got the more she couldn't help checking in with her owl.

You're sure? she asked it, already bracing herself.

It didn't bother to reply. She rubbed her eyes, not surprised. Its answer wasn't going to change.

A year. Time to put it behind her. Her uncle would agree with that, she knew, and so would her best friend Meaghan. They were the ones who'd had to put up with her moping, after all.

Olly packed the mice into Tupperware and piled them on top of matching containers of Christmas tree cookies and pastry wreaths and wedged the stack under her chin. She was ready to go.

Almost.

Olly paused at the window, careful to perch exactly where she couldn't be easily seen from the street. There was nothing outside except the usual blobs and pools of light from houses. The only movement was a lone group of tourists she recognized as the family who were staying up the street. Good. She was safe to get to the car.

Crisp air whisked the kitchen warmth from her cheeks and her owl perked up, rustling its wings hopefully.

We're not flying, she told it as she put the containers of food in the passenger seat. Her owl blinked unhappily. *Unless you think you can carry all of these over to the Express? Two tucked under each wing?*

It grumbled, unconvinced. Olly's nose wrinkled as it peered through her eyes at the plastic containers of baked goods.

You should throw those away, it told her, indicating with a curl of her own lip the sugar mice. *You got them wrong. They're all dried up, not lovely and squishy-crunch at all.*

Squishy-crunch is not what I was aiming for, so thank you.

Olly slipped into the driver's seat and pulled out. Here on the outskirts of town, the night was still. To one side of the street, the town glowed warm and bright; to the other, the snow and trees called to the wild part of her. She'd always felt that living on the very edge of Pine Valley township made sense as a shifter: a balance of her human and owl parts. And of course being on the outskirts meant there was so much less to watch out for. That tourist family were the only unexpected addition to the street in the last six months, and she'd watched them carefully enough over the last week to know their habits and feel confident they wouldn't surprise her.

She took the slow route towards the Puppy Express, dodging around the outside of town instead of driving through the center. There were too many uncertainties there.

You're not complaining about the wreaths? she needled her owl as she kept an eye out for sudden movement. *Or the trees?*

We won't be eating those, her owl replied primly. *The herbivores can have them.*

Olly shook her head, tucking a smile into the corner of her lips. *You know there's more animal products in the pastries than in the mice? Maybe you should have paid more attention while I was baking.*

But they're mice. *Mice are for* us. *They're—*

Her owl's psychic voice cut off as headlights appeared at the edge of her vision. Olly glanced across the intersection and regretted it at once. The other driver was in a truck, and the lights were high enough they flooded straight through her windscreen.

She winced, shielding her eyes with one hand, and as suddenly as it had appeared the truck turned around and drove off. It took the same turn she had been about to make, down the road that went either out of town or towards the Puppy Express.

Olly blinked until her eyes cleared. Her mouth was dry. She waited for her owl to berate her, to tell her that she should have been more careful, should have scouted out the route before she drove along it in her lumbering, *visible* car, there for anyone to see her and sneak up on her—but it was silent.

She licked her lips. Silence was worse.

"Must be another visitor," she said quietly. Her voice hung empty in the air. "Guess they got lost and didn't realize they got on the road out of town."

Her owl still didn't say anything. Olly frowned, swallowing until her mouth felt less like a desert. She'd been too blinded by the glare to see the truck clearly, but it had looked like—no. Flatbeds like that were common as dirt in these parts. There was no reason to believe it was…

Just in case, she checked with her owl.

Did you recognize the truck, or—?

No!

Olly's head hurt, but she got it.

She took a deep breath. This was what she had had to hold on to, these last twelve months of flinching at her owl's reactions: *understanding* it. Even if that understanding was just understanding that her owl was a skittish snob.

Olly?

Olly blinked. Her owl sounded… uncertain. *What is it?*

I've been thinking, her owl said, *about… last year. What happened.* It paused, embarrassed. *The mistake.*

Why? Olly's heart skittered against her ribs. *What is there to think about?*

She'd made a mistake. That was all there was to it. Whatever she'd thought Jackson was to her—

There was something *there.* Her owl gnawed over the thought. *Something not-quite. Something almost…*

And it wasn't enough, was it? For the first time in nearly a year, Olly let herself—let her owl—really feel what had happened last Christmas. When she'd opened her eyes, expecting with all her heart that the mystical mate bond she'd heard so much about

would suddenly spring into existence, and felt…
nothing.

Almost wasn't enough, she told her owl, fighting back tears. *He's not my mate and I can't be in love with him, he isn't—he isn't important.*

Her chest hurt with how much that last statement wasn't true, and she twisted the pain back before her owl could feel it.

It didn't say anything else about its thoughts, and Olly kept driving.

I just need to get through this Christmas, she told herself as she headed down the snow-lipped road towards the Puppy Express. *Then everything will be normal again.*

I can stop thinking about… him. After all, it's not as though I'm going to see him again.

3

JACKSON

He was halfway to the Puppy Express, driving through a tunnel of ice-tipped trees, when his phone started to buzz. Because he was an idiot, a bit of his heart leaped at the thought that Olly might be calling him. That she might have sensed he was close, and wanted…

Wanted to talk to me? His chest tightened. *Wanted anything in the world to do with me?*

He pulled over and checked the call notification. The screen read: Ma.

Jackson let out a sigh and told himself he wasn't relieved, or disappointed. He snorted. Hardwick, the closest thing he'd had to a friend in his new hometown, would have glared at him and told him that was two lies. One of the downsides of working with a lie-detecting griffin shifter.

He took the call. "Hey, Ma. Merry Christmas."

"Merry Christmas to you too, son of mine. Why's it so dark? Don't say I woke you up, it's not even seven yet."

Jackson frowned and pulled the phone away from his ear.

"That's better," his mother's voice piped through the speaker. Jackson winced at himself. Video call, not a phone call. He was really on a winning streak, today.

The video quality wasn't great, but it was clear enough for him to see the delight in his mother's face. Louisa Gilles was short and so fine-boned, people sometimes had difficulty believing Jackson was her son. The most they had in common was their brown eyes, but whereas Louisa's eyes were the soft long-lashed eyes of a doe, his were just… eyes.

His mother was calling from her kitchen. She must have propped her phone against the windowsill; he could see the island where he ate breakfast every morning growing up and, beyond it, the dining room with the table he'd built from a windfall tree when he was a teenager.

And covering every surface, bowls and pots full of steaming food.

"Keeping busy?" he asked.

She put her hands on her hips and surveyed the chaos. "Just a few things I'll be dropping off in the morning." Her chin had a familiar obstinate tilt to it.

"Would I be wrong in guessing the people you're dropping the food off to don't know about it yet?"

"Don't you go detectiving at me, my darling son."

"I won't go detectiving if you won't go stuffing casseroles down innocent people's chimneys."

"Jackson! Don't be ridiculous. What a waste that would be." She smoothed down her apron. "You know how people are around here. No one will ask for help even if their stomach's so empty it's wrapping around their spine. They don't want to be any trouble. Trouble! I'll show them trouble."

"I'm sure they're shaking in their boots."

"They will be by the time I'm done with them. Wobbling like jellies."

Jackson laughed. "I wish the criminals I deal with were more like you."

His mother's face went still. "Speaking of people who won't ask for help," she began, and then appeared to change her mind. "You did ask for time off over the holiday, didn't you?"

"I'm not that bad, Ma." Except that Thanksgiving had been a disaster. He touched his forehead absently. "I'll be there Christmas Eve."

"Well, I'm glad they gave you a few days off, at least. Now, what about your partner? What was his name. The griffin shifter." She frowned. "Oh, I'm terrible. Remembering a man's animal and not his name. How embarrassing."

"Hardwick. No, he's not much of a Christmas guy. But, yeah, I got the time off. The full week, actually." He turned so she could see the trees behind him, through the tiny camera on his phone. "I'm back in Pine Valley for a few days to sort out a few things, then I'll head down. Let me know if you want me to pick anything up—"

"You're in Pine Valley? I thought you were coming straight here!" She leaned closer to the screen, both hands braced against the counter.

It was a bit of a detour, he had to admit. His mother lived on a small farm that was closer to the town where he was trying to make his new home than to the mountains—close enough to cause trouble and far enough away to hide from it, she'd always said.

"I will, Ma. Christmas Eve to New Year, I'm all yours."

"Damn it."

Jackson blinked. His mother never swore.

Except when she was talking about…

"When he told me, I thought—hell." She stalked around the kitchen, arms folded. "I'd better come up there."

The hairs on the back of Jackson's neck prickled. "What for, Ma?"

"Don't you mind. He was talking some nonsense about…"

Jackson waited to see if she was going to say more, but she just stood there in the center of the kitchen, arms crossed, tapping her foot on the tile.

"Damn it," she muttered again.

"Ma, is this about—" He hesitated just long enough to hate himself for hesitating. "Andrew?"

"Andrew the ass," his mother muttered under her breath, and that was enough to almost make the whole ordeal worth it.

"What was that?" A car was approaching, its headlights wavering as it navigated the bumpy road. Someone else on their way to the Puppy Express party? Jackson checked that his hazard lights were on. The last thing he wanted was for his Ma to watch him be involved in a traffic accident from a hundred miles away.

She narrowed his eyes at him. "Never you worry."

"What do you mean, he's been talking nonsense?" The car passed. Instead of going down the road towards the Puppy Express, it took the turnoff onto the potholed Rabbit Road. Jackson frowned absently. He didn't recognize the vehicle; it was new-looking, shiny, with dark windows. Tourists, probably. Lost? Possibly. Rabbit Road didn't have anything to offer except potholes and, unless things had really changed over the last year, a secret hideout where some local teens hid stolen bottles of beer.

He felt suddenly, unreasonably uneasy and shook himself. If those were tourists, and they were about to get lost, they wouldn't have any difficulty un-losing themselves. Back up Rabbit Road and follow the lights to town; easy as that. No one would thank him for following them and interrupting. Besides, it was just as likely they were heading out of town for some sky-gazing or any of the other activities people did at lonely lookouts under the stars…

Jackson shook his head. His mother was still talking, and he'd lost track of the conversation.

Louisa tutted. "I told you, no detectiving. I'll sort this out. I'll come visit you! I haven't been to Pine Valley in so long. It'll be lovely."

"But, Ma—"

"But Ma nothing. You spent enough years telling me it's the most Christmassy town in the world, so now I'd like to see it."

"And this has nothing to do with my father."

Louisa stood so still that if it wasn't for the steam wreathing above the casserole dishes, Jackson would have suspected the video had cut out. Another set of headlights cut through the night. Not the same car—this one was coming from town and followed the road to the Puppy Express. Jackson kept his attention on his mother.

"He's talking nonsense, but—I thought you'd be here." She picked up the phone and held it so her face filled the whole screen. "If you do see him…"

"That'd be a Christmas miracle."

She gave him a very motherly look. "Just—take what he says with a grain of salt. Several grains of salt. The size of that Himalayan lamp you gave me. The tasty one."

"You know you're not meant to lick—"

"It was once." His mother looked prim, and only slightly guilty. "I'll see you soon."

Jackson said goodbye and dropped his phone back in his pocket. The conversation had left him feeling, if not better, then differently bad.

His mother must have gotten her wires crossed. Jackson's father hadn't seen the need to be a part of his life for the past three decades. Why would that change now?

As though he didn't have enough to worry about.

4

OLLY

Olly pulled up outside the Puppy Express a few minutes later. She'd passed the truck that made her owl go so strangely uninterested on the way there. Once again, her owl had carefully not paid any attention to it. was as though it had decided that instead of being anxious about new things, it was going to ignore them.

Good idea, she told it. *I'll get fewer chilblains if I don't have to run circles around every building before I go inside.*

Olly was just relieved not to find herself parking behind a tree and staring fixedly at some poor asshole's car until she convinced her owl it wasn't going to jump up and bite them. Taking her owl's lead, she didn't even glance at the truck in her rear-vision mirror as she drove away.

When she saw the parking lot, she frowned, and the strange truck flew out of her head. She knew she was late to the party—the sugar mice should have been done hours ago, but her owl had kicked up a fuss about being stuck inside at dusk and insisted on going flying, and that quick flight had turned into an inch-by-inch inspection of the town—but she hadn't expected… this.

The Puppy Express building was designed to look like a log cabin, but on a massive scale. Olly's uncle Bob had designed it and sometimes Olly wondered if he'd let his owl do the planning: everything about it was too big all over, like an owl sizing up a human residence. The front door was double-wide and had flattened more than one unwary visitor. Each window could fit four or five woeful huskies with their front paws on the sill, waiting for people to come and take them for a ride. The roof was covered with snow and the snow was spangled with tinsel and colorful lights.

Tonight, the massive front door and most of the windows were hidden behind an enormous pavilion. It glowed from within, and music filled the air. Dozens of cars were crammed into what was left of the parking lot with the tent taking up so much space, and they were squeezed in so tight she wouldn't be able to tell if someone was hiding between any of them. The parking area spilled back into the woods, where they'd plowed out some of the auxiliary space that was normally used for dog hitching and snowmobile storage.

On some level, she now realized, she had come expecting the usual office Christmas party and gotten… this.

Normally the Puppy Express office Christmas party was a low-key affair. But this year Jasper Heartwell had gotten involved and decided to combine it with his annual Christmas spectacle after the town council had nixed its usual venue. She had hoped that it wouldn't be as huge and loud as usual, because there just wasn't enough room here.

Apparently she'd been wrong. If there wasn't room, Jasper had simply made more room. He could have invited everyone in town. In fact, by the look of the parking lot, he probably had.

Inside Olly, her owl's feathers puffed up with anxiety. She bit back a sigh. So much for her owl ignoring things instead of freaking out over them.

I'm not freaking out! her owl hissed. *It's just… a lot of people…*

I know. And she felt the same. A stab of worry deep in her stomach.

She had to wedge her car under a tree at the very edge of the lot and even then, it took her ten minutes to convince herself to open the door and get out.

She was being ridiculous, she knew. But knowing it and making her fingers grab the door handle were two different things.

Her owl didn't like surprises. She wasn't in love with them either, and when it came to surprises at work…

She scrambled at the door handle. There! She was out. Cold air blasted her face and her shoulders tensed as she hurried around the back of the tree.

The parking lot was stuffed full. Okay. That meant she could check whose cars were there, and have some idea of who might be inside. But she still wouldn't know *where* they were inside and, after all, people could have carpooled. So she still wouldn't know exactly who, either.

All she knew for sure was that half the Puppy Express's employees definitely weren't there. There was no sign of Meaghan and Caine Guinness's cars, which meant their hellhound pack must not have arrived yet.

Her jaw ached with tension, and a sudden thought flashed into her mind: *What would Jackson think, seeing you more anxious about seeing your neighbors than seeing the hellhounds who terrorized you last year?*

He'd laugh at her, probably. Or…

She swallowed. No, he wouldn't laugh. Because he'd been the one who found her after the hellhounds broke into the Puppy Express and scared her senseless.

But he wasn't here. And neither were the hellhounds, not that they scared her anymore. They were a bunch of softies—in human form, at least. Who *was* here, going by the cars packed into the parking lot, were most of the shifter families that lived in Pine Valley. All people she knew. She could safely walk in and…

Still, she'd feel better if she knew *exactly* what was waiting for her inside.

She narrowed her eyes and, moving slowly, put down her stack of containers next to the tree.

Just one circuit, she told her owl. *Just in case…*

She didn't even know. But this was unexpected, and her owl was prickling at her, and she didn't want any surprises.

Music drifted through the night air as she picked her way around the building. She knew all the best vantage points for seeing in through the windows without anyone seeing her if they randomly glanced out. But… the tent. That was new. She'd have to think about it. Around it.

It all looked innocently festive. The main building was set up as a food hall, with the souvenir displays and cushy sofas pushed aside to make way for long trestle tables. Music flooded from the tent: dancing?

It was still a Christmas party. Just a bigger one than she'd anticipated. Her heart hammered against her ribs. A Christmas party! That was fine, right? She could go back to the tree, grab her Tupperwares, and…

…Maybe she would just finish scouting around the building first. To be safe.

Olly spotted her uncle Bob through a window and a tiny bit of her wariness unwound. He was dressed up as Santa and his red nose was more authentic than most Christmases thanks to the cold that had snuck up on him the week before. And—yes, there was Suki from the general store. She'd been on the invite list for sure. With all those special orders she did for dogfood, she probably made more off the Express than Bob did. And there were the Hawkinses, and that cat curled up by the roaring fireplace had to be Joanie.

And there was the new deputy. Olly was surprised to see him there. Sure, he was a shifter, but he spent so little time in Pine Valley she half-suspected he was deliberately ignoring the town. When Jackson was here—

Olly hurried to the next window before she could think too much about Pine Valley's previous deputy, and why he'd left.

Kitchen. From the size of the roast that bear shifter Hannah Holborn was carving, Jackson was about the only person who'd lived in Pine Valley in the last decade who *wasn't* invited. Except—no. Everyone she'd spotted so far was either a shifter or married to one, and Jackson was—was…

She made her way further around the building. As she reached the far side, something whined excitedly.

Olly's owl did *not* react. She would have been relieved, but she'd been expecting this, so her owl must have been, too. Her circuit of the building had brought her close to the kennels, and half a dozen sad noses were pressed up against the door, clouding the glass with their breath.

"Poor puppies. Everyone got invited to the party except for you?" She felt sorry for them: sure, they had the evening off, but they loved pulling festively decorated sleds around the forest tracks so much that that was more of a punishment than a vacation. Olly was about to unlock the door and scratch a few ears when the sound of two car engines roared over the music, and suddenly, she was no longer the most interesting person at the party.

Every dog in the kennels, from loopy Loony to old reliable Hoops, was suddenly trembling with excitement.

Be careful! her owl warned her, but Olly knew who she was going to find as she darted back around to the front of the building. She ducked and dodged around cars until she found where the new arrivals had crammed in at the edge of the parking lot.

She set her lips into a determined line. The hellhounds. And their new alphas.

Careful careful, her owl whispered.

They're my friends now, Olly insisted. *They're not a danger.*

Still…

Oh, stop it. Olly clawed back the urge to circle back into the safety of the trees. She wasn't the silly, frightened little girl she'd been last Christmas. She knew the hellhounds now, and trusted them and, more importantly, trusted their alphas.

"Meaghan!" she called out. Her owl screeched in dismay as a half-dozen people in various stages of getting out of their cars turned towards her. Mostly men, and one woman.

"Olly!" Meaghan sounded surprised, and delighted. Olly got a half-second glimpse of her curly dark hair and broad grin before the rest of her pack got out of their vehicles and mobbed around her.

"I'll take your bag!"

"Watch out, there's ice—"

"Is the air too cold? I heard you cough before."

"All right, that's enough!" Caine Guinness waded through the pack until he was at Meaghan's side. He was tall, with dark-red hair and an athletic build. One gesture from him and the other men scattered—briefly. They backed off a few feet, hovered, and jittered on the spot as though they were about to jump back into the fray.

"Oh, for…" Meaghan buried her face in Caine's shoulder and growled something that made him laugh. "And give me back my bag, Ryan!"

Ryan, a young man with hair like a wire brush, sheepishly held out her handbag. She grabbed it, thrust it under one arm and glared at him until his shoulders curled inwards.

Olly hadn't moved. *They're behaving very strangely*, her owl muttered suspiciously, and she had to agree. The hellhounds were always boisterous—they were all relatively new to being shifters and, like the actual Puppy Express puppies, they seemed to bounce between wild excitement and tail-between-the-legs misery at the drop of a hat—but this was different.

Meaghan smoothed down the front of her coat and walked over to Olly, her smile back in place. "Hey, babe. Merry almost-Christmas!"

She pulled Olly into a hug and Olly sensed a grumble of protective unease from Caine's hellhound. She raised one eyebrow at him over Meaghan's shoulder and he had the decency to look shamefaced. Her owl blinked rapidly. *Him, too?*

"I'm so happy you could make it." Meaghan gave her another squeeze and let her go.

"Of course I could make it," Olly said, confused. "When have I missed one of our staff parties? Even if it is a bit bigger this year…"

Meaghan looked uncomfortable. "It's just—well, with how you've been acting this year…"

Olly suddenly felt as though she was under a spotlight. Her owl hissed and she glanced around to see every one of the hellhounds watching her intently. Fire shimmered at the edges of their eyes.

All of a sudden, she was back behind the counter at work twelve months away, cowering in fear as the strangers' eyes burned straight into her deepest fears.

She wet her lips. "I think I'll do, um, I think I'll just go and check—do another circuit of the buildings," she stammered, and Meaghan made a frustrated noise.

"Hey! Leave her alone. If you start defending me from feeling worried about people, you can all sleep in the kennels tonight. Shoo."

The hellhounds ducked their heads guiltily and shuffled off. Olly got the feeling that if they'd been in their animal forms, they'd have had their tails around their legs. She relaxed.

"I'm sorry about that," Meaghan said to her in an undertone. "Are you okay?"

Olly nodded quickly, her eyes still fixed on the hellhounds, and Meaghan snorted in disbelief.

"Of course you're not. Bloody hellhounds and their freaky eyes. I can tell them to go home if they're going to ruin the evening for you."

"No, they're fine. It's just—you know me."

"Hmmph. Yeah, I do. I know that you and the hellhounds get on so long as they keep their beady eyes to themselves, and that right now they're having trouble…" She broke off and growled. "They *are* trouble."

Meaghan's grumpy at the hellhounds? Why? Olly's owl stared out at them through her eyes. And it was strange, Olly agreed. Usually, Meaghan had no problem with the pack.

Don't ask what's wrong, her owl urged her. *We can figure it out. Piece by piece.*

Caine strolled up to them, hands in pockets. "I hope you don't mean me, too."

Meaghan had been watching the hellhounds retreat. She spun around and tapped her mate playfully on the chest. "You, I can handle. But…"

His eyes flickered. But whereas the other hellhounds came out blazing with ferocity, Caine's hellhound's fire was warm and affectionate.

"Is something wrong?" Olly spoke before her owl could stop her.

Meaghan and Caine exchanged a look that Olly immediately interpreted as *Let's not tell her*, which did nothing for her worries. Or her owl's.

"It's nothing," Caine said, and Meaghan clicked her tongue.

"It's not *nothing*. They're all on edge, and as soon as one of them tips into having trouble keeping their hellhound under control the others get suckered in, too." She grumbled under her breath. "God save me from nervy shifters."

"I'm sorry being the alpha of a hellhound gang isn't everything you dreamed of," Caine murmured. If it weren't for the mischief in his eyes, Olly would have thought he was being serious.

Meaghan flashed him a look. "Being the alpha of a hellhound gang is nothing I *ever* dreamed of," she said. "And yet…"

Caine pulled her close. "It's not all bad, is it?"

"It has its moments," Meaghan admitted. "But right now…"

Every inch of Olly's skin was prickling. "Are their hellhounds—"

"They're no danger to you or anyone else," Caine said firmly.

"Just a pain in the ass." Meaghan reached over and squeezed her hand. "Come on. Let's head inside."

"I'll just do another circuit—"

"No." Meaghan tugged on her arm until she fell into step with her. "Come on, Olls. You can do this," she murmured in her ear. "No circuits, no spying everyone out. You're safe here. It's just a party."

"I hate parties." It sounded sullen, and teenagerish, but it was better than the truth.

Meaghan snorted. "It's all your shifter neighbors, getting drunk and singing along to carols. What's the worst that could happen? Wait… don't answer that."

Olly fetched her Tupperwares and held them in front of her like a cavity-inducing shield. The other hellhounds were straggling around the door, waiting for them. One of them—a pale-haired guy called Flea, who worked some shifts at the Puppy Express—caught Olly's eye and looked away, shoulders hunching. She hadn't seen any fire in his eyes, but just the glimpse of it before had sent warning bells screaming in her head.

The last time she'd gotten lost in their hellfire eyes, she'd panicked and run straight into the worst decision of her life.

She shook herself. That was last year. She knew the hellhound boys now, and she knew the hellfire was just part of what they were; nothing to be afraid of.

Meaghan might be worried about her, but she was fine. She had it all under control; she just needed to keep a close eye on things, and that would keep her safe. Get all the information, and make an informed decision. The way her owl had always done.

I just need to be less, less…

The urge to do another scout around the building and the tent itched under her skin and Olly sighed.

Less me.

No wonder Meaghan's worried.

Inside the tent, heat and sound hit Olly like a blanket. She shook her head, recalibrating her senses to take into account dozens of loud voices and music streaming from at least five speakers playing at least three different carols. Her loop around the building hadn't prepared her for the sheer onslaught of—*Christmasness.*

"Olly! Meaghan! Caine! And retinue!" Jasper Heartwell bowed extravagantly. "We were beginning to think you wouldn't make it! This makes a full house. Quick, someone tie the door shut before some poor human wanders in and sees Cec in his finery."

Cecil was one of Hannah's endless supply of nephews. The last time Olly had seen him, he'd been hiding from his aunt's latest matchmaking scheme. He must have decided hiding wasn't worth it, and was currently sprawled out in bear form in the middle of the tent.

Someone had tucked a dog plushie under one of his massive forelegs. Someone else or, possibly, the same someone, had also wrapped a length of tinsel around his head like a crown. Olly surprised herself with a giggle that felt as though it bubbled up all the way from her toes.

"...fire risk. Fire risk! Honestly. How is a Christmas tree park a fire risk?" Jasper's voice carried above the crowd, loaded with indignation. He hefted his daughter Ruby in the air and pouted at her. "You don't think filling the town square with Christmas trees is a fire risk, do you, cutey?"

"In the town council's defense, there were *several* fires last year," Meaghan pointed out. The rest of her pack, Caine included, ducked their heads guiltily.

"Only small ones!" one of the hellhounds protested.

"No one blames you for that," Jasper said, a rare serious look on his face.

"If you want to feel guilty about something, feel guilty about stealing our dogs every other day!" Bob called from across the room. The hellhounds hung their heads as he made his way through the crowd.

"It's not our fault! They keep picking up on…"

Caine growled something under his breath and Flea's eyes went wide.

"They just want to hang out!" he finished.

Olly strongly suspected that was *not* what he was going to say, or the real reason the sled dogs kept breaking out of their kennels and making their way to the Guinnesses' land. She shot Meaghan a questioning look and hid a grin as Meaghan responded with a *don't-you-dare-say-anything* glare.

She couldn't hide behind her Tupperwares forever. Which was the whole idea, after all. Bringing food gave her the perfect excuse to go and hang out in the kitchen and get her bearings—again—before she joined the party properly.

The tent was connected to the main building by a small canopy. Olly wedged the boxes under her chin again and wove her way past the trestle tables. The small kitchenette in the staff area was barely big enough for one person, but Hannah bustled out as Olly arrived.

"Getting your bearings?" Hannah asked, balancing a platter of sliced meat on each hand. "Or hiding out?"

Olly eyed the containers in answer and Hannah nodded understandingly. "I know how you feel. It'll be hibernation for me as soon as the vacation rush is over," she joked with a smile.

Olly's lips pinched tight. She wasn't hiding out. She just had to…

A new Christmas carol wove through the air. 'Last Christmas'.

Olly swallowed as the door swung shut behind the bear shifter. Talk about the most painful song to remind her…

She closed her eyes and focused on every noise *except* the music. Laughter. Conversation. The clack of cutlery and the clink of glasses as people made toasts. *Everything's fine.*

5

JACKSON

There it was: the Puppy Express. One main building, so big it made him feel child-sized, and behind it a warren of trails winding through the trees.

Jackson squeezed into a parking space and walked slowly through the crowded cars, his boots crunch-squelching in the icy gravel. A cacophony of Christmas carols filled the air and the fairy lights strung over the building and the billowing tent in front of it looked dangerously overloaded. If Jackson had had any doubts, this would have resolved them: Jasper Heartwell was definitely involved.

And so long as he concentrated on that, he could ignore the fact that Olly had to be somewhere inside.

He shook himself and shoved his hands deep in his pockets. Of course she was there. Probably perched in some corner, carefully arranged behind a piece of convenient cover and near enough to steal more than her fair share of canapes without anyone seeing. Enjoying herself making private bets about who would go where and talk to who next, and who would be the first to fall down drunk or fall headlong into a Christmas tree, and being so pleased with herself when she got it right that no amount of blank-mask self-control in the world could keep her from smirking cheerfully.

He pushed through the tent door.

"Jackson?" Abigail Heartwell stared at him. Abigail was small and curvaceous, a wellspring of level-headedness in contrast to her husband's flighty nature. Not that you'd be able to tell, from her party outfit. She was dressed as a Christmas elf, with stripy leggings and a pointed hat with a bell attached to the tip. Unlike the other Heartwells, she was one hundred percent human.

She had one hand outstretched as though she'd been about to grab the tent door, but when she saw Jackson she turned the gesture into shaking his hand. "It's been—gosh, a year?"

"Merry Christmas," Jackson mumbled awkwardly, taking her hand.

"Hah! Well, we're trying," Abigail said, wryly and mysteriously. She quirked one eyebrow at Jackson's confused expression. "Health and safety came down hard on Jasper's master plans after what happened last year."

For one terrible, stupid moment, Jackson thought she was talking about him and Olly.

Abigail went on. "He's had to beg and borrow party venues from all his friends, now that he's not allowed to fill the public spaces with trees and set them on fire. Don't worry, he's stopped short of stealing. So far."

She grinned at him and Jackson, feeling as though his brain was creaking as it caught up, winked at her.

"Don't worry. I'm on leave. And Pine Valley isn't my district anymore, anyway."

"I'll tell him to break out the moonshine whisky, then! Come on. Everyone's here—grab yourself a drink—"

"I'm actually just here to see Jasper."

"Oh." Abigail gave him a look that made him feel like she was measuring up his insides. "Is this about the house?"

"That's right."

"Well I'm not sure he's brought all the paperwork in his party suit," Abigail mused. She tipped her head on one side. "Where are you staying in town? I'll make sure he brings it by tomorrow. He should have a few minutes before…" She shivered dramatically. "They're doing a Christmas play. On ice, down at the rink. Dress rehearsal's tomorrow."

"That sounds…"

"I'm sure it will be superb, especially if Cole remembers the baby Jesus isn't meant to transform into a dragon and steal all the Wise Men's presents." She chuckled. "So, you're staying at…?"

"I'm not." He shrugged as she looked at him in surprise. "I just planned to be in and out of town tonight."

"That's hardly a visit." She narrowed her eyes. "So you're just here to tie up loose ends."

"That's the idea."

"Hmm." Her gaze slid past him. "Jasper!"

"Yes, my darling?" The dragon shifter swept up. He was wearing a Christmas sweater with a design of dancing dragons, decorated with flickering LEDs. The small girl in his arms was wearing a matching pinafore and squeaked happily when she saw Abigail. "Oh—hello, Gilles," Jasper said, catching sight of Jackson as he handed baby Ruby to Abigail. "You're here about the paperwork?"

Jackson ran one hand through his hair, just stopping before he revealed the scar on his forehead. "If you've got the time—"

"Not tonight." Jasper gave him a shining grin. "Sorry! It's all back at the lodge. Completely slipped my mind that you might be popping in this week. But if you're here… why not join us?"

Jackson cleared his throat. "I'm not sure that's a good—"

"Jackson Gilles?" Hannah Holborn's voice boomed into his ear a moment before she clapped a heavy hand on his shoulder. "Come skulking back, eh? What, didn't they feed you right in… wherever you went off to?"

"There's nothing there to compete with your pig on a stick, Hannah," Jackson told her, and she snorted.

"Well it's beef, tonight." She gave him a shove. "Speaking of. Why did you run off so quickly? We've missed you."

She doesn't know? Jackson bit down on the inside of his cheek and gave a noncommittal answer.

"Well don't just grunt at me. Go and get yourself a drink, then you can tell us what your new town's got that we don't."

It's more what it doesn't have, Jackson thought, making his way through the tent. People waved and grinned at him in recognition, and that felt—strange.

He ducked a drunken hug from an alligator shifter he'd once pulled out of a tree and hopped up the stairs to the main entrance to the Puppy Express building.

The air was warmer here: central heating competed with a crackling fire in the huge fireplace that took up pride of place on the opposite wall. Jackson scanned the room automatically, Abigail's wry complaints about fire hazards still fresh in his mind. The shop furniture was safely pushed against the walls, replaced by long tables that were groaning with food.

There was no sign of Olly. Not tucked behind any of the couches shoved against the walls, not lurking within sneaking distance of the food.

"Hey, Cole." Jackson waved to a dark-haired boy who was busily piling a plate high with slices of roast beef and layers of crispy roast potatoes. Forget fire hazards: a food avalanche was imminent. "Have you seen Olly?"

"Owl Olly?" Cole asked around a mouthful of gravy-covered potatoes.

"Yeah."

"No…" Cole started the syllable quickly, then dragged it out slow as though he was reconsidering. "But, um, she hides a *lot* these days. She was meant to come to dinner at our place a few weeks ago and Uncle Jasper said she was there but I didn't even see her."

Jackson frowned. "What are you talking about?" Olly was sneaky, but what Cole was saying sounded… wrong.

Cole perked up. "You should ask the hellhounds!"

"What?!"

"Yeah, because even if Olly can hide, they can find *anyone*. I'll ask Manu—"

"I don't think that's a great idea." Hellhounds? Hadn't they sorted that business out last year? The pack of hellhounds that had harassed the town and used their shifter fear-powers to terrify Olly had been under the control of some prick from out of town. They'd gotten rid of the prick and Jackson hadn't heard of any more trouble from the hellhounds, so he'd assumed they'd left.

His throat was suddenly dry. He'd *assumed*. He'd never checked. He'd left—left Olly alone, and if the hellhounds were still here…

"I need a drink," he croaked. There were no glasses on the table. Cole pointed helpfully.

"There's more cups in the kitchen!"

6

OLLY

Olly kept herself busy in the kitchen. She felt as safe there as if she was wedged into a knot in a tree trunk: there was only one door in and out, and she was very close to the customer service desk, where she could access all the security cameras for the building and grounds. She would know the *moment* anything unexpected happened. She would—

Her owl jumped suddenly, its eyes wide and every one of its feathers bristling.

Olly froze. *What is it? What do you sense?*

She could feel that her owl was sensing *something*, at the very edge of its range. But it wasn't sharing it with her.

Nothing, it muttered.

"Suit yourself." Olly's voice was tight. She glanced over her shoulder, checking the door was still shut, and tried to focus on not freaking out.

There's nothing to freak out about.

Then why won't you tell me—

Shh!

The air was heavy with the smell of cooked meat and fruity punch. Despite her unease, Olly's mouth watered as she opened the first container and the sweet scent of cinnamon pastries joined the other smells.

Her owl clicked its beak. *Close that! I can't concentrate on the—I can't smell the meat properly now!*

Olly rolled her eyes and grabbed a plate out of the cupboard. She arranged the pastries in a spiral pattern.

You didn't complain when I spent all afternoon baking. What's changed now?

Nothing! It ruffled its feathers. *Hurry up so the bear-lady can give us some meat.*

Olly snorted and moved on to the Christmas tree cookies. Outside, the texture of the conversation changed.

She was instantly alert. *What's happening?*

Her owl went completely still. Olly froze, too, one hand hovering over the basket of Christmas tree cookies.

People were still talking. She couldn't make out the words, but there was a general air of… surprise? No one sounded anxious or unhappy, though.

Did someone new arrive? she asked her owl. *Who is it?*

For a moment, her owl didn't reply. Then it shook itself. *Nobody important.*

Olly frowned. She'd thought everyone was already here—all the local shifters, at least. The thought that she'd missed someone on her circuit before was—and Jasper had said—

I said it was nobody important!

"Okay, okay, geez." Olly was so surprised at her owl's vehemence that she spoke out loud.

It's not *important,* her owl repeated. *What's important is—is—*

Olly curled her shoulders in. *You sound as confused as I am.*

I'm not confused! Her owl bristled. *I know exactly what is happening!*

Well, just tell me if there's anything I need to know.

There isn't!

Olly took a deep breath. Her hands were shaking. She pressed them against the countertop.

What's the matter with you? she asked her owl, and then looked down at her hands. *Or with me?*

She and her owl had always been so close it was sometimes hard for her to tell if her physical reactions were *hers,* or the bird's.

Things had been… weird… for the last twelve months, but some things stayed the same.

Are you worried about missing out on the bloody bits of the roast? You know Hannah always saves some for us.

Her owl didn't reply. Olly bit back a frustrated sigh. Really. Now of all times, her owl was going to make *her* do all the work of—

The kitchen door swung open, letting in a wave of noise. Olly would have turned around, but her owl was adamant that it had everything under control and Olly figured that if she let it have this one, maybe later it would explain to her what its problem was. She let her owl sort through the patterns of sound and scent. The buzz of surprise was gone, so whoever—

Nobody!

—had arrived couldn't have caused that much of a stir.

Another scent mingled with the smells of hot meat and alcohol and sugar. Olly breathed in slowly. A hint of leather and wood smoke, overlaid with…

Mint! her owl squawked. Was she imagining the hint of panic in its voice?

She didn't have time to think about it. Her owl focused in on the smell of the cookies, and Olly's eyes watered as the smell of mint and chocolate overwhelmed everything else. She shook her head, blinking, and wished not for the first time that she and her owl could take form at the same time so that she could glare at it properly.

Will you just stop, Olly growled at it, and turned around.

The world stopped.

The kitchen, the cocktail of smells, the noise of the party—everything disappeared. Olly didn't dare breathe because if she breathed now, without the scent of chocolate to mask it, she'd only breathe in *him*.

Jackson Gilles.

Nobody important, her owl had said. Oh God.

He was exactly as she remembered him. Or was he? Were his shoulders that broad before? His hair was messier; he always used to keep it trimmed short, and now it was so long it curled down over his forehead. His skin was a deeper brown than it had been last winter.

Not that any of that mattered. She wasn't in love with him. She *couldn't* be in love with him. This couldn't be—

"Olly."

Even his voice was the same. Rough. That hint of tenderness. She remembered, even though it hurt, even though her whole body tensed against her owl's inevitable disgust, that she'd thought kissing him would tease out the tenderness in his voice. Instead it had brought out the gravel, as though every touch of her skin to his had brought something inside him closer to breaking.

And it had.

7

JACKSON

Her eyes were wide with horror.

He looked away, hoping his own feelings didn't show on his face. That one glance was all he needed to confirm everything he should have already known. Twelve months of yearning, of hoping against hope… And just now, outside with Cole, the leaping, ridiculous thought that she might need his help. That she might need *him*.

Done. Over. And whatever the hell else he was doing here, he had the answer he already knew.

Olly didn't love him.

And he still loved her.

"What a mess," he muttered.

"What are you doing here?"

Her voice was thin. He forced himself to look at her again. Even if he couldn't bring himself to meet her eyes, he couldn't just ignore her.

She was completely still. Statue-like, and even not looking at her eyes he could feel them on him. Pinning him in place.

"I didn't mean to sneak up on you," he said, his voice a faraway rumble. She jumped as though she hadn't expected him to speak, despite just asking him a question. "I know you don't like it. I didn't know you were in here. Hannah, she said—"

He broke off. His excuses didn't matter.

Olly's cheekbones were sharper than he remembered. She'd lost weight. And her eyes were sunken, even if they still stung like knives to look at.

"Are you all right?" he asked.

"Why wouldn't I be?" Her eye twitched and he could practically hear her berating herself for talking without taking in the whole situation first. Because surely, if she'd had any time to think, she'd have realized why he thought she wasn't okay. She looked as though she hadn't slept in months.

She was off-footed. And it was his fault.

Jackson took a deep breath. He needed to control the situation, to find a way to give Olly back enough control that she didn't cut and run, but the words that came out of his mouth just sent it further out of hand. "For a start, you could hide a sack of presents in the bags under your eyes." Shit. He was *growling* at her, now? First he startled her and now he was telling her off. No wonder she didn't want anything to do with him.

He took a step forward. Gritted his jaw. *Do this right.* "Olly, you look like hell."

"Well, you look like—" Her lips pinched shut and her eyes flew around his face. They landed on his forehead and skated over his scar, and even though he knew there was no way she'd be able to see it behind his hair it still throbbed. "Why are you here?" she burst out. "Why couldn't you just stay *away*?"

Her voice cracked and Jackson's blood rose. He took another step towards her and she strained forwards, as though her feet were frozen in place but some part of her still wanted to—

No. That couldn't be real. He'd scared her, and now he was imagining things.

Jackson tried to make himself look as non-threatening as possible.

"Something's wrong here. I know it. Whatever's going on with you, you can tell me."

He was growling, still, and he hated himself for it, but Olly's pupils went wide. He swallowed.

"I can't," she whispered. "I really, really can't. I—"

There was a crash from behind him.

Jackson spun around, automatically putting himself between Olly and whatever had caused the noise. Yells of surprise filled the air.

The trestle tables were untouched. But outside…

Jackson swore as he strode forward.

The tent had collapsed. Cold air blasted through the front door and the festive party tent billowed and sagged like a swamped goose.

People were fighting to get free. Jackson breathed in the smell of singed plastic. Somewhere, Jasper Heartwell was shouting about small fires.

And in the middle of the giant mess was a gleaming, silver-winged pegasus. Its wings shimmered as though lit by something more than moonlight. It threw its head back, as though it was surprised to find itself in the center of such chaos, and its mane rippled like molten silver.

Jackson's stomach sank.

He should have paid more attention to his mother's warning. Mythic shifters weren't exactly common. Jackson had seen one pegasus, once in his life. This would make twice.

The pegasus caught sight of him and whinnied excitedly. It tried to canter towards them, got its hooves caught in the canvas, and tripped on its shining face.

Jackson turned away, back towards the kitchen. "Olly, I—"

He was too late. The moment he reached the kitchen door there was an explosion of feathers and Olly was gone, flying out through the window into the night.

Jackson watched her go, taking the newly broken pieces of his heart with her.

The shouting behind him got louder. He ran both hands down his face.

This isn't your problem, he reminded himself. *She doesn't want anything to do with you. You knew that already and now you know it for sure.*

Another crash. His eye twitched. *That? That is your problem.*

Jackson straightened his shoulders and strode outside.

He stepped onto the crumpled roof of the tent and something squeaked under his foot. He bent down and hunted around until he found the tent's entranceway. To his surprise, a long-haired sheep scuttled out, bleating.

He hadn't known there were any sheep shifters in Pine Valley.

Abigail stumbled out next, elf-hat askew and eyes wide. "Ruby," she said urgently. "She wanted to play with Cole—where did she—"

She tried to throw herself back into the crushed tent and Jackson held her back. "I'll find her," he said. Abigail put her hands over her face.

"I know she's not hurt," she said strangely. "I can feel it… here." One of her hands drifted to rest just above her heart. "Like with Jasper. And—oh!"

She spun around just as a plume of flame erupted from the tent. A tiny, brilliant red snout followed it, and then a larger black one.

"*Ruby!*" Abigail put her hands over her mouth. "Cole! Come over here at once, and stop burning things!"

The two dragons—one the size of a large dog, the other the size of a cat—popped free and looked around, apparently delighted. The black dragon's nostrils were trickling smoke. The little one looked at him and burped out another puff of flame.

"No," Abigail said firmly. "Jasper—"

Her husband battled himself free at the far end of the chaos and called both dragonlets over to him. Abigail sagged against the doorframe in relief. "At least *he* didn't panic and shift," she muttered to herself. "Oh, Mrs. Lamb—let me help…"

Jackson left her helping people stumble free of the tent. He could have stayed, pulling people to their feet as they crawled out the escape-route door, but that would have been ignoring the bigger problem.

He picked his way over the heaving canvas, careful to avoid any moving lumps, until he reached the pegasus.

"You picked a hell of a time for a family reunion," he growled at it.

The pegasus was still trying to find its feet. It clatter-fluttered towards him and he got a face full of silver feathers. The smell of whiskey was even stronger than the smell of burning plastic.

"How much have you been drinking?" Jackson gasped. "Come on—shift back, why don't you?"

The pegasus whinnied and slumped its head over his shoulder. His knees almost buckled under the weight. One of its wings thwapped the ground. The other almost took off Jackson's head.

Step by step, each more difficult than the last, he managed to lead it onto clear ground. The fallen tent buckled and slumped as the rest of the party pushed their way free, either through the flattened doors or ripping their way out with claws and teeth. A few shifted back into human form, shivered in the cold, and shifted back into their safely furred or feathered forms.

Jackson turned away.

"You sure know how to make an entrance," he muttered to the swaying pegasus. It hiccupped and stared at him with huge, confused eyes.

"Jackson." Jasper had the orange dragon in one arm and Abigail tucked under the other. He looked as close to unhappy as Jackson had ever seen him. "You want to tell us what the hell is going on here?"

Jackson took a deep breath. He gestured towards the pegasus.

"Jasper, Abigail… everyone."

He winced.

"Meet my father. Andrew Petrakis."

8

OLLY

*F*uck.

Cold crackled against the owl's claws as it landed on the frozen branch. Olly sank down inside its mind. If she'd had fingers, she would have been gnawing at them.

Fuck shit fuck.

She was in the best vantage point of the best tree on the best ridge above town and it still wasn't helping. No amount of perspective was going to fix this.

That didn't go right, her owl chittered, as disturbed as she was. *You said—but he was—what happened?* A wave of suspicion. *What have you been hiding from me?*

What have I been hiding? How did—whatever-that-was—crash into the tent without you even noticing?

Guilt and panic welled over her owl's suspicion. *I was focusing on—on—*

On what? Not telling me that he *was coming?*

She couldn't even think his name. Not yet. Her owl was right, she had been hiding something.

She'd been hiding everything.

What was that, anyway? she asked wretchedly. *That... thing. That crashed through the roof.*

I don't know. Her owl crackled with discomfort. It *hated* not knowing. *It was big and it had wings.*

I'll ask Meaghan—

No! We'll figure it out!

Okay, okay. We'll figure it out. By waiting until Meaghan or someone else brings it up, she added to herself, wishing she had a forehead to rub and knuckles to rub it with.

I heard that, her owl told her sulkily.

Olly groaned. Of course it had. Her owl heard everything that was in her head. Which was why she'd been so careful to—

I knew it! You are hiding something from me!

I'm not! Olly cast around for an escape. She had it at once. The same distraction that had let her escape the kitchen. *I just wish I knew what it was that crashed through the roof. It would make me feel safer if I knew what to look out for in the future.*

Yes! Safety! That's what's— Her owl hesitated. *Important?*

She breathed out, so hard her owl let out a puff of misty vapor. *Yes.* That's *what is important here.*

Her owl jumped on the problem at once. Images flickered at the edge of Olly's mind as it clawed over what it had seen of the chaos through the kitchen door, and the sliver of a glimpse as it had flown away as fast as it could.

While it was distracted, Olly concentrated. She hadn't done this before; she wasn't even sure it would work.

Instead of thinking, she hovered lightly over memories. Memories of her owl muttering to itself so quietly she couldn't hear it, and how it mentally turned its back when she was doing something disgusting like baking.

Slowly, with all the care her owl would have taken in stalking the movement and trajectory of prey, Olly un-stalked her owl.

The sensation was... odd.

Olly still had an awareness of what her owl was doing. Claws on icy branch, feathers wiffling in the breeze. But the sensations weren't as immediate as they usually were. It was as though she'd drawn a blanket around her mental self.

She remembered how her owl would rustle its wings or blink at her from inside her head, and drew her legs up into the blanket too, until she was completely burrito'd inside the cozy cocoon of... of... her-ness.

I love Jackson Gilles, she thought experimentally.

Her owl didn't respond. It didn't even hear her. Exactly as she'd hoped. Because her owl wasn't in love with Jackson.

But *she* was.

Fuck.

9

JACKSON

Wwhat was left of the party had moved inside, except for the gatecrasher, who leaned against a car and whinnied dismally to itself. Outside, doing his best to ignore his drunken father, Jackson was helping Jasper and Caine put out fires and fold away the singed tent.

"Almost done!" Jasper gestured to the black-scaled dragonlet and pointed at a smoldering patch of canvas. "There—can you unlight that, Cole? Since you probably lit it in the first place," he added in an undertone.

Cole bore down on the smoking fabric and sniffed it hard. The fire went out.

Like magic, Jackson thought, and snorted at himself. Of course it was magic. The kid was a dragon shifter. They were *all* magic.

"And that's everyone out. Come on, everybody—one, two, *heave!*"

They all hauled on the tent. The fabric folded, skidding across the frozen ground—and stuck.

"Not quite everyone out," Abigail remarked from the door. She was supervising their progress from what Jasper had announced was a safe distance. Her dragon daughter Ruby was snuggled in her arms, puffing smoke happily.

Jackson followed her gaze and pulled up the roof of the tent so he could see what was in the way. A massive brown bear was sleeping peacefully in the middle of the mayhem: one of Hannah Holborn's nephews.

Jackson's eyebrows shot up. "He's right where my—where the pegasus landed. Is he all right?"

Abigail shrugged at him, as though to say, *I'm not a shifter either, why are you asking me?*

"He's fine," Jasper announced. "Just sleeping." He paused and his gaze went vague for a second in the way Jackson had come to recognize as meaning a shifter was speaking telepathically. Then his face went red. "And he's told me to shut up and let him keep sleeping."

"I guess med school is even more exhausting than he let on," Abigail said dryly. She shot Jackson a shy smile and hoisted her daughter into a more comfortable position.

Jackson smiled back at her. Plenty of shifters forgot their human friends couldn't hear telepathic speech, or didn't bother letting them in on conversations. Abigail had better luck than he did training her friends and family to actually talk to her if they wanted her to hear what they were saying.

Olly's uncle Bob appeared at the door. He'd managed to escape the collapse without shifting, but Jackson thought he might have looked better if he had: his nose was red and raw-looking, and his eyes were bleary. "I guess that could have gone worse," he grumbled, and blew his nose. "What was that you said about no fires, Heartwell? When I said you could use the Express for your shindig, I didn't realize I needed to specify not to destroy the whole place."

"A Christmas pegasus crashing through the roof wasn't exactly part of the plan," Jasper retorted. "A Christmas *pegasus*! I'm going to be out of a job."

"I'm so sorry!"

A young woman ran through the crowd. Jackson had never seen her before, but from the way she dodged past Cole without a second glance, she had to be a shifter.

She had shoulder-length honey-blonde hair, and eyebrows shaped like crescent moons that gave her whole face an urgent, nervous look. "I'm so sorry," she repeated as she reached them. She had an English accent. "I was just parking the car—a bit further away than expected, but I didn't realize he'd had *quite* that much to drink…"

"You know my—him?" He gestured to where the pegasus was leaning against the Puppy Express building, absently trying to eat a string of tinsel.

She looked at him and her expression brightened. "Yes! And you must be Jackson. Phew! That's one good thing tonight, at least. I'm Delphine, your father's PA." She held out one gloved hand for him to shake. "Delphine Belgrave."

He was instantly suspicious. "PA?" He rubbed his face, then caught himself and shook her hand. Her grip was firm, through her bulky glove, and she held on a millisecond longer than was normal. He put it down to her still getting over Andrew's no-doubt hectic escape. "What's this about?"

Delphine pursed her lips. "I'd… better let him explain that," she said. Foreboding gathered in Jackson's chest. *If he's come back into my life after twenty-five years to introduce me to my new step-mom…*

He cleared his throat. "Right, well, that will have to wait. We need to get rid of all this mess before first shift tomorrow. Right, Bob?"

He turned away. He was itching for something to do, or else frustration would boil out of him. The young woman didn't deserve to be at the pointy end of whatever feelings he had about his father, and God, throwing heavy things into a tidy pile right now sounded like a great idea.

How could he have already ruined everything again?

A hand fell on his shoulder. Jasper. The reason he was here in the first place. He'd almost forgotten the house paperwork, on top of everything else.

"We'll be fine here," the dragon shifter said. "You—er—did you see Olly, earlier?"

"She left."

"Oh." Jasper looked too innocent. Pieces started to fall together in Jackson's mind, and he didn't like the picture they formed.

He opened his mouth to accuse Jasper of choreographing this whole thing—him coming back to Pine Valley, surprising Olly—and shut it again.

Jasper might have brought him here, but this was his mess. He needed to deal with it.

"If you're happy managing here, I'll get rid of the gatecrasher," he said, and turned to the pegasus.

"I'll bring the car around," Delphine said brightly.

Jackson's stomach would have dropped as he saw the car, but it was already firmly lodged in his boots. It was the same new-looking car he'd seen turn down Rabbit Road earlier. If he'd followed the sense of unease it had given him earlier, maybe he could have avoided this whole nightmare.

Well, this isn't awkward at all, Jackson thought once they were all on the road.

Getting Andrew into the truck had been easy enough. He'd been still dazed from crash-landing on the not-so-solid roof of the tent, and had tucked himself into the back seat with minimal fuss. Then he'd sat and stared voicelessly at Jackson and Delphine in the front of the truck while Delphine drove to their accommodation.

Jackson caught his father's soulful gaze in the rear-view mirror. "You know I can't hear you, right?"

Delphine stifled something that sounded like laughter. He glanced at her questioningly.

"Oh—nothing. I'm sure you're missing out on a scintillating conversation."

"Your duties as PA don't include translating?"

Delphine's eyebrows pricked upwards. "That isn't—er, that is, if he *is* speaking, he's speaking only to you. I'm not getting anything." A quick smile. He wondered if it was meant to reassure him, or herself.

"Given the bottles we found back there, I doubt he's making any sense anyway."

She winced at that. "I did wonder why he was so quiet these last few miles. I knew he was nervous about meeting you, but I didn't expect… oh, well."

"*He's* nervous? He's—" Jackson stiffened his jaw before he could say anything else. "Where are you staying, anyway?"

"Almost there." Delphine consulted the GPS on the dash. "He wanted a place quite out of the way, so he could go flying without anyone seeing him."

"Didn't stop him back there."

She winced again and he felt guilty.

"Just around this bend—ah! There."

The house loomed in the yellow glow of the headlights. It sat comfortably among the snow like it had sprouted up from the ground of its own accord and settled in for a good rest. Its empty windows promised a serene view of frozen trees, and it had a tall chimney that Jackson hoped someone had cleaned before the winter.

The worst thing was, he liked it. It was exactly the sort of house he'd like to live in one day.

"Here we are," Delphine said needlessly as she parked in front of the house. "Now we just need to get him inside."

Jackson would have suggested leaving him in the car, but even shifters weren't that immune to the cold. He didn't know why his father had decided to see him after all these years, but he wouldn't get any answers from an ice block.

Besides, how hard could wrangling one pegasus be?

A few minutes later, he knew exactly how hard it could be.

Six limbs, Jackson thought. *I'll never complain about herding humans into the drunk tank again.*

A wing buffeted Jackson in the face as he opened the back door of the car. A hoof followed, then another, then the pegasus got stuck.

"I'll try the other side," Delphine called. "Mr. Petrakis, your head's at this end, try coming out this way…"

"Or shift?" Jackson suggested.

Delphine shook her head as Andrew tried to get out through both doors at once. "It's an idea, but…"

The pegasus whinnied in desolate frustration. Jackson's jaw tensed.

"What's he saying?" he muttered, and tapped the side of his head when Delphine looked at him in confusion. "I'm not a shifter, remember?"

"Oh! Er. Nothing particularly helpful." She fumbled in her handbag. "I'll just, er, open up—"

Jackson bent down to look inside the truck as she hurried to the cottage door. Two soulful, sky-blue eyes stared back at him from a confusion of feathers and hooves.

"*Mwheeeer*," the pegasus declared, and exploded in a flurry of sparkling lights. "My boy!"

Jackson covered his eyes. He'd seen more of his fa—of Andrew today than he'd seen in the last twenty-five years.

He really wasn't in the mood to see even more of him.

"There-he-is. Issa. Jackson Petrakis."

"Gilles," Jackson grumbled as an arm landed heavily over his shoulders.

"Ja'son Petrakis-Gilles. Firs' fledgling. Never thought…"

Andrew's voice trailed off. Jackson yanked him to him feet, then braced himself and flung one arm around his torso to keep him upright as he stumbled. He felt wool under his hand and cracked his eyes open.

"How the hell did you get dressed that quickly?" he demanded.

"Eh?" Andrew stared dazedly down at himself. Gold glittered on his little finger. He wasn't dressed for the climate; his suit was wool, but it was still just a suit jacket, not something that would keep the mountain cold out.

But the most important thing about his clothing was the fact that he was still wearing it. Every other shifter Jackson had ever met lost their clothes every time they shifted. Mythic or plain old ordinary animal shifters, their clothes all suffered the same fate.

Though whether that fate was vaporized or just torn to pieces, he wasn't sure.

"Keeping my kit on? Jus' gotta… gotta not be lazy 'bout it," Andrew declared. "Warrathink, waste a suit like this e'ry time I shift? Pshh."

He swung around so quickly Jackson almost dropped him.

"Teach you all about it," he slurred. He patted Jackson on the chest and beamed blearily. "M'boy. Teach all… e'rything. Things. Important."

"Sure," Jackson said absently. Andrew nodded.

"Exc'llent. Good job. Don'… don' know what I was worried about." He puffed out his chest and one leg shot out from under him. "Argh!"

Jackson hoisted him back onto his feet. Andrew muttered to himself and straightened his jacket, and Jackson took the opportunity to look at his face properly.

The last time he'd seen Andrew Petrakis the man had looked like a giant. Two decades later, Jackson had two or three inches on him. It gave him the perfect perspective to see where their similarities started.

Curly dark hair. A solid jaw—Ma always called his *dependable*, which rankled now he knew where he'd gotten it. Even their eyes were the same shape.

It was like a punch in the gut.

"'Splain it all," Andrew slurred. "Pegasus. Fledg… lish… fledgish. Fledging. Firs'… ever. Important."

He kept muttering to himself as Jackson half-walked, half-dragged him inside.

"The bedroom's upstairs, I'm afraid," Delphine said as he closed the door. She was twisting her hands together, but her expression brightened when she saw him. "Oh, good, he's human again."

"Delphine!" Andrew cried out. "Have y'met… have you… my boy here." He gestured at Jackson and his eyes lit up. "Jackson! Have y'met…"

"Delphine?"

"Thassaone."

"Yeah, we've met. About a half an hour ago." Jackson shot an apologetic look at Delphine, but she just shrugged.

"Delphine Belgrave. Ver' good… old family. Lion shifters. Ver'… wings." Andrew stared intently into Jackson's eyes, as though he was trying to find the point of his sentence there. "Wing' lionsh."

"Lions?"

"Wiv wings!"

Jackson shook his head. "Winged lions, huh? I guess they would have wings, yeah."

"It's all in the name," Delphine added blandly. She caught Jackson's eye and shrugged.

Andrew's head swung between each of them. "Good. Good… Now…" He trailed off. The silence stretched and Andrew's face went contentedly blank, as though he'd forgotten he'd begun to speak at all.

"Time for bed, you think?" Jackson suggested.

"No, no… well, p'rhaps. Upstairs?"

Andrew craned his neck to look up the stairs. His eyes narrowed.

"Watch out!" Delphine called suddenly.

Jackson only had a split second to pay attention to her warning. He flattened himself against the wall, but not fast enough. Andrew shifted in an explosion of lights.

"You're not seriously going to—" Feathers filled Jackson's mouth as Andrew spread his wings. Something tumbled off a side table and smashed on the floor.

"Mr. Petrakis—"

The pegasus beat its shining wings. More crashing. It made it to the bottom of the stairs—and collapsed.

Another burst of lights, and Andrew was lying in a crumpled heap. "No 'nough room," he muttered, and closed his eyes.

Jackson exchanged a look with Delphine. To his slight relief, she seemed as embarrassed as he felt.

"We could take one arm each?" she suggested.

Andrew wasn't as asleep as he appeared, or at least not consistently so. As Jackson and Delphine half-carried him up the stairs he kept trying to launch himself forward, or sideways, or in one terrifying case, backwards.

"Just so long as he doesn't shift again," Jackson muttered to Delphine as he hauled Andrew onto the landing.

"No' a chance. Can' hear me, can ya?" Andrew slurred.

"I can hear you just fine."

Andrew waved one hand and narrowly missed hitting Delphine in the face. "Inna head."

"Yeah, humans can't do telepathy, Andrew."

Andrew muttered something he couldn't make out. "'S'early. 'S'okay."

"Right. Sure thing." He nodded to Delphine. "I can manage him from here. Can you get the door?"

The cottage bedroom was situated over the living room. The flue from the downstairs fireplace ran up alongside one wall, to take advantage of the heating, and the window on the opposite wall looked out into the trees. It was a classic Pine Valley view, with a hint of gold in one corner from the glow of the town itself and the stars a brilliant scatter of light above. In the morning, the sun would slip across the valley, inch by inch, picking out the white snow and black trees and rock in vivid contrast.

And Andrew would be too hungover to appreciate it.

Jackson dumped him on the bed and he promptly slid off it.

"M'boy." Andrew's hand clutched in the air about a foot away from Jackson's shoulder as he stooped to pick him up. "J'st like y'old man."

I hope not. Jackson heaved Andrew onto the bed and Delphine reappeared at the top of the stairs in time to grab his legs and pull them up. Andrew grinned contentedly at them both and promptly passed out.

"Well," said Delphine, straightening her sweater. "This is nice and awkward, isn't it?"

Her hair was a mess, with a single silver feather sticking out from it. Jackson ran a hand over his own hair and found a loose feather there, too. He gestured to Delphine and she finger-combed her hair self-consciously.

"I think I'll head to the hotel," she said. "He won't be up until late tomorrow, and that'll give me time to finish some work."

"You're not staying here?"

Delphine's eyebrows shot up. "Excuse me?"

"I meant—"

"There's only one bedroom. Your father's not that sort of boss, and even if he was, the only reason he brought me on this trip is..." She pinched the bridge of her nose. "Something I will leave to him to explain."

Jackson sighed. He didn't know much about Andrew's life other than that his business was the excuse he'd used for never having time for him, but he was pretty sure PAs weren't usually expected to hole up in tiny mountain towns with their boss over the Christmas holidays. "I'm sorry you got dragged into all this."

"Why?" Her honey-gold eyes bored into his. *Winged lion*, he thought, the hairs on the back of his neck bristling. *Yeah, I can see that.*

He shrugged. "I can't imagine ferrying your employer around the mountains and hauling his drunk ass to bed is how you want to spend your Christmas."

"Oh, I don't know." Delphine started downstairs. "One boozy boss and a nice drive in the snow ranks above a planeload of angry families and dealing with Heathrow at Christmas, in my books. Though…" She reached the bottom of the stairs and looked back at him over her shoulder. "I wasn't expecting anything like that party. Are shifters really so open here?"

"That depends. Off-season, the main worry is hunters, and maybe a few of the newer families who haven't noticed they're neighbors with dragons yet. Winter and summer is when people have to be careful. Folks come up for camping in the summer and skiing in the winter, and you never know who's got a camera or a phone out."

"But when it's just shifters, it's expected that people are going to be in their shifted form?"

"Within reason. Transforming into a mythical beast and crashing other people's parties is taking it a step too far." Jackson shrugged. "But most shifters aren't mythical and most folks on vacation aren't going to think twice if they see a bear in the woods. There are places in the valley that are private access only and if people are worried, they set a watch—"

Like Olly. His throat went dry. Olly always volunteered to keep watch. Her owl was the perfect guard, and knowing where everyone was and what they were doing always made Olly happy.

So how the hell had he managed to sneak up on her?

She couldn't have changed that much in a year, could she? Jackson's heart leaped, and he felt queasy. No amount of change on either of their parts could alter what was really important.

He shook his head. "Basically, if you want to stretch your wings, do it at night or someplace no one can see you."

"That won't be an issue." Delphine bit her lower lip. "I mean, my lion isn't quite as... excitable as Mr. Petrakis' pegasus. And I'm more of a town person, anyway."

"Not that Pine Valley's much of a town?" Jackson joked, picking up on the uncertainty in her expression.

She stared at him. "Sorry?"

"Never mind."

There was another awkward silence.

"You know, I'd really better get going—"

"I'll help you bring the bags in."

Jackson helped Delphine lug three massive suitcases out of the truck. He left them lined up in the hallway, said goodbye and just managed to stop himself from apologizing for Andrew's bullshit again.

It wasn't until the truck's headlights disappeared in the distance that he remembered his own car was miles away, back at the Puppy Express.

He thudded into the sofa in front of the fireplace.

A shifter wouldn't worry about—

He groaned and buried his head in his hands. Was that really his first reaction? That a shifter wouldn't be put off by an hours-long trek through snow in the middle of the night? If he had wings, or was sturdy enough, sure, but no small animal would think twice before deciding to curl up in front of the fire and wait out the night.

He pulled out his phone. Rideshare services hadn't reached Pine Valley yet, but the town did have a taxi. Singular. He could…

His thumb hovered over the screen. He could call the taxi, assuming it was still running this late at night.

Or he could face up to the truth he'd been running from for the last year.

10

OLLY

Olly flew high above the trees, one thought whirling around and around in her mind: *What am I going to do?*

It wasn't words that echoed through Olly's head so much as a churning flood of emotion. She'd kept everything frozen up inside her and now the spring floods had come.

And like all spring floods they were leaving destruction in their wake.

Her first year in Pine Valley, when her parents had suggested she move to the small town to help her uncle with his business and get some good owl time in away from the city, an avalanche had torn through the forest. She'd almost gotten caught in it, and had learned after that to keep watch for the warning signs. She'd put that lesson to good use in the rest of her life, as well. There were *always* warning signs, and even if they weren't warnings, they were good information. Knowing who was in a room before she went into it, or what people were talking about, just the shape of a social interaction in general before she inserted herself into it, made her feel safe.

But this last year, ever since the hellhounds, she'd gotten worse.

Except it wasn't just the hellhounds, was it? They were the cause. But the thing that had made her really feel the world cracking beneath her feet was what had happened with Jackson.

She flew for an hour before she could convince herself it was safe to land on her bedroom windowsill and claw the latch open. She let the curtains fall over the window and shifted, heart hammering.

There was no movement in the house. She was alone. Safe.

What was that about? Her owl's voice was brittle.

Olly bit back an hysterical laugh. What was she thinking? She was never alone.

The hellhounds? She tried to sound like she wasn't terrified out of her skull. To a creature that *lived* in her skull. *Just reminding myself they're nothing to be afraid of. They can't help their hellfire, and they're friends, not enemies.*

I know that! But… just after that… and what you were saying before, when we were perched on the best branch…

Emotions threatened to crash through her, more terrifying than any avalanche. Olly tried to hold them back. It hurt so much. It hurt her heart and her head because if what she was feeling was real, there was something terribly wrong with the world.

Her owl's feathers puffed out. *You're hurt?*

I'm not—I can't be…

Like before. You're hurt like before?

This was worse than being spotted by someone else before she saw them. Her own owl was interrogating her!

What do you mean, like before? I'm not—I don't—I'm fine.

Nothing's wrong?

Olly covered her face. Nothing *could* be wrong. None of this could be happening. And nothing *could* happen, because there was no way Jackson could still have feelings for her after what she'd done to him last year.

Nothing's wrong, she told her owl.

Right. Good.

And that was wrong, too, because her owl sounded *relieved.* And being relieved meant it had been worried in the first place, and why would her owl be—

I'm not worried! Everything is fine!

Her phone beeped.

Olly froze, her eyes snapping to her dresser. She'd left her phone there that afternoon when she started baking. Who could be trying to contact her?

Bob wouldn't bother with a phone when he could telepath her. Meaghan might—Meaghan and Abigail were the main reasons Olly even had her phone, these days—but…

She checked the notification. New message from Jackson Gilles.

Oh, God.

What? What is it? Oh. Just him. Her owl's voice was heavy with suspicion. *The… not-important one.*

Why do you keep saying that?

You said it.

Olly groaned. *I've spent the last twelve months thinking—* She pounced on the thought before it could get any further. *If he's not important then there's nothing wrong with me seeing what he sent, is there?*

She opened the message. It was only a single line:

Sorry about today.

Her skin felt electric. **What specifically?** she wrote back.

I feel like I should say "everything".

She snorted. Everything? He couldn't be blamed for her owl refusing to acknowledge him, and then her freaking out when she finally did see him. Or whatever or whoever had crashed the party, or her using it as a distraction while she fled like a terrified bunny rabbit after Jackson got the jump on her.

Better start with sorry for sneaking up on you.

Olly blinked. It was as though he'd heard her thoughts.

I should have heard you coming, she wrote back.

For a few long, painful minutes, there were no new messages. Then her phone buzzed in her hands.

I left my truck at the Puppy Express. I'll be around tomorrow morning to pick it up. Figure you should get some advance warning this time.

The next message came only a second later, as though he'd tapped it out and sent it before he could change his mind: *And maybe we can talk.*

Talk. The word was like ice water trickling under her collar. Because they *hadn't* talked. Not after—what had happened—and not when Jackson had left. And not in the twelve months since.

Olly's gut twisted. What did they have to talk *about?* He knew the most important thing. She'd gotten everything wrong. He wasn't her mate and regardless of how she felt, that meant she had nothing to offer him. Nothing true or real.

I don't think that's a good idea.

She sent it, and waited until the moon had crossed the sky. He didn't reply.

II

JACKSON

3 DAYS BEFORE CHRISTMAS

He had left calling the taxi too late. And he couldn't bear to look at his phone, anyway. Not with that last message blasted across his mind's eye.

I don't think that's a good idea.

If he needed any proof that he wasn't wanted here…

He spent the night on the sofa, alternating glaring at the fake coals in the gas fire and snatching whispers of sleep. Every time he closed his eyes, his dreams were disturbed. It was as though something was looming behind him—or maybe inside him.

Either way, it left him frustrated and uneasy.

Andrew didn't wake up until the cuckoo clock in the kitchen squawked twelve. Jackson was in the kitchen, already on his third cup of coffee.

He had considered leaving before Andrew woke up, but part of him felt responsible for the bag of bones he'd dumped onto the bed the night before. A very small part, which shrank every time the cuckoo went through its routine.

Whoever designed it must never have heard a real bird before. It was the most annoying—

"Someone wring that bird's neck!"

—it was probably important to someone's cultural heritage, Jackson thought, and grimaced at himself. How long was he going to keep this up, putting himself opposite to Andrew just to prove to himself that they were different?

The cuckoo clock was a monstrosity. Houses were houses, whatever they looked like. He had happily gotten on with being as tall as he was and having a tangled mess of hair and sturdy jaw for decades before he learned it was his father he'd gotten them from.

"Where the hell am I? What's this? What—Delphine! Delphine? Why's there—"

Thuds and groans accompanied Andrew's journey from the bedroom. From the sound, he found the door by falling into sections of the wall until one of them gave way.

Jackson rubbed his face. "In here," he called.

He was answered by several thuds and more swearing. The kitchen door remained untouched.

He gave up rubbing his face and rested his forehead on his hand. *Who would have guessed it. All those shifts looking after the drunk tank were to prepare me for running into my dear old pa again.*

"Kitchen!" he called, just as the door sprung open. Andrew's face appeared in the gap. Last night, he'd been ruddy, the classic top-of-the-world drunk with every inch of his brain fizzing as the alcohol bounced around inside it.

This morning, he was gray.

"Kitchen," he gasped, staggering against the doorframe. His eyes unfocused, then focused. "Coffee."

"In the—" Jackson began, but Andrew was already lurching towards the counter. He sagged against it, and managed the coffee machine with surprising deftness. Jackson tried not to be impressed, especially when he saw that Andrew's eyes had fluttered shut again.

"Nothing like a good coffee to bring you back to the world of the living," Andrew announced suddenly, fumbling along the counter until his hands found a cup. "Ain't that right, Del—no—wait…"

He turned slowly. One of his eyes popped open, and the other followed gummily. Both widened when he caught sight of Jackson.

"My boy!"

For one terrifying moment, Jackson thought he was about to surge forward, but at the last minute he collapsed back against the counter and raised his coffee cup to his lips.

"D'you know what a hell of a time I've had trying to track you down?" he said, and took a gulp of coffee that made him hiss. "Months—no idea—and a place like this?" He shivered. "Those *were* dragons I sensed last night, weren't they?"

Jackson nodded, then realized Andrew's eyes had gummed themselves shut again. "The Heartwells? They're dragon shifters, yeah."

"God!"

"They weren't too happy about you barging in."

"Barging in? Barging in? I never barge—oh." His forehead creased. "Now that you say that, it is coming back to me…"

He groped his way to the kitchen table and sagged into a seat.

"Not the best introduction," Andrew suggested after a few seconds.

"Probably not," Jackson agreed.

"Ah, well. Had to be done. Couldn't—needed a bit of courage. Make it through." He upended his coffee cup over his mouth and then stared, dazed, into, as though bewildered that it was now empty. "More coffee."

He hauled himself back to the coffee machine.

Jackson sat back, observing. He wasn't angry, and it was hard to be humiliated when the only other person around was busy making an ass of himself.

What did Ma ever see in you? he thought, and immediately felt guilty.

Andrew was still muttering to himself. "No way around it—help along. A bit of help along. So's could…" He stopped and spun around. "I did tell you, didn't I? Why I'm here?"

To pat my shoulder and make sure everyone whose opinion I care about knows my father's a complete loser? Jackson opened his mouth—and closed it again.

Not everyone. Olly was already gone by then.

And whatever else his father—Andrew—had come here to achieve, he'd at least stopped Jackson from making the mistake of chasing after her.

"Sure," he said out loud.

"Good! Good." Andrew sounded uncertain. "And you met Delphine?"

"Your PA?" Andrew seemed to expect him to say more. "She seems nice."

"Nice." Andrew's voice echoed his, hollowly. "Ah, well."

He staggered back to the table, fresh coffee in hand. "I definitely told you," he repeated, half a question, half seeming to want to reassure himself. "Yes."

This isn't going anywhere. Jackson stood up. "There's breakfast things in the fridge," he said, having already rummaged through it while he was waiting for Andrew to emerge.

"You're going?" Consternation oozed across Andrew's face. "But… I just got here! Surely you have questions…"

"I have a lot to do."

Luckily, or unluckily, his father was hungover enough not to argue. And had a driver on speed-dial.

"You're quiet this morning." Delphine peered through the windscreen as she navigated the road to the Puppy Express.

"Huh," Jackson grunted, and she laughed.

"God. You're really nothing like your father, you know that?"

The road opened out to the parking area in front of the Puppy Express building. There was hardly a trace of the chaos from the night before: the broken tent had been packed away, and any ice that had melted from the dragonlets' small fires had frozen over again.

To Jackson's relief, Delphine pulled in directly in front of the building. There. Olly knew he was coming, and now she'd be able to spy on him to her heart's content. If that was all she wanted from him, then he would happily give it to her.

"Nothing like my father?" he echoed as he stepped out of the truck. "That's the best news I've had all year."

"I'll try to remember not to tell him that." Delphine looked amused. "Though you might find—never mind. Will we see you later?"

Jackson paused, one hand on the door. "I don't think so," he said slowly. "Look, Delphine, it was nice to meet you and maybe in time I'll be able to say it was nice to see Andrew again. If only to confirm what I already knew. But I'm not in the mood for a father–son reunion. I have other problems to deal with right now."

Delphine leveled her gaze at him. "What sort of problems?"

She wasn't very good at making questions sound casual. Jackson shrugged. "Just tying up some loose ends."

"Oh, yes. I meant to ask you. I spoke to the woman at reception at my hotel, and she sounded surprised that you were in town. What brought you back? Do you—" She hesitated, and the part of Jackson that was assessing her as a suspicious deputy silently congratulated her on not tipping whatever the hell hand she was trying to play.

"Same thing that made me leave," he muttered, and the hairs on the back of his neck prickled.

He glanced at the Puppy Express building just in time to see a flash of movement behind one of the windows.

"*Oh.*" Delphine's half-moon eyebrows shot up. "Well, if you change your mind, you know where to find him."

"I'll keep it in mind," Jackson drawled, with no intention of doing so. "Thanks for the ride."

"You're welcome. See you later."

Like hell. Jackson remembered his manners in time to keep the words from slipping out. He shook his head at himself as Delphine drove off. One day in his dad's presence, most of it with Andrew unconscious, and he was already regressing to teenagerhood? Talk about making up for lost time.

He shoved his hands into his pockets and they bumped up against his keys—and his phone.

I should have called her the moment I got back into town. Cleared the air between us. Acted like a goddamn adult. Now…

Now, it was too late. He'd already gone ahead and ruined everything, jumping her like that last night. If there was one thing Olly hated it was surprises. She always made sure to check out any room or building before she went inside, so she knew what to expect.

And when she was the one already inside, she kept an eye on the windows and doors to see anyone who was coming by, so she could get the jump on them when she came out to say hi. Which meant that if that had been her in the window just now then she'd made it clear she didn't want to see him. Same as last night.

I don't think that's a good idea.

His chest ached and he forced himself not to watch the Puppy Express windows as he trudged towards his truck.

He had his keys in his hand. His truck was right there. He was damned sure Olly must have already seen him coming—she never missed anything.

That prickle of unease on the back of his neck again. He almost felt like someone was standing there, breathing cold air on him.

Keys. Truck. There was no reason for him to go inside, except…

Something here didn't fit.

Olly always watched from the windows. That was normal. But she wasn't *watching*, this time. She'd glimpsed him and disappeared.

If that had even been her.

And if it wasn't…

He was already marching up to the front door. He didn't know what was worse: the possibility that something *was* wrong, and he had a reason to storm in on Olly like this, or that he was making it all up and had no excuses, no reason except the yearning tug in his heart, pulling him to the last place he'd seen her.

Like a criminal returning to the scene of the crime, he thought, scowling. *Or a dog biting at a wound so it never heals.*

Olly would laugh at that. The Puppy Express had special, festive cones for when their dogs needed a bit of encouragement not to bite themselves crazy. Or maybe she'd just think he was pathetic, since it was his own cursed fault that he—

Anyway. He wasn't a dog. Olly liked watching how shifters betrayed their animal sides when they were in human form, but he didn't have an animal side and she didn't like him.

That was all there was to it.

So if he did have this all wrong, and he was just bothering Olly when she didn't want to be bothered, it wasn't like she was going to like him any less.

He pushed the door open.

The air inside was warm, but not warm enough to account for the beads of sweat that broke out on his forehead. What the hell was he doing? For just a second, he felt like he was back six months ago, letting his need for action overwhelm his common sense. That same buzz in his ears as though he'd lost concentration for one second and—sure, he probably wasn't going to be shot at this time, but this might just be worse…

A jolly Christmas carol rang from the speakers, making his shoulders hunch. He glanced towards the counter and despite everything, despite the crystal-clear knowledge that he was the last person Olly would want to see, a smile started to curl around—

Olly wasn't there.

The confusion of hope and guilt and self-loathing that had been writhing inside Jackson swept away. Olly wasn't behind the counter. Instead, there was a man who had no right to be there.

Sullen expression, heavy jaw, shoulders like a linebacker. He couldn't remember the guy's name, but he'd recognize him anywhere.

He was a hellhound shifter.

Jackson's blood boiled. "What the hell do you think you're doing here?" he demanded, striding towards the hellhound.

"Hi, welcome to the Puppy—hey!" The hellhound backed away as Jackson got closer. "What's your problem?"

"My problem? Let's start with you." Jackson bit off a growl. "Where's Olly?"

The hellhound's jaw jutted. "Who's asking? Hey, you're not allowed to come back here—"

Jackson stormed around the counter. Hellfire flared in the shifter's eyes. It sparked a deep and primal fear in the back of Jackson's brain and he paused, breathing heavily.

He knew this trick. He'd seen the effects of hellhound terror before. Last year, when this asshole and his friends had tormented Olly.

"Where is she? If you've hurt her again—"

"What? Who? Olly? I don't know, out the back?" The hellhound's eyebrows lowered menacingly. Every word he spoke sounded like it was being dredged up from a tar pit. Fear simmered across Jackson's mind, primal and… distracting.

I'm missing something. Again.

"I said, you're not meant to be back here." The hellhound shifter moved forwards and it took all of Jackson's bloody-mindedness not to back off as his fiery gaze hit him full force. Every self-hating thought he'd ever had, every bump in the night he'd been afraid of, simmered like hot oil across his mind. "You'd better—"

His gaze went hazy and unfocused. Jackson caught himself on the counter as the hellfire onslaught stopped.

"You'd better…" Something broke behind the hellhound shifter's eyes. His shoulders slumped. "Seriously? You want me to… shit, alright, alright." He focused on Jackson again and said in an embarrassed monotone: "You'd better tell me… who that woman was who dropped you off outside."

His expression said *I dare you to start shit over this.*

Jackson sighed. Without the hellfire, the hellhound shifter looked like a normal guy in his early twenties.

"Olly, I know you're around here somewhere," he called out, ignoring the hellhound shifter. "Come on. Can't we just… talk?"

There was no reply, either from Olly or the hellhound. Jackson glared at the door that led into the employees-only back room, and then at the shifter.

Who looked as though he'd rather be anywhere but here.

"What's your name again?"

"Manu."

"You want to tell me what the hell is going on here?"

Manu shuffled his feet. "She doesn't want to see you," he muttered. His eye twitched. "Um, and she says… Maybe you should use your eyes before you run in somewhere and start…" He broke off. "Um. You get the idea. Sir."

Jackson stared at him. Properly, this time.

He'd been so quick to action after he saw the shifter that he hadn't paid any attention to what he was actually *seeing*. The guy was wearing a Puppy

Express uniform. Right down to the name badge with a grinning husky on it.

"You work here?"

The hellhound shifter nodded gloomily.

Jackson's frown didn't grow any lighter. Olly's uncle was *employing* a hellhound shifter now? After what they'd done?

"Since when?" How much had changed in Pine Valley since he left?

"Since—" The shifter's expression became pained. "I'm telling him!" he muttered under his breath. To Olly, Jackson assumed, and his scar ached. Where was she? "Since last summer. I guess we all needed jobs, and the boss and Caine didn't want us hanging around being useless and Olly doesn't do so well at front of house, you know, and—"

"I don't know, actually." Jackson's fingers twitched. His first impression *had* been right. Something was wrong here. "Olly's worked here for years. This is her home turf. She might be watchful, but she's not the sort to hide herself away."

He punctuated that last sentence with a suspicious glance at the door. Behind it, something clattered.

"That's it," he growled. "Something's wrong here. I'm not going to wait around and—"

The door creaked open. Olly was just visible behind it, staring out through the gap. Her mouth was pressed into a thin, determined line.

"Um, she says, what are you even doing here—" Manu began, miserably, and she shot him a sharp look. By the way his shoulders shot up, he felt that look right through the back of his head.

"Okay, so, I'm just gonna go… tidy some shelves…" Manu muttered, and slunk off.

Jackson stared at her. She didn't stare back. Her eyes were fixed on one of the windows behind him, and her fingers kept twitching on the doorframe as though she was one wrong word from disappearing into the back room again.

The air between them felt tight.

"Olly," Jackson began, his voice edged around with an awkward burr, and it was as though someone had taken a crank and twisted the air until it was ready to crack. Olly's chest hitched.

Something is *wrong.*

Her face was too pale. The shadows under her eyes were even deeper than he remembered from the night before and her lips were almost colorless.

"What's wrong?" he half-whispered. It came out too rough.

Olly's eyes flickered, but she didn't look at him, and she didn't answer.

"Olly, this is… Something's wrong. I know it is. You've got hellhounds working here, and you're not even front-of-house anymore?" He stepped forward, lowering his voice. "If someone's making you act like this…"

Olly let out a bark of something that sounded almost like laughter. She lifted one hand to cover her face as though she was trying to grab hold of the sound before it got out.

"The only person who makes me act like anything is *me*. Don't you know that by now?"

Her eyes flashed to meet his and jerked away just as quickly. It was only a split second, but that was long enough for Jackson to see the expression in them. She was confused, and frustrated, and… hurt.

He paused, searching for the right words to connect the uneasy feeling in his gut with whatever instinct had dragged him in here in the first place, and Olly jumped into the gap.

"What are you doing here, anyway? You're not deputy anymore, you can't just barge in and start giving orders to people."

"I came to pick up—"

If he'd had any doubts Olly had scouted out the whole situation already, her next words confirmed it.

"That's your truck outside?"

Jackson nodded and he saw her file the information away.

Her lip quivered. "I didn't even recognize it. I thought—but then, I thought, you couldn't possibly have come back—I should have looked more carefully—" Her head jerked. "That doesn't matter. It's outside, you could have just picked it up. You didn't need to come in here. There's no *reason* for you to come inside."

No reason? All the guilt Jackson had been holding onto for the past year welled up inside him. Did she really think he'd let go of everything he felt for her? "What if I wanted to see you?"

She went completely still. She still wasn't looking at him, but her eyes hardened, clouding over like glass and just as brittle.

"Why would you want to do that?"

Her voice gave nothing away, and that was all Jackson needed to know. Olly was quiet, but she braided her emotions into her words, even when she didn't speak above a whisper. This flat tone wasn't her.

Frustration twisted with guilt in Jackson's chest. He'd left Pine Valley because he'd thought it was the right thing to do. For them both. What was the point of everything he'd gone through in the last year, if it hadn't helped her?

"I don't know, Olly. Maybe because I still care about you."

"Despite—" Olly's face twisted and she raised her hand again to hide it. "Despite everything? Despite me being *me*?" And then, in a whisper that was at once reassuringly familiar and discomfortingly ragged: "I'm not ready. I can't even think about this now, let alone talk about it. Please."

Her eyes went hazy. He knew what that meant: she was talking to another shifter telepathically.

Or listening to one, he amended as her expression tensed. And it was bad news.

Olly bit her bottom lip. Her eyes flicked past Jackson, to where Manu was hovering awkwardly. The hellhound's expression mirrored hers, right down to the way both their gazes kept flickering in and out of focus.

"Flea," Olly muttered. "Oh, God, this is the last thing I need."

"What?"

"It's trouble. One of the tour groups—"

"The couple," Manu interrupted. "Olly, I can't go out there. Not if he's freaking out this badly. Our hellhounds…"

"I know." Olly was completely still, locked in thought.

"Then we'll go. You stay here and man the shop, and Olly and I will go sort out whatever's wrong."

"Don't be stupid, she can't—"

"Yes I can." Olly's voice cut like a knife. "I'll go."

"But—"

"I *will*. I have to stop all this—I have to do better. Get better. Be less myself, or more my old self, or…"

She stuck her chin out and made for the back door as though she wanted to make a grand exit. Jackson's chest twisted as she stopped in the doorway as though she'd walked into a wall. Her shoulders rose like hackles and she pushed forward.

Manu grabbed Jackson's shoulder as he followed her. "Be careful," he muttered.

Jackson was about to shake him off, or swear at him, but something in the hellhound shifter's voice stopped him. It was fear. Not the fear of hellfire, but a normal, human concern.

"I mean be careful *for* her," Manu added, tripping over his words. "She's still—last year—if Flea loses control of his hellhound and looks at her, she can't snap out of it like most people do—"

"Why do you think I'm going with her?" Jackson pushed him off roughly and headed after Olly.

Flea had to be another hellhound shifter. Jackson cursed silently. If Olly couldn't shake off the hellhounds' magically terrifying gaze, why did she *work* with them, for God's sake?

The yard was filled with the barks and howls of agitated dogs. Olly was in the garage, half-hidden behind its open door. Even though she'd just walked through the yard, she was scouring it with eyes as hard as diamonds.

Jackson frowned. *She's half-panicked over whatever is going on and still can't go outside without checking the area first.* A grim certainty lodged in Jackson's chest. There was no way he was leaving here without finding out what was wrong.

12

OLLY

The Puppy Express wasn't all dogsleds—Bob had a couple of snowmobiles, too. Olly and Jackson were on one now, roaring along the track and following Flea's telepathic yelps of unease.

Hellhound! her owl hissed. *We're going straight towards him!*

Yes, well, that's the idea, Olly muttered back. Her owl scratched unhappily, keeping its suspicious attention on the road. And as annoying as that was, at least it meant its attention wasn't on Jackson.

Jackson, perched behind her on the snowmobile. His big, solid body nudging against hers every time they hit a bump in the track. Jackson, who'd turned so instantly protective when he thought she was hurt…

Her stomach hollowed out. *I shouldn't have let him come.*

What? Her owl turned its attention back to her, quick as a whip. *Why not? You told me he's not important, but now you're—*

Luckily, Flea's voice burst on top of anything else it might have said.

Come quick! Please!

We're on our way! she reassured him.

What am I missing? her owl muttered. *There's something you're not telling me. Something I can't see.*

Olly swallowed. *I can't tell you right now.*

Then how can I keep you safe? Flea won't say what's happening and now you won't tell me what's wrong and—corner ahead! Her owl tightened its claws around her ribs.

I see it. She'd run this track a thousand times, on the dogsleds and the snowmobiles, so she wasn't worried about missing the turn. She leaned into the easy curve of the track, and her owl clamped down on her.

Corner! it shrieked. *Can't see past it!*

Olly gasped and almost lost control. The snowmobile fishtailed and Jackson leaned forward, his body heavy against hers as he grabbed the handlebars. Olly shrank in on herself. Her owl's fear echoed in her skull.

Can't see past it—can't prepare—can't know what to do, what's going to happen—

Her pulse thudded in her ears as Jackson righted their course. They turned the corner. There was nothing there: just trees, and snow, and inside her head, Flea's urgent cries.

Jackson cut the engine. "Are you all right?"

His voice was deafening in the sudden silence. Olly drew in a ragged breath that only seemed to half-fill her lungs.

Are you alright? she asked her owl.

It hunkered down low inside her and didn't answer. Flea's cries for help were still knocking against her skull.

"Keep going," she forced out with the little air she'd managed to suck in. She grabbed at pieces of Flea's words, knowing Jackson couldn't hear him. "They're at the lake. Sweetheart—Sweetheart Lake. It's a mile, maybe a bit more—"

"I know where it is." Jackson pulled her around to face him, not roughly, but her skin still burned under her clothes everywhere he touched her. "It's you I'm worried about."

Don't be. "I've got it under control," she said, hoping it wasn't a lie and knowing it was. Meaghan was right. *Jackson* was right. Something was wrong with her, seriously wrong, and it had taken him coming back for her to see it.

What's wrong? her owl demanded. *You have to tell me!*

I almost crashed! She bit her lip. *You were so scared about all the things you don't know, that I almost—* Olly shook her head. She couldn't think about this right now. Out loud, she said, "Please. Let's just go."

"All right." Jackson didn't hide how reluctant he was. "But I'm driving."

She slid onto the seat behind him, hesitated, and wrapped her arms around him as he set off. He was too tall for her to see past, so she had to rely on her other senses. She strained her ears so hard her jaw ached.

Her owl scratched for attention. *Why did you let him drive?*

Because you almost made us crash!

We couldn't see where we were going! If we don't know what's in front of us and around us and, and about us, something might sneak up on us!

So it's better that we wipe out? Olly gritted her teeth.

There was a hesitation, then her owl said, *I'm sorry. I didn't mean to make us crash. I just needed to know what's ahead. I always need to know what's ahead.*

Yes, she thought back fiercely, not ready to give up on being angry yet. *I know! All year, you haven't let me do anything without checking and checking and checking every goddamn thing, and it hasn't done anything except make my life worse! Even my best friend thinks I've gone crazy. And Jackson…*

She could feel it already: her owl gathering itself up to say, Oh *him, he* doesn't matter, and she couldn't bear it. Not while she was sitting here pressed against him, her skin still warm from his concern for her,

her heart aching for everything that had happened between them.

But it works, her owl insisted. *If we have all the pieces of information beforehand, we know what to expect. Nothing has snuck up on us all year!*

Jackson did! Olly couldn't stop herself. *You tell me when a tourist sneezes three blocks away but you didn't even tell me he was there in the kitchen, staring at me?*

Him? He—but he— Her owl seethed. *You said he wasn't important!*

Well, he is!

The Sweetheart Lake rest stop was in a small clearing overlooking a mountain lake… or pond, really; it wasn't that large. This time of year, it was frozen over, and made a romantic backdrop to the picnic table and Puppy Express mailbox, where visitors could post cards or letters to be delivered by dogsled on Christmas Eve.

Flea had set out earlier with a young couple who'd been so wrapped up in each other that Olly's uncle wouldn't have let them take a sled out without a guide even if they'd asked. She doubted they'd heard a word of Flea's safety talk. She was surprised *they* were the group causing trouble, and not one of the boisterous families that had booked in today. How the hell did two people cause trouble when they couldn't even tear their eyes off one another?

She waited for her owl to say something sarcastic, but it was unusually quiet. It hadn't said anything since she told it Jackson was important. She didn't want to think about what that might mean. She just hoped it didn't figure out the truth. There was too much going wrong with this day already without her owl confirming what she already knew: that love or not, she and Jackson could never be together.

We're almost here, she called out to Flea. They were coming up the last twisty bit of the trail, choked with brush and trees, hiding their view of whatever had happened at the lake. Olly leaned forward so she could peer over Jackson's shoulder. She told herself it wasn't so she could press herself closer against him, as though she was squeezing as much contact from him out of this situation as possible.

"Any idea what we're getting into here?" Jackson called over his shoulder.

"No," Olly called back over the engine's roar. "Flea just keeps yelling about something being wrong."

Jackson snorted. "Yelling in your head, you mean. We're the loudest things here. I can't hear a thing other than this machine."

They came around the last turn. There was the lake, snow-covered ice stretching clean and pristine under the winter sky. There were the dogs, milling around next to the picnic table, still hitched to the sled, as if they'd simply been abandoned. No people were in sight at all.

Jackson braked and cut the machine's engine, and abruptly the only sound was the barking and whining of the impatient dogs, who were now getting tangled up in their harnesses trying to get to the newly arrived humans.

"Where the hell is everybody?" Jackson asked. Olly started to dismount to catch the dogs, but he caught her arm, keeping her on the machine while he looked around for danger.

Look out! her owl shrieked at her.

Olly wrenched free and leaped off the snowmobile in a pure instinctive reaction, so fast one of her feet got caught on the running board. Her owl tried to shift and make her run and hide behind a tree at the same time. She stumbled over feet that suddenly didn't feel the right size or shape and found herself ass-deep in snow at the side of the picnic area. Jackson hastily slid off the machine after her.

"Olly! What happened? Are you—"

"I'm sorry! It's just me!" Flea bounded up from behind a snowy bush. His winter coat was caked with snow, and in the shadow of the hood, his eyes were hellfire red.

Olly had managed to hold on to her human form, but that didn't stop her from flying back to twelve months ago, when she'd first seen Flea and the other hellhound shifters.

Terror rolled over her. Terror that made no *sense*, but nothing made sense, because she hadn't seen the men approach, hadn't heard them come into the shop—the bell above the door hadn't rung, the door was still *locked*, she hadn't opened up yet, how had they gotten in?—but they were in, and their eyes were like windows to every secret fear she'd ever hidden herself away from…

"Olly! Olly, can you hear me? It's okay. You're not—get away from her, you're not helping!"

Jackson. Jackson's voice, heavy with concern and sharp with an edge that didn't cut into her but *around* her, as though it was carving a protective space around them both. She drew a shaky breath. It was so familiar. Why was it familiar? She tried to push herself up, using the counter as support, but there was no counter, she was outside, her gloved hands crunching on snow…

That was it. She knew why it sounded familiar. Because *that*, the shop and the counter and the hellhound shifters who moved so quickly between shapes she couldn't keep count of them, was then, and *this*, sitting in the snow with the winter air sharp on her face, was now. Two separate occasions.

And Jackson was there in both, wrapping himself around her like armor.

She drew a ragged breath and opened her eyes. The first thing she saw was Jackson's face. His eyes pulled her in, warm and brown and oh God, she was lost and found at the same time.

He's not—

Olly clamped down on her owl before it could utter another syllable.

"Say something." It wasn't not an order, or a plea, but something in between that tugged at Olly's heart.

She wet her lips. "Did I scream?"

"Do you ever scream?" His lips outlined a smile, but his eyes were still deep with concern. "You went quiet. Too quiet."

I'm always quiet. The words didn't make it out of her mouth.

"This is why I couldn't go out there and tell them myself," Flea moaned from somewhere behind her.

She met Jackson's eyes. Met them properly, not letting herself sink in but keeping a distance that let her ask a silent question that didn't need any shifter telepathy, and see his answer.

He nodded and her heart fluttered. Everything felt old and new at the same time. Even this. Just *looking* at someone and letting herself be looked at back, instead of ducking and hiding.

With Jackson's silent understanding giving her strength, she twisted around to find Flea.

Her owl bristled. But there he was, hunched over a good six feet away, all anxious gangling limbs and guilt and, most importantly, *dark* eyes.

He's not a monster, she reminded herself, breathing easy, *and he's not here to hurt me. I should have known…*

She bit her lip. She'd had all the information she needed to figure that it was Flea jumping out of the bush, not some stranger and not some monster from her nightmares. Her owl should have known that, too. It had all the same information he did. Including all the *hundreds* of times Flea and the others had crept nervously up to her and apologized for the effect their hellfire terror had on her.

"I'm sorry!" Flea blurted out as he saw she was looking at him.

"Just tell us what's going on," Jackson said, glancing at the lake and the dogs. The dog team had given up on anything interesting ever happening again, and were mostly lying down. At least Flea had had the sense to set the sled brake when he'd stopped the dog team, so they hadn't gone anywhere.

"They broke the rules," Flea moaned. Fire burned in his eyes, angry and righteous, and he covered his face with his hands. "It keeps happening. Whenever my hellhound sees someone doing something *wrong*, it takes over. I couldn't do anything. I panicked and hid."

"Oh!" Olly said, because suddenly his panic made sense. Jackson was looking puzzled now. Turning to him, she explained, "Hellhounds sometimes go after wrongdoers. Meaghan told me that."

"I don't want to hurt anyone," Flea whimpered, hands still over his face.

Olly patted his shoulder. It was hard to be afraid of him in this state, and she could feel her own panic receding. "You won't," she reassured him. What would Meaghan say in this situation, or Caine? "You have it under control. You're going to be okay."

"Okay, that part makes sense," Jackson said. "So what rule did they break, exactly?"

"The one about not leaving the picnic area," Flea murmured.

Olly and Jackson looked at each other, and Jackson broke into a grin. "Are you seriously telling me," he said, "that all of this panic is because they went for a *walk*?"

"The trails can be confusing in the winter, and not all of them are well groomed," Olly pointed out. "They could get lost. We'd better go find them."

"Not actually a problem," Jackson remarked, and he pointed across the lake.

The couple had just emerged from the trees. They were hand in hand, and their giggling carried across the lake.

"There's a ski trail that loops around the lake," Olly said. "They're on that." Even her owl had relaxed. There was no danger. No one was in trouble.

"Hey!" Jackson called, waving to the couple and then cupping his hands around his mouth. "Get back here! Visitors aren't allowed on the trails without going through the safety seminar! Right?" he murmured in an aside to Olly. "I assume that hasn't changed since I've been gone."

The couple simply waved back, as if they thought Jackson was merely being friendly.

Olly nodded. "Yeah, they aren't supposed to go out there without a safety seminar and a map. It's not that dangerous, though. I mean, it's a groomed ski trail, not the middle of—*What are they doing?*"

The couple had started out onto the ice. Even from here, Olly could see and hear it creaking and settling. Behind her, Flea moaned a deep moan that was almost a growl.

"Keep it together!" Jackson snapped over his shoulder at the hellhound. "If you shift, that's not gonna help! Hey! You! The ice isn't safe—get back to the trail!"

He waved his arms vigorously, but all that happened was another cheerful wave from the tourist couple. They clearly saw nothing wrong.

"And this is why we have a safety seminar," Olly muttered. Inside her, her owl was going wild, wanting her to shift and fly out of reach of danger. *There is no danger to us,* she told it sternly. *The danger is on the ice.*

"Get off the ice!" Jackson bellowed across the lake. "It's not safe!"

"In a minute!" the man called back. "Got something to do first!"

With that, he went to one knee in front of the woman.

Under other circumstances, it would be very romantic. The frozen trees and snow-covered banks of the lake made a lovely backdrop. But the cricking and cracking of the ice was becoming louder.

"Get off!" Jackson yelled one more time, and shook his head. "Idiots. They're gonna get themselves killed. Flea, *stay there.*" The hellhound was inching forward, looking one panic attack away from shifting. Olly quietly put herself on Jackson's other side.

"Can't we get them off the ice?" she asked.

"More people going out onto the ice is just gonna make it worse. What I'm gonna do," Jackson said, "is circle around to where I can get to them from the trail. Flea, you've got blankets in the sled, right? Start getting them out. If they fall in, we're going to have some hypothermic tourists on our hands."

Flea turned back to the sled, and that was when things went wrong.

The dogs assumed that their driver coming back meant it was time to go again—and there was nothing sled dogs loved more than running. All of them jumped to their feet and flung themselves into their harness. The sled brake—a metal claw underneath the sled that dug into the snow to stop the sled from moving—pulled loose under their combined efforts, and suddenly the sled lurched into motion.

Straight forward. Which right now was pointed at the lake.

At Olly and Jackson.

Olly was frozen in place. She couldn't move, paralyzed with her owl's panic and indecision. *We need all the information—figure the angles—decide which way to go—*

Then Jackson pushed her out of the way. She tumbled into the snow, and looked up just in time to see the excited dogs slam into Jackson. Under most circumstances, the worst that would've happened was that he would have been pushed into the snow by a bunch of overly friendly dogs who had obviously forgotten in their tiny dog brains that they were hauling a sled behind them, but in this case the whole mess of them—Jackson, dogs, and sled—went hurtling out onto the ice.

And through the ice.

Farther out on the lake, there were screams, but Olly only had eyes for Jackson as the ice broke under him and he plunged into the winter-cold water with a half-dozen thrashing dogs on top of him.

"Jackson!" she screamed.

Her owl's indecision was gone. All either of them could think about now was helping Jackson.

"Call the dogs back!" she shouted to Flea, not daring to look back at him in case she caught his eye and got caught in hellfire terror again. "You can talk to them, right? Get them out of the water!"

Flea's guilt and confusion burst against her mind. She shook it off and ran into the freezing lake, sloshing through the half-ice, half-water until she could grab hold of the lead dog's harness. Poor lovely Missus, one of the older and most sensible Puppy Express dogs, was whining as she fought her own instincts to get out of the water, the hellhound's desire to help the tourists warring against her own growing panic as the sled harness tangled around her and her team.

"Jackson!" she screamed. Where was he? He'd hit the water—where? *Owl, help me!*

I think—I think— Her owl's thought stuttered in her mind. *He should be—there!*

With a yell, Jackson surfaced. He was a few yards away, waist-deep in freezing water and soaked through. Behind him, the tourists were screaming and thrashing as they struggled with their soaked clothes and floating chunks of ice in the bitterly cold water; once the ice had started to break under Jackson and the dogs, it had all gone down in a chain reaction.

But Olly's gaze caught on Jackson, like a finger on a jagged splinter. She had already started toward him in the water before she was dragged back by Missus, who wanted no part of going deeper into the freezing water.

"Get the dogs out!" Jackson told her. "I've got ice-rescue training. I'll get them."

She'd be no use to him if the panicking dogs dragged her under; she knew that. The faster she got them out, the faster she could help Jackson. "Go!" she urged the dogs, and half-waded, half-swam back toward shore, dragging Missus. "Hike. Hike!"

"Hike" was the sled-dog command for "Run," the sled dogs' favorite command in the whole world. Their legs pumped like pistons, and they heaved themselves out of the water into the snow, where Olly thrust Missus at Flea.

"Got her?" She looked back without waiting for an answer. Jackson was farther out in the lake now, thrashing his way toward the flailing, yelling tourists.

He had ice rescue training, but so did she; it was standard for Puppy Express employees. She wasn't going to leave him out there alone. "Flea," she said, her teeth already starting to chatter as she stood in her soaked clothes. "Get the dogs tied up, *securely* this time, and then follow me. We need to make a human chain to get them to shore."

She didn't realize until she had already waded into the water that she hadn't been afraid of him at all. Not even slightly worried. It had never occurred to her that he wouldn't obey her order. Out in the lake, Jackson was helping the tourist couple to shallower water, one at a time.

"Take them as I hand them to you and help them to shore," Jackson called, floundering toward her with his arm around the panicking woman.

Olly took the woman from him, and turned around—with only the slightest hesitation—to hand her off to Flea, who helped her ashore. "Some romantic getaway!" Olly heard her say as they floundered out of the lake.

Jackson was on his way back with the male half of the couple. Between the two of them, Jackson and Olly helped him onto the shore. He was shivering, his teeth chattering, and seemed to be struggling against them, trying to go back.

"What are you doing, man?" Jackson demanded, giving him a shake. "You'll drown out there!"

"Ring—gotta get the ring—"

"Forget the ring, Rick!" the woman exclaimed. At the sled, now secured again, Flea was bundling her into blankets. "You almost got us killed with your 'romantic' proposal!"

"I know—I wanted… be perfect," he forced out. "For you."

The woman softened and put her arms around him. Olly didn't dare look at Jackson, didn't want to risk meeting his eyes again and having another of those moments of shared understanding.

"Here," Flea said, handing blankets to each of them. He seemed a little more confident now that things were relatively back to normal. "You two are soaked, too."

"There's not room for all of us on the sled," Jackson said. "Get them back to town. We'll be behind you on the snowmobile."

Flea nodded and untied the dogs. They surged into motion; getting wet didn't bother them in the slightest, with their thick water-shedding fur to protect them. The sled raced off among the trees. Olly watched them disappear.

Olly opened her mouth. The words *We should follow them* were on the tip of her tongue.

And then Jackson took her hand. Hesitantly. Carefully. As though he was as nervous as she suddenly was.

He was a blur at the edge of her vision, wreathed in plumes of vapor where his breath hit the frozen air, but her skin burned where his hand was touching hers.

"Are you alright?" he asked.

She didn't say, *You're the human, I should be asking if you're* alright, even though she definitely should have. She didn't reassure him or wave away his concerns. Because she wasn't alright. Not even close.

And she absolutely didn't say the next words that appeared in her mind, blossoming like the first buds of spring pushing their way through the frost.

God, I love you.

Her owl peered at her, then out through her eyes at him, then back at her. *What? What did you just say?*

Olly bit her lip.

What do you mean, you love him?

You never noticed? She could have sobbed. Instead she felt as though every bone in her body had turned to stone. She ached with stillness. *What about last Christmas?*

Last Christmas? Her owl wasn't moving, either. Olly's brain lurched. Her owl was stalking-still, and it was stalking *her.*

Last Christmas we decided he wasn't our mate, it said firmly. *He was… interesting… but there was nothing there. And the only thing you've said since then is that you're* not *in love with him,* her owl accused her, and it was true, she'd been so careful—*But this means…*

You said he wasn't our mate, Olly reminded it helplessly. *What else was I meant to do?*

He's not. A pause. *I can't have gotten that wrong. I would have known! Everyone says—everyone knows—that you don't know until… But… I was getting everything wrong… and you just said, you said, getting things wrong, that's nothing new…*

Out in the world outside of Olly's head, where the air was biting into every inch of her exposed skin and sending sharp claws everywhere the water had soaked in, Jackson moved closer to her. His breath swirled like fog around her.

She closed her eyes.

You're hurting, her owl said, its voice half-wondering, half-aghast. *This is what's been wrong all year? You've been hurting and you didn't tell me?*

It doesn't matter!

It does *matter. All this because…*

It broke off suddenly. Olly trembled. She could guess why it had fallen silent; Jackson was right in front of her.

She could hear him. Smell him. She wanted to open her eyes. She wanted to never open her eyes again. She'd gotten everything wrong, first last Christmas and every day since, and now her owl knew just how broken to pieces she was and if she opened her eyes now, if she looked at Jackson now, really looked at him, then he'd know, too.

"Olly, you don't look good. I know it's—" He broke off and swore. "I know it's none of my business. I know I can't fix things between us but at least let me—"

Fix things. Olly's owl ruffled its feathers uneasily. *Fix this? It's not broken. I wasn't* wrong. *I'm always right. I… I wanted to be right, to make sure you would be happy…*

I was happy, Olly thought miserably. *Because I was in love with him. Until I found out I wasn't meant to be in love with him, and now…*

You still are! You're in love with him and you've been in love with him all this time and you told me it wasn't important! Olly felt like she was being pecked to pieces from the inside out.

It's not like that—

Yes it is! Her owl ruffled itself up to its maximum size. *He* is *important. And all my carefulness all year hasn't helped at all, has it? It hasn't fixed anything. You were scared by the hellhounds, and I thought being extra, especially careful would show you there's nothing to be scared of…*

It wasn't the hellhounds that left me like this. She hadn't hidden this from her owl, at least; she'd only just figured it out herself. *It was realizing that Jackson wasn't my mate. I was so sure, and then, when he wasn't… How could I be sure of anything, after that?*

"Let me help," Jackson whispered. "Tell me what you need and I'll do it."

I need you, she didn't dare to say, and her owl screeched in alarm.

You what? But you… But we… Oh. I got it all wrong. Her owl sounded wondering. *Now I know what to do, though! I'll fix everything!*

Images flashed in her mind. The moment the man fell through the ice. The speed and angle of his arm as the ring box flew out of it.

You're in love! That's what made you happy! If I'm going to make you be happy again—

Olly twisted away from Jackson and dove into the lake. Her owl was in control now, driving them both. Cold swallowed her whole.

"Olly!" she heard Jackson yell behind her.

"I know what I'm doing!" she shouted back, or tried to, but her lungs were seizing up with cold, and it came out as a breathy gasp. *You know what we're doing, right?* she thought at her owl. *What ARE we doing? Is someone still in the water?*

Down. Her owl was brutally insistent. *We need to get the ring. It's there. I know it. They fell through here—his arm jerked—the angle…*

Her owl pushed them down. She kicked through the water. It was easier in some ways, swimming under the surface, but it was so incredibly cold.

We're going to be all right, her owl thought at her. *We can hold our breath much longer than this. Let's see, left forty degrees, now turn—*

Her owl might be right about holding their breath, but it was so *cold.* Ice water was pouring through every gap in Olly's clothing and she wasn't sure which direction was up and her owl was doing *math.*

There!

Olly kicked out, kicked down. She thrust out one hand, groping with fingers that rapidly went numb. Something square-ish settled into her palm, and she closed her fingers around it.

*Yes! Because humans, and love, so you need—*Her owl was pleading now. Actually *pleading.* Olly felt as though her brain was splitting in two.

Can we get out of here now? She struggled to kick herself up toward the surface. Her arms and legs were leaden with cold.

It's like flying, her owl's voice echoed in her mind, and for the first time she sensed a quaver of uncertainty in it. *Arms and legs instead of wings and water instead of wind but—oh.*

What? Olly thought at it desperately.

We're moving slower than I expected.

Olly's lips parted in shock. Cold darted between them, sharp as a knife against her teeth.

I might have been… wrong.

Her head hit something solid. Stars flared in front of her eyes and winked out one by one. Water filled her mouth.

We're under the ice. Oh fuck oh fuck. How did we—

Her owl was very still inside her. *Oh. Whoops?*

13

JACKSON

He saw where she went under.

There wasn't time to be scared. Years of training kicked in. Scouts. Mountain rescue volunteering. Working as a deputy, in the mountains where the biggest killer was the cold.

Jackson blocked out everything except *next step, remember process, there's a proper way to do these things, remember your training.*

She hadn't come up yet.

Jackson knew this pond. He'd been here in mid-summer, when the chilly water was a draw, not a death-trap.

He knew the water here should only be chest-deep on Olly. If she hadn't come up—

He moved automatically. Into the water. *Breathe through the rush of cold. Relax; don't let your body flinch. Focus.* His foot hit a submerged branch. *Keep moving.* Panicking now wouldn't help anyone. Wouldn't help her. Wouldn't help him help her.

It must have only been a few seconds, but it felt like eternity. He knew why: adrenaline. Shock.

Knowing didn't help when he reached the edge of the ice and Olly wasn't there.

Roaring filled his ears. The evening was closing in, but there was enough light that he should have been able to see Olly's blonde hair or the flash of her pale face beneath the surface. But there was nothing.

Don't panic. Don't even think. Next step.

Jackson took a deep breath and ducked under the water.

The light from the grotto barely penetrated beneath the surface. The ice glowed blue-white and beneath it—black.

Jackson had worked winters before. He'd volunteered with search and rescue teams during high school and kept it up on the job. He'd considered being a ranger, at one point, but you didn't need to go deep into the wilderness to save people from the great outdoors. Knowing what the merciless outdoors could do to a person was the kick in the ass he needed if he ever found himself whining about convincing some drunk idiot to sleep it off indoors, or follow up a missing person report when his own bed was calling to him.

He'd never lost anyone in Pine Valley, but he'd pulled bodies from thawed rivers before and—

He cut the thought off and buried it.

The water's not moving. This was a pond, not a river. If Olly had lost consciousness she wouldn't have drifted far.

He searched the blackness. Nothing. Nothing, oh God, and all his training was telling him to surface and take another breath but he couldn't stop, couldn't leave her here if she was—

Something pulsed in his chest.

He moved without thinking. Strong strokes in water that was trying to sap the life from his limbs. He collided with Olly so fast they both overturned in the water, her feet kicking against his ribs, then his arms were around her and he was kicking up. Ice. Thick. He braced himself against the lakebed and thrust up with his elbow. Once. Twice.

Crack!

The ice gave. Jackson burst through it. Air burned his mouth, his lungs. It was the only sound in the universe. Olly's body was heavy. Limp.

No no no—

Jackson wasn't even sure the voice in his head was his. It didn't sound like him. But he wasn't hearing right anyway. He hauled Olly through the water and dragged her onto the shore, babbling out loud.

"Olly, don't do this to me." That was something from his training, wasn't it. Talk to the person. Reassure them. The words mattered less than the tone of his voice. "Don't you dare fucking die."

Okay, the tone of his voice probably wasn't going to help.

He grabbed her, held onto her. Her head fell onto his shoulder. Cold. Everything was cold. Was she breathing? He had to start rescue breathing if not. Desperately he listened for a hint of air through her parted lips.

And then Olly choked. Gasped. *Breathed,* her eyes flickering open, wide, searching for his, her gulping breaths the most beautiful thing he'd ever heard.

"You're all right," he said, "you're fine, I've got you," stupid words, but tone was what was important, a reassuring tone, "God, Olly, I thought—"

He gulped.

I love you.

He could say it. If tone was what was important, not words. But those words were unforgiveable even if she couldn't hear them.

"Let's get you somewhere warm," he muttered. "Back to the Puppy Express."

She was shaking, too out of it to respond. Her face was icy white. Jackson licked his lips, which were suddenly numb.

It was too far. She needed warmth and shelter right now. Not when they got back.

But there were ski cottages and warmup cabins scattered throughout the valley. The nearest was close enough that Bob spent half his time at the bar complaining about it ruining the ambience of the Sweethearts trail. He could take her there.

"It'll be all right," he said, bundling her onto the snowmobile and starting the engine. "I'll look after you."

Idiot words. Nonsense.

The cottage was empty. Windows dark, snow around it untouched. Jackson drove right to the door and brushed snow away from the step.

Bless Pine Valley, he thought as he found a key attached to a magnet shaped like a dragon. *And bless Jasper Heartwell.* When he'd first moved here he'd thought the locals were insane, leaving keys out where anyone could find them. But locked doors were as good as a death sentence out in the mountains. Leaving a key out was being a good neighbor who wanted their neighbors to stay alive.

He barged through the door with Olly limp in his arms.

It was cool inside. Not the frigid, lifeless cold of the air outside, but close. No one had been around yet that winter to turn the heating on.

But the power was still on. Bless Jasper Heartwell, again. He cranked the thermostat and carried Olly through to the bathroom.

Undressing her was the least sexy thing he'd ever done. He pulled her boots off. Her socks were soaked through, as was her sweater when he peeled her jacket off. She was wet all the way through to her woolen underlayer.

"But you're still shivering," he told her, running a towel briskly over her limbs. One of her hands was clenched white-knuckled around something. "And holding onto this, this…" He frowned. She was holding a ring box. Her fingers were clenched so tightly he couldn't open them.

She jumped in for that?

He shook himself. "Shivering. Grip. Two good signs. But you're not talking, and that's—that's—"

His mind went white.

"Bed," he said, jolting himself into action. "Warm you up."

There were emergency supplies back at the Puppy Express. Heat packs. A phone. Other shifters, who could call the doctor even without a phone. All the things Olly needed to keep her safe, to make sure she didn't—

Bed. The bedroom was upstairs. He took them three at a time, Olly too quiet and too cold in his arms.

There was an electric blanket on the bed, just as he'd hoped. He turned it on high and slid Olly between the sheets, bundling them around her. It wasn't enough.

He pulled his clothes off, noticing for the first time that he was shivering, too.

"Olly, can you hear me?" He slid in beside her. His body didn't feel like it was his own. He buffed her hands between his to warm them and tucked them into her armpits, then wrapped his arms around her. "Olly, please. Say something."

She stirred. "Jackson…"

14

OLLY

It was like a dream. Water sloshed around outside her boots and waterproof snow pants, and nothing else. Like an echo of sensation. Then an icy finger slid down one side of her boots. And another.

Something was wrong. She couldn't still be in the water. Could she? That was the last thing she remembered, true, but…

There was a distant sound, like wind whistling across a chimney-top. Breath. Her own? Yes. She was breathing.

That wouldn't be happening if she was still in the water.

But she felt… odd. The sound of rasping breath was *hers*, she was almost sure, but it was strangely distant. Was she in her owl's form? That would explain… something.

Her head spun, if it was her head. She felt as though she was clawing through darkness, but without claws or hands. Or eyes to see the darkness. Or her owl's eyes to see the darkness through. But if she didn't have those, then…

She wasn't sure she had a head to shake to try to clear it but when she did, her mind exploded in a kaleidoscope of nauseating lights. She stopped and waited for things to start making sense. They didn't.

Where are we? Olly asked her owl.

There was no reply.

Olly went completely still. *Owl?*

A skitter of claws in the shadows. The tension in Olly's lungs eased. So she had lungs, too. *There you are. What's happening? Why do I feel so strange? Are you—*

Why are you asking me? Her owl's voice was thin and ashamed. Olly frowned.

What do you mean?

You shouldn't ask me anything. I almost got us killed. I'm sorry. I don't want to hurt you anymore.

Her owl's voice grew fainter. Distant. Olly chased after it. *Owl, what are you—*

"Olly, wake up! Olly, can you hear me?"

Olly fell back into her body with a thud. "Jackson?" she tried to say, but the word didn't make it the whole way out. Her teeth clacked together.

"You're awake. Thank God. I thought—"

He broke off and Olly forced her eyes open. For a moment, they wouldn't focus. Panic rippled through her.

She had no idea where she was or what was happening.

"Where—" she began. A shiver shook through her body, so intense she couldn't speak through it. And she still didn't know where she was or who was there and—

"Hey. I've got you." Strong arms wrapped around her. Jackson. Oh, God, Jackson. Another shiver ripped through her. "You're safe. We're in one of the cottages along the edge of Rock River. It's just you and me."

Relief rushed through her and something else, too; something bright and dangerous like the sun breaking through the clouds. Olly blinked hard until her eyes started to focus and as soon as they did it was as though the whole world snapped into shape around her.

She'd felt Jackson's arms around her. Now she felt every individual hair on them. On his *bare* arms. His bare arms around her …

Her eyes widened. "Why am I naked?" she hissed.

Jackson's cheeks reddened. "Your clothes were soaked," he said gruffly. Olly shivered at the gravel in his voice. "You were freezing. We both were. I…" He pulled away, briefly, then wrapped her up in his arms again, ducking his head and murmuring something about *body heat.*

"We were in the water." The pieces were all there in her head, Olly just had to put them together. Easy. Or it would have been if Jackson wasn't right there, warm and solid and too… too good to be true. "You—you followed me in? After…"

Her stomach lurched. She'd jumped in the water. Her *owl* had jumped in the water, with her body. It had screeched something about being in love, and making things right, and jumped into the lake after that stupid engagement ring.

"Did I at least manage to get the ring?"

"Yeah, you did." Jackson managed a weak laugh. "And you jumped into the lake to get some stranger's engagement ring. Why?"

"My *owl* jumped in," Olly said automatically. "I mean—it jumped in, but in my body, because it can't fly underwater, and it was useful having… fingers…"

"At first I thought—" He caught himself, his mouth twisting. Olly stayed perfectly still. He was obviously trying to keep his thoughts out of his words and off his face—but he didn't hide the way his arms tightened protectively around her. "I don't know what I thought."

Her chest suddenly felt very stiff and tight. "I jumped in to get the ring. My owl thought it was important. Because—because…"

Oh.

Was *that* why her owl had jumped in the lake?

She felt as though she'd been standing staring at a cliff at the end of the world, and had only just remembered she could fly.

You idiot, she thought, fondly. She didn't know whether she was talking to herself or her owl. Both, probably.

Jackson's voice was a worried, wondrous rumble against her chest.

"You're warmer now, you're awake, you're going to be all right. Power's on, so we've got heat, we just…" Jackson looked away and cursed. "I'm doing this all wrong. Words aren't going to help, are they? Even if you had a reason for… what you did… I have to do things your way. "

She didn't understand what he meant until he unwrapped himself from around her.

Jackson slipped out of bed and stood on the floor in the middle of the room. He took a deep breath. It shook, slightly, and Olly's eyes swung to him like they were on magnets.

"I should have known better than to chase you down. Just one more mistake in—" He winced and didn't meet her eye. "I know you need to scope things out before you let them into your life. And I'm not saying I get to be back in your life, but…"

His voice trailed off. He shrugged helplessly.

"I'm not going to force you to tell me what's happening with you, Olly. But I know the only way you're going to let me in is if you know what you're getting yourself into. So here we are. Look as long as you like, ask me any question… I'm all yours."

Olly sat up, eyes wide. She drew the blankets around her like she was huddling beneath her wings.

Jackson stood still at the end of the bed. Bare-armed, bare-chested, bare… everything. Almost.

She *knew* Jackson. Or she had, last year. And he knew her and she knew what he was doing, right now.

Not pushing. Not cornering her. Letting her find her own weird, fucked-up way back to trusting him.

He didn't know that it wasn't *him* she needed to figure out how to trust.

Jackson didn't meet her eyes. He stood there like a man on the gallows. Like she had any right to judge *him*.

Olly swallowed. Normally her owl would already be judging him, of course, but it was still strangely silent.

It was just… her. Just her and him.

She slipped her feet to the floor and padded over to him, still wrapped in one of the comforters. It was like carrying around her own safe, snug tree knot to hide in.

She didn't have any right to judge him. But he was right. She hadn't let herself *see* him, not really, and forget her owl, *she* wanted that. So she walked around him. Slowly, her eyes devouring every detail.

He'd put on muscle. He carried himself differently—heavier. Like there was a weight on his shoulders.

She frowned as she crept behind him. She had a pretty good idea what that weight might be, and it made anger flicker inside her.

She was still frowning when she made her way back in front of him. This was easier, feeling his eyes on her. And harder, because even though knowing he was watching her meant she remembered to keep her expression still, she didn't know how long she could keep up the act.

Maybe it was a good thing he'd been gone so long, after all, or maybe it would have been easier if he'd stayed in Pine Valley and she'd had day after day of looking at him and trying to make her heart make sense.

She would never know.

She didn't look into his face. Not yet. She looked at his hands first. She picked up one, then the other, turning them over and exploring the familiar calluses. The tiny scar on his thumb, the rough skin on his knuckles because God forbid he use hand cream like a normal person. His wrists and forearms. His upper arms, the sweep of bone and muscle at his shoulders. She stood close, letting her breath whisper across his skin. He shivered.

She looked up at his face.

He'd grown his hair out. She'd noticed that already, but now she saw why.

He grabbed her hand as she reached to brush his hair aside and look closer. "Don't—"

"You said I could look."

He grimaced. "I did."

She pushed his hair aside gently. A pink new scar ran across his forehead, from above his left eyebrow to the hairline at his temple. "What happened?"

"A work thing."

She waited, because if he was still the Jackson she knew, he'd fill in the details for her.

"I got shot."

"*What?*" She grabbed him, as though she could reach back in time and drag him away from whatever idiot situation he'd gotten himself into to get himself— "Shot? Who shot you? Why? When?"

"I—"

"Tell me!"

"Wait, wait." He was still holding her hand. It felt very good. "I'll tell you, but let's do it in bed okay? We're both still chilled. No need to get hypothermic again while standing around and talking in a cold bedroom."

He had a point. She let him pull her to the bed, and as he did, she became aware of something that had been going on for some time; she had just been too distracted to notice. Normally her owl would have alerted her, but her owl was apparently not speaking to her right now.

Olly! Olly!

Flea? she thought back at him.

Oh, thank goodness. You're okay! You didn't come back! I was just about to go out looking.

The idea of Flea showing up at the cabin and finding them both naked in bed made a bubble of laughter rise up in her. *Don't worry. We both got soaked, so we decided to hole up in one of the shelter cabins rather than try to make it back on the snowmobile. We're going to dry out here and then head home.*

"Olly?" Jackson said. She held up a hand.

Oh good. I'll tell the others, Flea said, his mental voice growing distant.

Thanks.

She looked up at Jackson, wrapped up in the blankets with his skin pressed against hers. "Flea," she explained.

"Oh, right. The, uh…" He touched his forehead. "Telepathy thing. Better than telephones, I bet. Did you tell him, um…" He hesitated.

She felt a blush rise to her cheeks. "I told him we decided to dry out at the cabin before heading back. I think that's all he needs to know."

"Fair enough."

Beneath the blankets, her skin was warming against his. This close up, she could see the scar clearly. It was so obvious now that she noticed it. "I think you were about to tell me what happened to you."

"Yeah." He put his hands over hers, under the covers. "So, I guess where it starts… well, I never really had much training for the deputy job here. I just kind of fell into it. Mostly because nobody else wanted to come this far into the mountains, least of all the actual sheriff. I was basically a glorified shifter babysitter."

"That suited us."

"It suited me, too." He brushed his fingers over hers. "But I guess I'm meant for it, because I fell into it again as soon as I left. At a bigger sheriff's office, this time. With an actual budget. More colleagues. And bigger problems." He let out a heavy breath. "There was this griffin shifter, Hardwick—we ended up working together a lot. Everyone knew we worked well together. But they didn't know he was a shifter, of course. It was nice for him, being around someone he could share his secret with. We became friends."

He paused and took a steadying breath, and Olly waited. This, at least, she was good at: the patience of an owl, absorbing all the information, trying to understand.

"It happened when we were busting a drug dealer in this old warehouse by the docks. Hardwick and I went in first. We did that a lot, because Hardwick has shifter abilities; he's stronger, faster, and he can tell when people are lying. He said it's a griffin thing."

He paused again. The words came hard, each sentence forced out past a moment's indecision.

"But I was distracted."

"By what?" Olly asked softly.

The answer was almost too quiet to hear. "By thoughts of you."

Sick guilt choked her. He'd been shot because of *her*?

"No!" he said quickly, reading the shame on her face like an open book. "Don't blame yourself. It wasn't you, Olly. It was me. I ran from the mountains, ran from you. But I couldn't leave you behind. I thought about you all the time. I woke to thoughts of you and dreamed of you at night."

He paused again. She squeezed his hands in wordless encouragement.

"Right before I went in, Hardwick turned to me and said, 'Are you good to do this?' I said yes; what else was I going to say?" His mouth twisted in a faint, unhappy smile. "Hardwick just looked at me, and he said, 'You're lying. If you need to take a backseat on this one, partner, tell me now.'"

"But you didn't," Olly whispered. *Because admitting something's wrong would mean admitting you couldn't handle it. It would mean admitting how out of control you were.*

Her owl shuffled uncomfortably inside her.

"No," he said. "I didn't. I told Hardwick again that I was fine, and he looked away, and I knew right then that he knew I'd been lying to myself for months. How could he not know? But he backed me up, like he always did. He didn't say a word, just went in at my side, like always. And then... then the shooting started..."

His hands felt cold in hers. She stroked the backs of his hands with her thumbs, and tried not to let her gaze keep being drawn to the scar at his temple.

"This one guy, he almost got the drop on Hardwick, because Hardwick was too busy covering me. Hardwick knew how out of it I was. He could see it better than I could."

"Did Hardwick..." she began hesitantly. "Is he—"

Jackson shook his head. "No, he's fine. I took the shooter out before he got my partner, but I took a bullet in the process."

Took a bullet. Such a simple phrase for something so awful. She could almost see him lying on the warehouse floor, with blood all around him, splattered on his clothes and his beloved face.

"You could have died." It came out choked.

"But I didn't." He almost smiled. "Left me this dashing scar. At least that's what Ma calls it."

She managed a tiny grin. "Your mom's sense of humor is worse than yours."

He shook his head. His hair fell back over his forehead, hiding the scar. Without thinking, she reached out and brushed it back again.

"I had a lot of time to think in the hospital. Like I was making up for all the time I spent *not* thinking. About you. About the situation here. Leaving things the way I did... We never even talked. I never told you—" He broke off. His expression tightened. "I almost got Hardwick killed because I couldn't admit that I was too distracted, too *fucked up*, to be working that job that night."

"It's not your fault." A sudden flash of insight, the kind she used to get all the time, back when she and her owl were working together rather than against each other. "Hardwick told you the same thing, didn't he?"

"Yes," Jackson admitted, looking away.

"You're still friends."

"Maybe. I haven't really seen him much since the shooting, except when he came to see me in the hospital. I just walked away." His smile was more like a miserable grimace. "Like I do."

"Oh, come on," she said. "Hardwick's not going to blame you for that. He knows you had to go away to get your head together."

"Really?" He hesitantly raised his eyes to hers, and she was caught off guard by how neatly she had trapped herself.

"Yes," she said, feeling around the edges of the idea. Forgiveness. For herself. For him. It felt strange, and yet... right.

"I thought leaving here was the right thing to do, too. Leaving without even talking to you, or telling you I still—" He shook his head, a sharp jerk. "I told myself that if I wasn't your mate, then there was no point in me sticking around. It'd only hurt us both, and you… didn't have any use for me."

"No." It burst out, faster than thought. *No, never.*

"No?" A brief glint of humor failed to cover up the heaviness in his eyes. "What would you have done if I hadn't run away? If I'd stayed, and begged you to keep me?"

"I'd have done the right thing." She licked her lips, trying to convince herself. "Told you to leave. Because you deserved better than someone who knows they're not fated to be with you."

The lines deepened at the corners of his mouth—a mouth meant for smiling, turned down now. "How do you know what I deserve?"

"Because I know you! Because you're brave, and kind, and you listen and watch people almost as much as I do, but you do it so you can help them. You deserve so much more than I've given you." She had both her hands on his face now, caressing the prickle of stubble on his jawline. "I should have talked to you then."

"How? I'd already run away." The sad curve of his mouth deepened. "I'm not your mate, Olly... Am I?"

She hunted within herself. She didn't even know what it was meant to feel like, this mate-bond everyone was so obsessed with. She just knew she didn't have it. All her feelings for Jackson hadn't transmuted into some magical connection. And she'd been so shaken by that she hadn't let herself see what they'd stayed.

Love. Normal, everyday, wonderful love.

"No," she whispered. "So we were both right. The right thing was for each of us to let the other go."

He seemed to become smaller, his shoulders rolling inwards. Olly grabbed them and this time, she couldn't stop her fingertips digging in like her owl's talons. Holding onto what was hers.

She met his eyes. "I want to do the wrong thing."

15

JACKSON

Olly's words echoed in his head.

"You do?" he said. He shook his head. "No. I must have heard you wrong."

Olly pressed her lips together.

"I didn't hear you wrong."

She shook her head.

"But—" He wanted to hold her. Twelve months of confusion and longing honed to a knife-sharp point of need inside him. He pushed it down, same as he'd been doing that whole twelve months and telling himself he wasn't. "That's impossible. You said it yourself. I'm not your mate."

"No." She slipped her hand into his. "And I still love you."

Her eyes widened as though she'd surprised herself. Her free hand flew to her mouth.

"I can't believe I just said that. I can't believe I spent a *year*…" She tore away from him and spun away, then turned back to him, her eyes blazing. "A year! Being miserable, and telling myself I wasn't, telling myself everything was happening the way it was *meant* to, so what I was feeling couldn't be real, couldn't be *important*…"

Something in Jackson's chest, some secret part of his heart or soul or whatever the hell it was non-shifters had, fluttered and then stilled, as though it was waiting for the other shoe to drop.

Olly paused. Her eyes flicked sideways, the way they always did when she was checking with her owl. She frowned.

"But how is that possible?" Jackson didn't want to ask, but he had to. The look on her face… "Your owl—"

"It was trying to help." Her expression was a muddle of confusion and tenderness. "All the time. I thought I needed certainty so that's what it tried to give me. And I never let it see how unhappy I was, so…"

"It threw you into a frozen lake!"

"I already told you why. It thought it had a good reason."

"How is a *ring* a good—"

"Where is it?" Olly's eyes flashed. She reached under the bedcovers, feeling around. "I'm sure it's here somewhere. I had it in my hand, I know I did…"

"What's so important about that damn ring?" he asked, half-laughing as she hunted through the bedcovers.

"It's not the ring. It's what it represents. Aha!"

She sat up, holding one closed hand in front of herself.

"What are you doing?"

Her lips twitched. He wasn't sure whether she was laughing, or trying to stop herself from crying. "I told my owl how unhappy I'd been, and why. I told it I was in love with you. And it went to get me this." Her eyes were shining, and he still couldn't tell: tears of happiness, or sorrow? Her voice dropped. "It wanted to fix things."

She was clutching the ring as tightly as she had been when he pulled her out of the water. He hadn't even been able to open her hand, then. Now he gently uncurled her fingers, one by one. The tourists' engagement ring glittered on her palm.

He swallowed. "That's not going to fit on any of my fingers," he managed to say.

"We can't *keep* it!" She snatched her hand away and dropped the ring on the bedside table. "I'm an owl, not a magpie."

"Didn't you just tell me your owl's the one who picked it up?"

"We're going to return it," she said firmly. "It's the right thing to do."

His heart hammered in his chest. "I thought you wanted to do the wrong thing?"

Olly stared up at him, her gaze long and searching and no longer confusing. She was happy and Jackson felt a corner of his heart open up to the possibility that he might be, too.

"That's different," she murmured. "I'm still going to do everything wrong when it comes to you. Even though it's not fate, even though I'm not meant to… I love you."

"I love you too."

His voice hung in the air. One heartbeat. Two.

Then Olly was kissing him. Her lips were still cool; Jackson wrapped both her arms around her and kissed her until they were both panting and the icy water was a distant memory. When the kiss broke, they were both lying down—he didn't even remember when that had happened—with the blankets tangled around him.

"Twelve months," Olly grumbled, her breath hot against his cheek. "Twelve—what was *wrong* with me?"

She kissed him before he could answer, then kissed him until he couldn't remember the question, her body hot and straining against his. He ran his hands down her sides. It had been so long since he'd seen her, touched her…

He hissed as her hands found a fresh bruise on his side.

"Where did that come from?" She outlined it, her fingers so gentle it somehow hurt more.

"Pond," he replied shortly. "You kicked me."

"No!"

"Good thing you did. I couldn't see—" He shook his head. "Let's not talk about this now."

She shivered and he rolled over, holding her close beneath him. Her chest rose and fell under his as he nuzzled her neck, brushed wet strands of hair away from her skin and then kissed her again until she gasped with need.

He moved down her body, inch by inch, rediscovering her. He laid gentle kisses on her nipples and harder ones on the crease between her hips and her belly. He nipped lightly at the top of her thigh and her leg jumped.

Olly moaned breathlessly. Her hands roved over his shoulders, the back of his neck, her fingers tangling in his hair as though she didn't know whether she wanted to pull him back up and kiss him or push him further down.

He went down.

He kissed the hot wetness between her legs, and flicked his tongue out to caress her clit. She gasped, both legs twitching.

"Is this good?" Jackson asked, his voice a rumbling murmur against her heat.

"Oh God." It was exactly the answer he'd hoped for. He kissed her again, sliding one finger between her slick folds, and had to hold her leg down with his other hand.

"No kicking," he warned her, and pressed her mouth against her clit as he repeated: "No kicking… be careful…"

This was heaven. Olly's body strained tight as a bow. He slid another finger inside her and she moaned.

"No more. Please. Come back—up here—"

Jackson relented. Olly's eyes were shining. Her lips were red and wet, the surrounding skin roughened from his stubble. He touched it, a silent apology, and she closed her eyes, tipping her head back.

Jackson froze.

Olly's eyes flew open. "What's wrong?"

Everything. Jackson swallowed. "It's nothing. I…"

"*Jackson.*"

Jackson's head dropped onto the pillow beside her head. He couldn't bear to look her in the eye. Couldn't bear the caring concern in her voice. When she realized why he'd frozen—

He lay above her. She was still trembling; he was shaking, still buried deep inside her, still holding her safe in his arms as they both gave themselves over to breathless climax. This was it. Everything had led to this. Every late night together watching the stars, the quick looks that had gotten longer, silent questions eventually given voice... They were together and for the first time Jackson could remember, everything in the world felt right.

He *felt right.*

Then she opened her eyes.

"I'm sorry," Olly whispered, back in the present. "I should have thought."

She touched his face—gently, cautiously. Her fingertips rested just next to his scar.

"I should have realized," she continued, her voice edged with irony, "that recreating the moment I broke your heart might be a bad idea."

"It's not your fault." His voice was tight.

"I should have *thought.* I had all the—it's not even a case of having all the pieces! It doesn't take an owl shifter to see the problem here!" She groaned. "I'm sorry. God. What a mess."

Jackson rolled onto his back. She kept her hand in his hair and didn't complain when he pulled her close, winding his arms around her as they lay nestled together in the tangled blankets.

"I don't think either of us were doing much thinking," he admitted. "Not with our brains. This isn't—we can't—"

"I want to." She watched him, waiting, her heart in her eyes. "You're the only man I want, Jackson Gilles. Even if we're not mates. Even if it's not *fate*."

His chest twisted. Yes, he'd been hurt. He hadn't needed to hear her say he wasn't her mate that night twelve months ago – it had been clear in every line of her face. In the way she'd pulled away from him, as though even his touch horrified her. And then she had said it, neatly shutting the door on paradise and throwing away the key, and she might as well have taken a pickaxe to his heart.

But she'd been hurt, too. Her own soul had betrayed her. That had to cut deeper than…

"You're sure?" he said, like an idiot. Olly would think he was—

But of course Olly wouldn't blame anyone for checking and double-checking.

She gave him a brief, understanding smile. "Yes. I'm sick of lying to myself. I'm not going to lie to you, too."

"I can't lie to myself anymore, either," he admitted. "I told myself I would never come back here. Then when Jasper called about his paperwork, I told myself I wouldn't see you. That I'd already shut the door on my broken heart forever and there was no point opening it again." His mouth twisted. "See how well that worked out."

"Didn't it?" Olly wriggled around until she was pressed against his chest.

Jackson wrapped his arms around her. She was warm, and soft, and everything he'd thought he'd lost forever.

"No more broken heart, right?" she whispered.

He knew Olly too well to miss the double question. He pulled her close.

"It's healing."

"Good." She nuzzled close against him. "Mine, too." Her tone went completely dry. "Piece by piece."

He snorted and buried his face in her hair. It was still damp, and smelled like pond water, but her own scent was there beneath it, sweet and wild.

Olly. *His* Olly.

He slid his hand down her back and she tipped her head up. "Hmm?"

"Just checking. Either you're warming up or I'm freezing as well."

She huffed with amusement and grabbed his hand. "You don't feel cold to me."

"Well, the same rule applies. If you're still freezing, I'd feel—"

She snaked one foot up and pressed it against his inner thigh. He bit back a shriek. "All right! I'm not freezing. Or I *wasn't*. Your foot's like ice."

Jackson reached down and wrapped his hands around her foot until it started to approach above-freezing temperatures. "You should have said. We need to keep all of you warm, after the lake."

"I just think they remember being the only bit of me not covered in feathers, even in human form." Olly shrugged and wriggled her toes. "You can keep doing that, though."

"Hmm." He found her other foot and gave it the same treatment. She gazed at him, one hand resting on his cheek.

"Thank you," she said softly.

"What for?" He massaged her feet. "Saving your life?"

"Oh, that." She wrinkled her nose, and then her expression tensed. "I mean giving me another chance. I won't let you down this time. I promise."

"Olly, you didn't—" Jackson's hands stilled and he knew, he just *knew*, that whatever he said now it would come up against Olly's steely obstinacy. So instead of arguing, he said: "And I promise not to run away this time."

"You didn't—"

"And you didn't let me down." He let go of her feet and took her hand. "We were both confused, and both hurting. But we can't start over if we keep dragging up what we did wrong last time."

"So you admit I was wrong."

"Only if you'll admit I was a coward who ran away rather than face up to my own feelings." Jackson's ribs tightened.

"You're not a co—ugh. I see what you're doing." Olly rolled on top of him and lay with her chin propped on her hands, scowling down at him.

"Good," he grumbled, smiling at her dissatisfied expression.

"And worse, I actually get it." She sighed, blowing a loose strand of hair off her face. "Is this what it means to be grown-up about things?"

"I'm afraid so."

"Ugh." She smiled, but there was a shimmer of sadness in her eyes. "I always thought that finding my mate would be the next big life stage for me. The official tick-box for being a real adult."

"Because having your own apartment and job, that's just kid stuff."

"You know what I mean."

And he did. He'd thought it, too. That being Olly's mate would mean finally stepping up and making something of his life.

Olly cradled his face in her hands. "Stop it."

"Stop what?"

"Whatever you're thinking about. You're being mean to yourself." Her fingertips traced a pattern along his jaw. "You get this line, from the corner of your mouth."

"Do you want me to tell you what your face does when you're self-recriminating about something?" he retorted.

"Don't you dare." A fleeting grin crossed her face. "You don't need to, anyway, because we're not going to do that. We're being adult about it. No sulking over the past. Agreed?"

"Sounds like a good rule." She lowered her lips towards his, and paused. Her face was close enough to his that her eyelashes brushed his cheek. "Speaking of adult things…"

Jackson's skin heated up, and it had nothing to do with the electric blanket warming the bed. "Hmm?"

Olly's fingertips were like sunlight on his face. "We could try things differently. This time around."

This time around meaning not looking back to last year's disaster, or the one ten minutes ago?

"Hey!" Olly tapped his jaw. "Rules, remember? But I, I understand if you don't want to…"

He pulled her down towards him and kissed the rest of her words away.

16
OLLY

Her head was spinning when Jackson finally stopped kissing her.

"Just to check," she said, her voice muzzy, "that's a yes? Wait. Or a no? If you don't *not* want to…"

He kissed her again for that, which she really should have seen coming.

"I just wanted to check…" she mumbled teasingly against his mouth.

He bit down on her lower lip, softly, and a jolt of arousal shot down her spine. "Have you gathered enough information?"

"More than I did last—"

Jackson growled deep in his throat. "Now who's breaking the rules?"

She buried her hands in his hair, holding his head in place as she gazed down into his eyes. "I'm not sulking," she said, and it was the truth. At last. It wasn't only the kisses that were making her lightheaded. "I've got all the information I need. More than I did last time. This time, I know exactly what I'm getting into." She wriggled against him and the hard ridge of his cock pressed against her thigh. "I'm not making a mistake this time."

That damned line appeared at the corner of his mouth again, and was gone again so quickly she thought she must have imagined it.

"I love you," she said, just in case she hadn't been imagining it, and some part of this gorgeous man was still trapped in whatever dark shadow came over him sometimes. "You're everything I want."

"And you're everything I've ever wanted." His hand hovered an inch away from her cheek, as though despite the desire sizzling between their bodies, he was still holding himself back. "We're going to make this work."

It wasn't a question, but she answered it anyway: "Yes."

He caressed her cheek, his callouses scraping against her soft skin. "My Olly."

Olly's heart leaped into her throat. "My Jackson."

He was *hers*. Not her mate, not her owl's preferred extra puzzle piece of soul, but *hers*.

And she wasn't going to lose him again.

She stretched out, pressing the length of her body against his. He had changed, in all the small and important ways she'd noticed earlier, but this was the same. His strong, hard body. His hands, warm and rough on her body.

Jackson's eyes were dark, the deep brown of his irises almost swallowed whole by his pupils.

"You said we could try things differently." His voice was like river stones tumbling in the spring thaw. "What did you mean by that?"

His hands were on her waist. His thumbs made small, slow circles above the dip of her hipbones. Small and aggravatingly tempting.

"This time I'm not waiting for fate to take control," she murmured, matching the pace of his thumbs with her hips as she ground them in a circle. Jackson's breath hitched. "*I'm* taking control."

She rocked her hips against him again. He moaned and tangled his hands in her hair and kissed her and heat flowed through every inch of her body.

"This is a good cure for potential hypothermia," she mumbled, and Jackson bit off a curse.

"Actually, it's not advisable to—"

She bit down on his earlobe. Gently.

"—physical exhaustion… dehydration…"

She bit down very slightly harder. "Do you want me to stop?"

"Biting me?"

"This." She ground her hips against him again, moving up his body until his cock slipped between her thighs. "Or maybe both." She nibbled on his ear again.

"I can see I'm going to have to keep your mouth busier." He dragged her face to his and kissed her until her whole body strained against his, tight as a bowstring. Desire pulsed inside her.

"Keep my mouth busy?" She kissed him back, running her teeth along his lower lips, then moved down his body. She ran her hands over every inch of him she could reach, shoulders, pecs, abs, following each touch with a kiss.

When she reached his cock Jackson bucked his hips up and gasped. His hands scrambled against the sheets. "God, Olly—"

"Well, you did say," she pointed out dryly, and wrapped her hand around his thick length. She smiled at him and lowered her lips onto him.

Jackson pushed himself up on his elbows. His eyes met hers, hot with helpless pleasure.

Then they drifted downwards to where her lips were kissing the tip of his cock.

His chest hitched. Heat surged in Olly's veins, red-hot.

This *had* to be where she'd gone wrong last time. She'd lain back, let Jackson focus on *her*… and missed out on this. The utterly overwhelmed expression on his face was more vulnerable than she'd ever seen him.

And hornier. And just really, really fucking hot.

She kissed him again, slipping her lips over the thick head of his cock. Salt burst on her palate. She swirled her tongue around and the sweet tension between her legs tightened.

"Oh, God, Olly…" Jackson's voice was all gravel.

"Jackson." Hers was liquid heat.

She lowered her head, tasting him, running her tongue along his length. Jackson clenched his fists in the sheets. His hips jerked upwards and she sucked him deeper into her mouth. God, this was… this was… *he* was…

She sat up, so fast he was still groaning from the loss of her mouth when she straddled him. Her legs were trembling. She positioned herself over his cock.

Jackson's eyes met hers. God, she was so wet already. Desire coiled through her, a fire ready to run wild.

She pushed herself down just as Jackson thrust up.

His cock slid into her, filling and stretching her. She gasped. Every inch felt like he was about to stretch too much but she didn't stop, *couldn't* stop, until the insides of her thighs were resting heavy on his hips. He filled her completely and it was too much but God, too much was just what she needed.

"I'm sorry," Jackson gasped. "I should have—slower—"

"Slower?" Olly rocked forward, hard. It felt so good her heart thudded in her ears. "Like this?"

Jackson made a noise that was half groan, half gasp. She moved faster, grinding against him, and the noise that ripped from his throat made her fingers curl against his chest.

Need thrummed inside her, a fire stoked with every new breath she took. God, even *breathing* was enough movement to send sensation sparking inside her, that glorious feeling of too much and perfect and—oh, shit, if she wanted this to last any time at all she really should—

"Olly." Jackson's voice was rough. Pained. His fingertips dug into her hips and his cock jerked inside her, its urgency as clear as the need on his face.

Olly dragged his shoulders up and kissed him. Sitting like this, in his lap as he wound his muscular arms around her, his cock pressed inside her at a new angle. She muffled her cry in Jackson's shoulder.

His voice rumbled against her chest. "I've been dreaming about this. Every night. You. The way you…"

He slid one hand up to caress her breast and her breath hitched.

"Just like that," Jackson murmured, running one thumb across her nipple. "You're so still and careful, all the time, and seeing you like this drives me wild."

Olly grinned widely. "Really?" She bucked her hips and Jackson's eyes closed.

"God. Yes."

"Like this?"

His eyes flew open again as she pulled herself off him and sank down again. It felt incredible. Slick and hot and full. She let her head fall back. Jackson was right, she hated when people saw her, hated when they saw what she was thinking or feeling especially, but this was different. *He* was different. She couldn't hate him and she couldn't hate *this*.

It was way too fucking hot, for a start. Feeling him. Touching him, tasting him, hearing him…

Jackson groaned deep in his throat as she rode him again and again.

"Or this." She nibbled on his earlobe again and he growled at her. She caught the tip of her tongue between her teeth, catching back a giggle and the impulse to bite harder.

Pleasure was building inside her, ready to pop. And it wasn't just the physical *everything*, even if the everything was very very *very* everything, it was—she felt… safe.

Sensation exploded inside her. Every muscle in her body clenched exquisitely and suddenly released, leaving her light-headed and then twisting tight again, each new wave soaring higher and higher.

She buried her face in Jackson's neck, breathing him in, wishing there were words for what she was feeling but she couldn't have said them, anyway. She could barely gasp.

Jackson came with a groan that reverberated against her breastbone. His breath was hot on her skin, his hands strong and firm on her waist and the back of her head. His passion enveloped her and she sank against him, falling back to earth and back to *him*.

She gulped in breaths. *Safe.* Of course he was safe. He was the best man she'd ever known. The best *person*. She would trust him with her life.

She was the one who wasn't safe. The one who couldn't be trusted. She couldn't even trust herself.

She pressed her face against his shoulder, putting off the next moment as long as she could.

"Olly…" Jackson was panting. His fingers ghosted through her hair. "You… that was… are you all right?"

Guilt squirreled in her gut. She raised her head and rested her forehead against his. Her lips curved and she couldn't stop herself from smiling. "I don't think I've ever been happier," she admitted, and it was true, even with the knot in her stomach.

"Nothing changed." His tone was wary.

The knot in her stomach twisted. If he'd been a shifter, she might have been able to sense what he was hiding. If he were a shifter, they might be mates now, bound by more than…

Jackson sounded like he'd swallowed a burr. "It's still just… us."

He twined his fingers between hers. Even though he was still buried deep inside her, there was a strange new intimacy in this touch.

Olly let out a breath that was far too close to a sob. The knot in her stomach dissolved.

"Just us. Just everything I want."

How could she have wanted to put off this moment? She should have done this a year ago.

The answering smile on Jackson's face was all she needed to make things as close to perfect as they could get.

"We're really going to do this," he said. "Make a go of it together." His expression softened.

"You'd better believe it. Because I love you and I'm not letting you go again." Olly kissed him. He fell back, pulling her with him, and they tangled together in their nest of blankets.

Hours later, Jackson stopped kissing her and frowned. "It's dark," he announced.

"No, really?"

He gave her an exhausted look and she grinned. "Good thing we're already in bed then, isn't it?"

"We should…" His jaw firmed. She knew that expression, and guessed what he was going to say before he opened his mouth again. "We should head back to town. Make sure everyone's alright. It would be the responsible thing to do."

The corner of his mouth twitched downwards and Olly placed a finger on it. "What if I want to stay right here?"

"We should at least let everyone know you're safe."

A chill went down Olly's spine. She tried to hide it, but the sudden alertness in Jackson's eyes told her she'd failed.

She looked away. "If any of the other shifters had picked up on what happened to me out—out on the ice, they'd already be here. Right now, you're the only one who knows I threw myself into the lake and—"

"And that's bad enough?"

She pressed her face against his chest. "I didn't mean that. I mean… I want it to just be us. Just for a bit longer. I've had all year without you, and I don't want this to end. Not yet."

"You want me all to yourself?" he asked gruffly.

"You know I do." She rolled on top of him and pinned him in place, one elbow either side of his head. "I'll check in with my uncle, let him know I need some time off."

"Right before Christmas?"

"Yeah, I know, but…" She wriggled against him. "For some reason I *really* want to be selfish for a while."

Jackson looked pleased, and looked like he was pleased despite himself. She wriggled again and he threw his head back.

"All right. You make a very good point." His hands glided over her butt. "We'll have a romantic night together, starving in an abandoned ski cottage."

"We won't starve. People always leave some supplies in the cupboards, even if it's just a tin of beans."

"The sexiest meal of all, right there."

"I could go hunt us a rabbit if you like. There's plenty around—"

"Beans it is." Jackson went slightly green and Olly laughed. "You're right, though."

"About what?"

"Not doing what we *should* be doing." He stroked her back, a long, sensuous caress. "None of this is what we *should* be doing. But I wouldn't give you up for the world."

She smiled and kissed him. But later, when he was asleep, she couldn't help worrying.

Here, alone with each other, things were simple. Once they got back into the real world… that's when things were going to get difficult.

She clenched her fists with determination.

No matter what, I won't lose him again.

I can't.

17

OLLY

2 DAYS BEFORE CHRISTMAS

The next morning, Olly and Jackson raided the cottage's cupboards. Her owl was still lying low: even the prospect of a tin of beans for breakfast didn't taunt it into making a scathing remark.

"What do you think of the place?" Jackson asked, with that off-the-cuff casualness that always meant he had an ulterior motive. Olly stirred the beans on the stove and considered her answer.

"It's definitely a cottage," she said.

"Hmm."

She looked around, inspecting the room more carefully. "It's warm," she said. "That's impressive, given no one's stayed here for a long while. Or I assume that's the case, given the expiration date on those beans and the fact there was nothing else in the cupboards." Steam began to rise from the beans. "This is one of the Heartwells' places, though, so that explains it. Jasper wouldn't let any of their properties fall into disrepair, even if my uncle does wish the Heartwells would let him knock down all the tourist cottages this close to our trails."

"It'd be a shame to demolish it, though, wouldn't it? It's a nice place... solid bones..."

"I think it's a particularly good place to not die," Olly said firmly. "And for everything else we did last night. And this morning." She lifted the pot. "Beans are ready!"

"Oh, good. Great!"

After a leisurely breakfast—it was amazing how long you could take to eat a single tin of beans when you were in love—they drove back to the Puppy Express, crushed together on the snowmobile more tightly than was probably necessary.

Bob called out to her telepathically just as they were pulling in by the kennels. *Olly! Where have you been? Manu said—*

Oh, shit. That was right. Despite reassuring Jackson that she would touch base with her uncle, she'd fallen asleep in his arms without bothering to let anyone know she hadn't fallen off the edge of the Earth.

I'm fine, Olly said quickly. *You know me.*

Yes, that's why I was worried. Fond frustration batted against her mind like a wing. *Manu told me about Flea's issue yesterday. Sounds like the rescue didn't *go so smoothly. I figured you were hiding until you could dry your feathers off.*

Olly bit her lip. *Something like that.*

She felt happier than she remembered being in a long time. Still, a worry gnawed at the back of her mind. She knew that being with Jackson was the right decision. She just wasn't sure her uncle, or the other shifters, would feel the same.

Are you in today? she asked Bob.

Work? No. This bloody cold. I'm giving myself one day in bed. Not that you need me around with the hellhounds on board.

They arrived at the Puppy Express. Jackson cut the snowmobile's engine and frowned. "Quiet today," he said. "Where are the dogs?"

Olly passed the question on to Bob—but without saying who had originally asked it.

Dogs? Mother of… if those hellhounds have stolen the dogs again…

I'll look after it, Olly reassured him. *You get some sleep.*

And give me some time to figure out how I'm going to explain this to you, she added silently. *Any ideas?* she asked her owl.

There was no reply. Just a shuffling sensation as though her owl was rustling its feathers.

"I guess I'd better leave you to your work," Jackson said. He reached for her and hesitated.

She folded herself into his arms. "Why? Do you think you might have a negative effect on my productivity?"

He grinned bashfully. "About as bad as you used to have on mine."

"I thought you did a great job keeping the Puppy Express a crime-free zone."

"Until last year." Jackson's expression turned serious. "We haven't talked about the hellhounds yet. Can you trust them, after what they did?"

"That was a year ago."

"Yesterday, just one look at that Flea guy made you freeze up."

"They're alright, Jackson. And *I'm* alright." How could she explain? "It's like getting sick off, off tequila, and then never being able to stomach it again. I got hit so hard by their hellfire last year that I still get it worse if I see it now."

"So why do you have to see them at all?"

"It's not their fault. Don't argue, I know how that sounds." She blew a stray strand of hair off her face. "They're the most pack-oriented shifters I've ever heard of. If their alpha says jump, their heads hit the ceiling. And their last alpha *made* them all shifters. That's even more power."

"You're telling me I should hate the barman, not the tequila?"

"Something like that." She grinned. "Anyway, Meaghan is their alpha now. Or Caine is, but since she's his mate, it's basically the same thing."

"Meaghan Markham, who caused trouble since the day she moved into town?"

"I knew you'd remember her."

"That's not actually reassuring," he said seriously, but his eyes were sparkling so much she couldn't help kissing him.

Eventually, though, she had to tear herself away. "I'm going to have to work again today after all. Bob's off with the plague. See you tonight?"

"Dinner?"

In front of everyone? Her initial instinct was to balk, but she'd spent twelve months not being brave enough to get what she wanted. And she wanted Jackson. All of him, public and private. "Yes?"

"I'll pick you up, then."

"In my two-days-old work uniform? I'm going to go home and change first. I'll meet you there." She tipped her head back. "I just need you to tell me where 'there' is."

"Hannah's? Seven?"

"I think I could manage that." She kissed him again, to seal the deal.

Olly trailed after Jackson as he got into his car. As he disappeared around the bend, her owl finally raised its head.

It worked! her owl said. *You're happy now, aren't you?*

…Yes, she admitted. Her owl shuffled happily around inside her. *But he's still not my mate, you know.*

Her owl ruffled its feathers. *True. That's… hmm.*

Hmm what?

Just hmm. Her owl blinked. *For now.*

"Well that's not unsettling at all," Olly muttered. Her owl's feelings became muted in her mind. *Are you hiding something from me?*

Don't worry. I just need to think it through.

Fine. Be like that…

What could her owl be hiding? There clearly wasn't any point asking it. It wasn't like it had even told her what it was doing yesterday, before it made her jump into the lake after that ring.

She groaned. The ring! It was still back at the cottage, forgotten on the bedside table. She would have to return it another day. Hopefully the tourists hadn't cut their vacation short after what happened at the lake.

She didn't do a full circuit of the building before she went inside, but she did catch sight of Flea through the window. He was standing morosely behind the desk.

She pushed the door open and Flea looked up. There was no hint of hellfire in his eyes and Olly changed course. Instead of finding a perch behind one of the postcard or plushie displays, she walked over to the counter.

"Olly!" Flea cried out. "You're back!"

"Sure am." And hoping to avoid questions about where she'd been, so she quickly changed the subject. "I hope the tourists aren't planning to sue us."

"No problems there! We got the doctor to check them out, and Manu sorted them a free dinner at Hannah's. The ring's still missing, though, which is *their own fault for not obeying the*—er, um, I mean which is really a *shame*." He glowered at nothing, which Olly knew extremely well was the only option people like them had when they wanted to glare at a creature that only existed inside their own heads.

"They haven't left, then?"

"Oh, no. They're staying in town until the day after Christmas."

That was good news for her plan to return the ring, at least. "What about the dogs—"

"Oh, God! Sorry!" Flea spun around and faced the far wall, covering his eyes.

Olly fought her owl's urge to duck down behind the counter. *It's just like a bad hangover*, she told herself. *The hellfire can't hurt you and look, he's not even looking at you.*

The hellhounds had powers that shouldn't exist. but once you got past the fact that they *did* exist, she found that she could handle their magic, after all. At least while his back was turned. Her shoulders straightened.

"Right. Flea, where are the dogs?"

"I'm not supposed to tell you!" He paused. "Well if *someone* stopped going freaking psycho every ten minutes—!" He looked up, saw Olly staring at him, and went bright red. "Sorry. My hellhound…"

"Sounds a lot like my owl," Olly said understandingly. "I told Bob I'd go get them. I'm guessing they're over at Meaghan and Caine's, same as usual?"

Flea nodded morosely.

She raced up the stairs to the staff changing room and flung the window open. Cold air wrapped around her limbs as she quickly undressed and shifted.

She leaped from the windowsill and her owl swooped upwards, catching the warm air from the Puppy Express chimney and soaring over the trees. The sight stopped Olly's worries dead in their tracks. Winter had always been her favorite time of year—her plumage blended in so well—wait, was that *her* thought, or her owl's?

Questions were still tumbling through Olly's mind when the sound of dogs barking filled the air. The trees gave way to a small clearing with a house in the middle of it. The "lost" Puppy Express dogs were leaping around the building. One of them jumped up at the front door, trying to scratch its way in. When they caught sight of the owl, they turned as one and barked at it.

So loud, her owl sniffed. *What do they have to bark about? It's only us. They should see that* before *they decide to bark. Also, they should hide. Don't they know they're in trouble?*

It's not their fault, Olly reminded her.

True. It's their *fault.*

Manu and another of the pack, Ryan, appeared at the door. They were both in human form. The dog who'd been jumping up slipped past them into the house and Olly's owl tutted. *Did they really not see that coming?*

One of the hellhound boys waved at her. *Hi Olly!* He yelped as the other one smacked him on the side of the head. *Er, sorry about the dogs…*

Olly sent them a brief don't-worry reassurance and circled overhead. She'd been to Meaghan and Caine's dozens of time since they moved in together, but she still wanted to get her bearings before she landed.

Or maybe her owl did. Or maybe her owl did but only because it wanted her to feel safe that it, and therefore she, knew what they were getting themselves into.

Either way, her head hurt.

Meaghan and Caine lived a short distance out of town. It made a lot of sense. Human visitors wouldn't bat an eye at seeing an owl swooping around the edge of town, like with Olly and her apartment, but a pack of fire-eyed hellhounds needed a bit of privacy. Just as the Heartwells had their lodge further up the mountain, here, the Guinnesses had their camp.

The camp had started off life as one of several luxury cabins a decent drive from what in Pine Valley counted as the bustle of town. The original architect, who had designed a modern, fashionable construction, all angles and glass would probably not approve of the renovations they'd made.

This architect had heard about insulation and granite countertops but not such complex cold-weather concepts as "needing a garage". Caine had added one, and then a small outbuilding beyond it, and then, confirming Olly's suspicion that the cabin was meant as a home for the small pack that was by then sticking to Meaghan and Caine like glue, they had moved the outbuilding several hundred yards to the far end of the section. The result was like a nest built up over seasons and generations, despite the house only being a few years old.

Olly flew down to the window Meaghan and Caine always left open for her on the upper floor. The barking intensified as she approached the house. The "stolen" dogs were all ecstatic to see her, even if they didn't identify her or Bob as their alpha anymore. Not since Caine came to town.

She shifted and pulled on the spare clothes Meaghan left in a drawer for her, then tiptoed downstairs. She already knew where she would find everyone—she'd spotted them through the windows while she was flying. Downstairs in the living room.

Olly knocked on the living room door to let them know she was there, and Caine opened it. He looked as shamefaced as the dogs outside.

"It's hard to run a sledding business when all your dogs go missing," she reminded him, deadpan.

"I am sorry," he said, rubbing the back of his neck. He glanced towards Meaghan, who was sitting on the sofa in front of the wood burner. The dog who'd snuck in earlier was draped over her lap, but it was the almost-imperceptible change in Caine's expression as he looked at his mate that made Olly catch her breath.

Her owl made the special, disdainful hiss it saved for hellhounds. Olly turned around and saw Manu and Ryan try to burst through the door behind her at the same time.

Caine dropped his head into his hands. Meaghan sniggered.

"Come and sit with me," she called to Olly.

"I really need to get back to work," Olly protested, already moving to the sofa. She squeezed herself into one corner and tucked her feet up under her. "And the dogs…"

"I'll take them back." Caine winced. "It's my fault they're here, after all. We got some good news yesterday, and my hellhound…" He paused and exchanged a worried look with Meaghan, who grinned mercilessly back. "Are you going to be upset if I say my hellhound called the whole pack together and that includes the Puppy Express team?"

"If I was going to be upset, I would have been upset the first time it happened," Olly reminded him. "*Bob* is upset. Though just about you calling them away. I don't know if he knows about the whole part-of-your-pack thing."

"Fair enough." Caine ducked his head, then looked at Meaghan again and straightened. Something passed between them, communication on a level of intimacy Olly could only dream of. "But this is—we have big news."

He moved to Meaghan's side and she squeezed his hand. Her eyes were dancing.

Her owl fluttered its wings. *I know this! I know what they've been hiding!*

Yes, but shh, Olly replied.

But I know! And we didn't even have to ask!

Caine flushed. "It's—we—Meaghan…" He looked at her and deflated. "You already know, don't you?"

"Of course she does." Meaghan squeezed his hand.

Of course we do! Olly's owl squawked. *Tell them! Tell them I figured it out!*

Olly blinked slowly, all innocence. "I have no idea what you're talking about."

What? Yes we do!

"And even if I did—" Olly cleared her throat. She'd spoken more loudly than she intended, as though she was actually trying to speak over her owl. "Even if I did, I'd want to hear it from you both."

She pulled her knees up and put her arms around them. Her owl was glaring at her from the inside, which was always a strange sensation.

But I know this, her owl insisted. *I figured it out!*

I know, but… this is a human thing.

It wasn't that she thought it was wrong. Her owl was seeing the same things she was—the shy pride on Caine's face, the fact that Olly was Meaghan's closest friend in Pine Valley and what that meant to humans and how humans communicated good news—and it *had seen* the same things she'd seen over the past few weeks. All the little clues.

Meaghan pulled Caine down so he was perched on the back of the sofa, and wrapped one arm around his waist. She leaned into him, her head resting against his side.

Her owl ruffled its feathers. *She's preg—*

"I'm going to have twins."

What?

"What?" Olly slapped both hands over her mouth. "Oo mff *twins?*"

"You didn't know? Hah! You didn't know!" Meaghan crowed.

Olly wrenched her hands away from her face. "How could I?"

"Well, you figured out I was pregnant, right?"

"Yes, but—" Olly gestured randomly. "I couldn't have figured out you were… Twins!"

"I know!" Meaghan burst out laughing as Olly threw herself across the sofa and hugged her. She smelled like woodsmoke and the herbal tea she'd started drinking instead of coffee. *Another thing I should have noticed,* Olly thought, letting Meaghan go and hugging Caine.

I noticed, her owl muttered.

"Congratulations," Olly said, hoping they both understood how heartfelt the sentiment was. Her face hurt from the grin stuck to it. "How long have you known?"

Caine and Meaghan exchanged another of their perfect-understanding looks.

"Two weeks? Two weeks," Meaghan said. "At least that's when I started getting suspicious."

"And my hellhound started acting like every shadow was a potential threat," Caine mumbled, his cheeks going pink. Meaghan bit her lower lip, which did absolutely nothing to hide her satisfied smirk.

Which must be why the others have been on edge, too, and he keeps accidentally calling our sled dogs over to strengthen the pack, Olly decided.

Caine met her thoughtful gaze and nodded. "...and it hasn't *stopped* thinking everything's a potential threat. Which is why I keep stealing the dogs. Sorry. They must sense that I'm worried about... *everything*... and—"

The hall door burst open. A sea of huskies flooded through it, yelping urgently. Olly curled herself up in the corner of the sofa, giggling as the dogs leaped up onto the seat and her owl hissed disapprovingly.

"I'm not totally sure how being buried in dogs is meant to protect me, but I'm happy to try it," Meaghan announced from beneath a wriggling blanket of happy dogs. "Bleh—enough kisses, Loony."

Loony got one more lick in and then let Meaghan push her off her lap. Another dog immediately took her place.

"I didn't mean to let them in!" Manu said from the door. "I just—er…"

"Wanted to come check on me, same as the huskies?" Meaghan deadpanned. She gave Caine a meaningful look and he jumped into action.

"Olly, how would your uncle feel about having a few extra hands around the place today?"

"Er, I guess he—"

"Great. We'll head straight over. I'll take the dogs back and deliver a few helpers at the same time."

"What about Flea?" Olly asked, remembering what he and Manu had said about tipping each other over the edge.

"His hellhound will behave if Caine's there," Meaghan reassured her.

Caine ducked to kiss her. When he straightened, every dog in the room—and the human-shaped hellhounds, too—jumped to attention. "I'll be back for lunch?"

"Come back *with* lunch," Meaghan replied, and pulled him down for another kiss.

Olly's smile half-dropped. Meaghan and Caine were so perfectly in tune with each other. And Caine was in tune with his hellhound. It might think about things differently, and its over-the-top protectiveness clearly left Caine slightly bemused, but it wanted the same things he wanted.

"I should really get back to work too," she said, starting to stand up.

Meaghan thrust out one foot and kicked her in the back of the knees. Olly sat down with an *oof.* Her owl fluffed out its feathers in absolute disgust. If she'd been paying more attention, she could have avoided the kick.

"Stay," Meaghan said plainly. "Or else I'll be left here *alllll* alone and then you'll never get the huskies back to work."

Olly narrowed her eyes. *This feels suspiciously like a pre-arranged plan,* she thought as Caine called out to his pack to get in the truck. "You don't need to send all the guys away," she said, testing the waters. "I'm sure the other hellhounds can drive themselves. Caine could stay."

"Nah. It'll do them all good to run around a bit. Honestly, recently they're more like hell-*sheep* than hellhounds. Following me around all the time. Or—you know that thing that cows do? Just standing around watching you? And I suppose it's only going to get worse."

"They don't go hellfire on you?" Even being friends with the hellhounds, and even knowing they didn't mean it if their hellfire spilled out, Olly didn't like the idea of them gathering around, staring.

"Yeah, but in a sad, dumbass way, not in a scary way. I think being mated to their alpha makes me immune."

"I wish I was immune."

Meaghan leaned forward, her face suddenly serious. "They haven't been bothering you, have they? I told them to be careful around you. I know you say you're 'fine'"—she made quote marks with her fingers—"but if you need them to back off…"

"From what? Working with me?" Olly shook her head. "I'm dealing with it."

"You're dealing with a lot, is what you're dealing with." Meaghan raised her hands. "And with Jackson back in town and that freaking pegasus shifter crashing the party last night, you know, I figure you're feeling extra… you."

"Ha ha."

"Seriously, Olly."

Olly shook her head. "No, I'm fi—I'm dealing with it," she amended, as Meaghan raised her fingers in quote-marks again. "Wait. Pegasus?"

"The guy who crashed through the big tent?" Meaghan stared at her. "You *missed* that? Damn it, I was hoping you'd be able to give me all the gossip. Caine got the pack to bundle me up and take me home as soon as stuff started looking crazy."

She pulled a face, but Olly knew her well enough to see through it. "So your pack is super overbearing and over-protective, but… you don't hate it."

"God no." Meaghan propped her head on one hand and gazed into the fire. Outside, an engine started and the dogs started to bark with excitement. A strange, wistful expression passed over Meaghan's face as the noise faded into the distance. "They're incredibly annoying and ridiculous and I love having them around, even when they're doing everything they can to piss me off. Because they're never *trying* to piss me off, they're just…" She sighed, her eyebrows drawing together. "I spent so much of my life feeling as though I was on the outside. Like even looking in was too much to ask for. And now I'm meant to be the 'alpha' of a pack? It might be weird as shit, but there's no way I'm going to abandon the boys after what they've been through." She wrinkled her nose. "Listen to me. 'Boys'. Manu's only three years younger than I am!"

"They're all new to shifting, though. Baby shifters." Which was why she couldn't blame them, either.

"And I'm no shifter at all, but here I am, the boss of them all." Meaghan shrugged. "Cup of tea? Or coffee? And don't you dare say you'll get it for me. I haven't been able to do anything for myself all morning."

She bounced up before Olly could protest. Olly sank back into the sofa as kitchen noises filtered through the house.

Meaghan sauntered back in, looking far more satisfied than making a cup of coffee should merit, in Olly's owl's opinion.

"Don't look at me like that," Meaghan said, handing Olly her cup. "You've no idea what a pain it is to have someone leap to attention every time I lift my little finger."

"Still with the not hating it?"

"Heck yeah." Meaghan nestled back into the sofa. "So… I couldn't help but notice you didn't jump up on the ceiling when Manu and Ryan burst in before. You're looking better, too. What's changed?"

"Maybe I got a good night's sleep?" Olly's cheeks heated up. She hadn't slept that much, actually.

"Mm–hmm." Meaghan raised one eyebrow. "And the truth is…?"

"Jackson's back," Olly blurted out. She wrapped her hands around her mug.

"That's…" Meaghan pursed her lips, searching Olly's face. "…Good? Bad? It's so hard to tell with you."

Hah! Olly's owl crowed.

"It's good. I hope."

"But…"

"What?"

Meaghan leaned forward. "That's what's coming next, isn't it? It's good, you hope, but…" She sipped her drink and made a face. "Ew. Maybe I should have let one of the boys make this. How can I get *tea* wrong?"

Olly fidgeted. Meaghan's eyebrows shot up. "What does your owl think about all this? I remember last Christmas—"

"Don't." Olly hunched down into the corner of the sofa. "You don't need to remind me. I made a mistake last year."

"About him not being your mate?"

"No. I was right about that. The mistake was thinking I don't love him."

Meaghan gave her a slow look, then shrugged. "Cool."

"Cool? Is that all you have to say?"

"Uh, I'm happy for you?" She raised her hands. "Look, Olly, I'm still new to this. If you'd have asked me last year, I would have said soulmates didn't exist, but I wouldn't have said two people couldn't fall in love and be perfect for one another *without* being soulmates. And you and Jackson just… work." She poked Olly with one toe. "So, you and Jackson. What's next?"

"I… don't know." Olly frowned. "We're going to dinner tonight?"

"Have fun," Meaghan said, smiling at her. "I'm happy for you. Jackson's a sweet guy, and I hope you guys have a good time." She hesitated. "Just keep in mind it might be a temporary thing, okay?"

Olly bristled. "What do you mean?"

"Seriously?" Meaghan gestured, slopping tea onto the floor. She cursed and put her cup down, then fixed Olly with a stare that was equal parts exasperated and worried. "Olly, he's not your mate."

"I know that!"

"Which means somewhere out there, someone *is*. Have you thought this through? What will you do if you find your actual soulmate?"

Cold gripped Olly's heart.

"I know I've only got a year of this whole shifter business under my belt, but... I am a shifter's mate. When I first saw Caine, it hit me so hard I didn't know if I wanted him, or wanted to..."

"...Stuff him in the back of your truck and kidnap him?" Olly suggested weakly.

"Hey, we both know what happened. No need to rub it in." As though unconsciously echoing her words, she started to rub her stomach. "But even though I didn't know what it was, it was *powerful*. And Caine says it was even more than that, for him. It was undeniable."

Olly swallowed. "I know."

"Cool." Meaghan swatted her arm. "Now get out of here and go have a good time on your date."

Sure, after you threw a bucket of cold water on it. But she knew Meaghan was only trying to help. And the worst part was, Meaghan was right. Shifters could fall in love with people who weren't their mates. It happened. But those relationships generally didn't last.

Meaghan thought Olly's relationship with Jackson was just a fling. A good time for both of them, but not forever.

She couldn't bear that thought.

She'd only just found her happiness. She didn't care what was *meant* to happen—no one could make her feel like Jackson did. Like she'd found a tiny piece of the world where she fit perfectly. She couldn't let anything or anyone take it away from her.

But if her owl identified her mate, it was all over.

I won't! her owl reassured her. *I won't let it happen!*

Can you even stop it? Honestly?

I can try, it said, its voice small.

"Hey," Meaghan said. "You okay?"

Olly clenched her fists. This was probably a bad decision, but…

"Yes. I'm fine. I'm going on a date with Jackson, and it's going to be *fun.*"

She would manage this. Somehow.

18

JACKSON

Jackson was standing outside Hannah's Grillhouse. Under the streetlight, so Olly would be able to spot him easily.

He ran a finger under his collar. His shirt felt too tight all over. It had fit fine when he tried it on in the store, but now he felt like a sausage about to burst out of its skin.

He undid the top couple of buttons. It helped with the throttling, but not the worry that if he breathed too deeply he'd be picking buttons out of the gutter.

Have I put on weight? Olly said my shoulders looked broader…

His stomach swooped. Thinking about the night before still made him sweat.

He'd almost lost her again. First in the pond and then when he froze up. His heart's desire had been in his arms and he'd almost screwed it all up.

She wants me. He waited for his stomach to stop lurching. *She chose me.*

And now here he was. Standing under the light outside the Grillhouse like a sitting duck so that she could take her time scoping out the situation before she—

He was keeping a lookout too, casually, and when a woman with her head down walked past him so close she almost walked *into* him, he did a double-take.

"Olly?"

"Jackson!"

The woman's head snapped up. Olly stared up at him, her eyes wide and somehow guarded.

She didn't look as though she'd forgotten their date. She was wearing her usual fur-lined coat over a tight dress and what he hoped were fleece-lined stockings. Her face was made up, or at least, her eyelashes looked darker than usual and he was pretty sure her lips weren't usually berry red.

She looked amazing. But the hood was pulled too far down over her head—she wouldn't have any peripheral vision. And she'd almost run straight into him.

"You weren't looking where you were going?" Jackson asked, surprised.

Olly's mouth worked silently. Eventually she gave an embarrassed grin. "Worrying too much about dinner," she admitted.

"If you'd rather go home—"

"No! I mean, home later, yes," she amended. "Food first."

He slipped his arm into hers. "You look beautiful, by the way."

"Really?" Olly looked down at herself, her face glowing. "I thought it might be a bit much…"

"You're making me feel underdressed."

Her eyes flicked over him and he got the uncanny feeling that she hadn't looked at him until then. For Olly, that was highly unusual.

"You're wearing a shirt with sleeves?" she asked, and he nodded. "Then you're already doing better than most guys in this town."

"One benefit of not dating a shifter." Jackson spoke in an undertone. "I'm less likely to bust through all my clothes."

Stop looking for problems, he told himself. *Wait for them to find you. If you go looking, half the time you'll be the one making the problem.*

His pocket buzzed and he bit back a sigh. Speaking of problems… Andrew had been trying to call him all afternoon. God knew how he had found Jackson's contact details but he'd made the mistake of picking up the first time so there was no point pretending he had the wrong number.

"Phone call?" Olly nodded towards his pocket.

"Nope." Jackson rejected the call and turned his phone off.

"I can't believe your phone survived yesterday."

"Waterproof case," he said, and slipped it back into his pocket.

She narrowed her eyes. "Mine's only water-resistant. And totally dead now. I'll have to borrow one of the work phones without Bob noticing."

"What?" Jackson guessed before she answered. "You haven't told him?"

"He was off sick today. And…" She sighed and bumped her head against his shoulder. "You and me is going to be big enough news without adding 'and also, my owl jumped into a frozen lake to steal someone else's engagement ring' to the mix."

"But you are going to tell him about us?"

"I thought *we* could tell him." She squeezed his arm. The soft breath she let out as she leaned against him made his blood run hot. "Later. After dinner and after after-dinner."

He held the door for her. "Sounds good to me. Especially that after-dinner." In between dodging Andrew's calls, he'd planned something for after they left the Grillhouse.

The restaurant was warm and cozy. It had a small indoor area and large courtyard out the back, with braziers burning merrily to keep diners warm. At the far end was a firepit where the evening's roast was being prepared. The restaurant's owner, Hannah

Holborn, waved them through to the courtyard. The smell of crackling pork wafted through the air.

And the hairs on the back of Jackson's neck didn't stop prickling.

Stop looking for problems, he'd told himself. But something wasn't right. Instead of watching all the other diners carefully, like she normally would, Olly seemed to be going out of her way *not* to look at them. She almost ran straight into one of the waiters.

"Let's sit here," she burst out, flustered. She grabbed a chair at a table in the middle of the courtyard, which was strange enough on its own, but the chair she'd chosen was facing the wall. She wouldn't be able to keep an eye on anyone from there. Well, anyone except him, if he sat opposite her.

"Everything okay?" he asked her as they sat down.

"Yes!" she replied. Too quickly, he thought. He felt bad for being suspicious, but…

Before he could pry any further—or get his act together and *not* pry any further—one of the waiters appeared at his shoulder.

"Hey, folks, what can I—oh, hey, Olly. I didn't realize it was you. You know your usual table's free, if you want to move to it?"

Jackson saw relief flash behind Olly's eyes as she recognized the waiter, and the way the corners of her lips tucked down with determination as she shook her head.

Stop being such a suspicious bastard, he told himself.

Olly smiled. "No, thanks, Brian. This is fine."

"Oh, well, in that case, I can get the kitchen to do your usual—"

"Actually, I was thinking I might try something different?"

"…Sure thing."

Jackson turned in his seat to glance at the waiter. He looked like he was having trouble keeping up and although Jackson could put some of that down to the dinner rush, some of it had to be that Brian was noticing the same thing he was. Olly was acting strangely.

And he knew how much she hated it when people noticed something about her.

He cleared his throat. "What's tonight's special?"

Brian jumped to attention. "Uh, there's pork belly…"

"Sounds great. I'll have that, and whatever beer you've got on tap."

"Me too," Olly added.

"Uh, but we're not allowed to serve it undercooked—"

"Then I'll have it cooked the normal amount." Olly's cheeks reddened. "And a beer."

Brian opened his mouth and Jackson could already see the question in his eyes, so he got in first. "Can we get some sides with that?"

"Uh, there's roast potatoes, sweetcorn, beans…"

"Yes," Olly said firmly. "*Extra* well cooked."

Brian hurried off, still looking puzzled, and Jackson sat back.

"Trying something new?" he asked, raising his eyebrows at Olly.

She shrugged. Just for a moment, something in the tightness of her shoulders and the way her head ducked down made her seem more like her old self. Then she straightened her neck and looked Jackson in the eye. "That's the idea. I decided I'm going to let go of some bad habits that haven't actually helped me as much as I thought."

He reached across the table to take her hand. "Bit early for letting go of bad habits, isn't it? New Year's a week away."

"But you're here now." Her fingers twisted around his.

Her eyes stayed locked on to his as Brian returned with their drinks. Jackson's throat was dry. He cleared it and lifted his glass.

"Here's to being your new bad habit," he said. His voice was rough, even though he'd cleared his throat, but Olly's eyes lit up.

"I hope so," she murmured, tipping her head back and smiling at him through her eyelashes. "Maybe you'll even end up being a good habit."

"Maybe." Jackson tapped his glass against hers and a shiver went down his arm. Because of the cold beer, he told himself as the shiver lodged itself in his chest. He took a deep breath and something trembled behind his ribs. "Wouldn't bet on it."

"That's exactly what I'm doing." Olly's lips flattened into a stubborn line. "If you can take a risk on me—"

She broke off as Brian appeared with their meals. Two slabs of pork belly with crackling an inch thick and piles of roasted vegetables. Jackson's stomach rumbled as the waiter placed his plate in front of him.

Olly prodded her pork belly with her fork. "This looks… good?" Her eyes drifted sideways—but not sideways enough to look at anyone else in the restaurant—and she frowned. "I'm *sure* it's good," she said, more firmly.

"Your owl's having doubts?"

Olly wrinkled her nose. "It thinks if something's not still bleeding it doesn't count as a meal."

That got them both a few disgusted looks from the tables either side. Jackson's own stomach wasn't too happy about the visual, either.

Olly caught his eye. "Sorry." She prodded the crackling again. "It *does* look good, though. Even if it's not leaking."

"God, Olly…"

She smirked at him and he glared at her until she laughed out loud.

Olly speared a slice of pork belly. Crackling crunched as she bit into it. "Oh, God, this *is* good," she muttered. "I can't believe I've been missing out on this my entire life." She peered up at Jackson, her eyes dancing. "Do you want to know what my owl says about it?" she added in an undertone.

He groaned and rubbed his forehead. "Go on. You can't ruin my appetite more than you already have."

"It actually likes it. Because it's crunchy and squishy at the same time and that's almost as good as fresh—"

"—And that's enough." Jackson raised his hands. "Are you trying to turn me vegetarian?"

"Is it working?" She eyed up his plate. "How much worse do I have to go before I get your share?"

Jackson picked up his fork. "Worse enough for us to get kicked out of here before I give up one bite of this belly."

Olly sniggered and sucked the fat from another piece of crackling. She grinned and crunched down on it. "Mmm," she moaned. "Almost as good as mouse bones…"

"You'll have to try harder than that."

"Really? Because you haven't touched your meal yet."

She was right. He was holding his fork, but that was as far as he had got. And not because she was putting him off.

His chest felt as though it was about to burst. The crawling emptiness, the constant feeling that something was missing from his life—he'd been a fool not to see it for what it was. He'd missed Olly like she was a part of him.

And now that he had her back, he wasn't going to let anything take her away from him.

"I'd be happy to take it off your hands," Olly suggested innocently.

Jackson grinned and cut into the succulent pork belly. "Try the vegetables before you start stealing my food."

The look Olly gave her vegetables was exceptionally owlish. Jackson snorted into his beer.

"All right…" She nibbled gingerly at a string bean. "What do you think?"

Olly's mouth twisted. "Maybe my bad old habits weren't all bad."

Jackson tried one. The string bean was lightly steamed, and crunched perfectly between his teeth with a hint of salted butter. "Tastes fine to me."

Olly took another mouthful. There was a distinct lack of crunch. She grimaced.

"Let me try that." Jackson tested a forkful of beans from Olly's plate. They were practically goo.

He forced himself to swallow them. "You did ask for everything well cooked."

"I think this is what put me off greens in the first place." Olly made a face.

"You or your owl?"

"Mommy, why does that lady have an owl?"

Olly's went completely still. She stared at Jackson, a hint of panic in her expression.

A little girl sitting at the next table had turned around in her seat and was gazing wide-eyed at them both. "Why do you have an owl?" she asked Olly.

"Because she's a witch," Jackson declared easily. He reached across the table and took Olly's hand again. She gripped his fingers fiercely. "Like in Harry Potter."

"Mommy, can I be a witch and have an owl? For Christmas?"

Jackson squeezed Olly's hand. She made a *phew* face and moved her chair around the table until she was sitting next to him. She pressed her face against his shoulder and groaned.

"Maybe I should go back to freaking out about things *before* I do them," she muttered into his shoulder.

Jackson wrapped one arm around her. "You're not going to put the whole shifter world in danger of discovery just because a little girl heard you talking about an owl."

"Hmm."

"She'll go away thinking you're a witch, and her parents will go away thinking you're a crazy person."

"*Hmm.*" Olly sounded both satisfied and extremely unsatisfied at the same time.

Jackson rested his chin on the top of her head. "We wouldn't have this problem if I was a shifter."

Olly tensed. If he hadn't been holding her, he didn't know if he would have felt it, but there was no way he would have missed the frustration in her voice.

"No, we would have a worse problem. Trust me, two or more people sitting staring at nothing and saying nothing is *way* weirder than talking about having some animal living inside you." She breathed out heavily. "As someone who has spent a lot of her life sitting staring at nothing and saying nothing all by myself, I know what I'm talking about."

She raised her head and looked directly into his eyes. "Stop wishing you could change."

Jackson frowned. Olly's gaze sliced straight through to his innermost fears. He felt like a rat in a lab. *Is this what she's avoiding when she says she doesn't like being looked at?* "I don't—"

"I love you just the way you are."

She kissed him. Her words had been urgent, almost angry, but her lips were soft and warm. Jackson pulled her close, tension easing from his body as she melted against him.

"Mommy, *ewwww*, look at those people!"

Olly pulled away, cheeks burning. "I just thought of another benefit my usual table has."

"A tad bit more privacy?"

She groaned and closed her eyes. "Something like that." She was about to say something else when a group of tourists pushed through the courtyard doors.

Jackson scanned them absently. Half-a-dozen men in their late twenties or early thirties; friends or colleagues on a pre-Christmas getaway, he guessed. He looked back at Olly.

Her eyes were still tightly closed.

"We can ask to move tables," he told her, but she shook her head.

"It's fine. I can—" She sighed and cracked one eye open. "I'll just make sure I keep all my attention on you," she said, and pecked him on the lips. "You and all this food."

"Glad to hear you've got your priorities straight." He was beginning to put the pieces together. His chest felt tender, hollow and full at the same time.

"True. I should have said the food first."

She wrinkled her nose at him in a mischievous grin and turned back to her meal. Jackson realized he was hesitating, and forced himself to do the same.

Olly caught him up on the local news as they finished their meals. Jackson was surprised at how much he'd missed—and how much he regretted missing it. He'd though being the human deputy in a town half-populated by shifters had been more frustration than it was worth, but he had to admit, it had had its good sides.

He watched Olly's face light up as she talked. "…visitors kept complaining about things going missing. Jewelry, mostly. No one wanted to blame the hellhound boys, but the new guy suspected them. He kept them all in lockup overnight. Meaghan was *pissed*, especially when things still went missing while they were in the cells."

"Walls can't keep hellhound shifters in," Jackson pointed out.

"Yeah, but Stringer was watching them, too. They didn't go anywhere all night and stuff *still* went missing."

"Jewelry." Jackson sighed and chuckled. "It was the Heartwell kids, wasn't it?" Dragon shifters, gold. It made sense.

Olly snorted. "Congrats, you just figured out in less than a minute what took Stringer *weeks*."

"I can't say I think much of my replacement."

"Well, he's not based in town like you were. He lives down in Hutton and only comes up when there's a problem."

"But with the number of visitors Pine Valley gets, the town needs someone around to keep an eye on—" Jackson shook his head. "I'm telling you what you already know. Again."

"We need someone who can catch problems as they happen."

"Even if he's not a shifter?"

Olly narrowed her eyes. "Stringer's a shifter. It doesn't make him any better at his job. Or anything that requires thinking more than half a step ahead."

"Now you're just trying to make me jealous."

It was a joke, but Olly went pale. Her eyes stayed fixed on his, but…

Jackson's jaw tightened. She wasn't looking *at* him, so much as she was not looking at anything else. Or any*one* else.

He caught hold of the feeling rising in his chest and shoved it back down.

Olly had chosen him. He couldn't let his own fear, his own *weakness*, ruin that. He needed to stop thinking up problems where there weren't any.

And he needed to stop *making* problems. What had he been thinking, inviting her out to dinner?

He picked up her hand and kissed it. "Want to get out of here?"

19

OLLY

Olly relaxed as soon as she was in Jackson's truck. Too much, perhaps. She slipped off the seat down into the footwell.

Jackson raised his eyebrows at her as he got into the driver's seat. "I didn't think you had that much to drink," he deadpanned.

"I just need a minute."

Jackson nodded as he put the truck into gear. "A minute out of everyone's sight, or a minute with everyone else out of sight?"

Olly pressed one hand against her stomach. It was still in knots from dinner. "You noticed?"

He nodded, and she sighed and dropped her head into her hands. "I just—" *Don't want to hurt you, ever again.*

Even with her head in her hands she could feel Jackson's eyes on her. Warm and gentle.

"Changed things up a bit too fast?"

Olly bit her tongue. "Yeah. That's it."

She rubbed her forehead. Her owl had been silent all evening. Silent and smug and determinedly looking no further than her next forkful of food.

She was relieved it was supporting her, and hollowed out by the effort it was taking her owl *not* to peer at everything and everyone that moved in the restaurant.

"Going out for dinner was a mistake," she muttered. "I mean—not going out with *you*, but..."

She swallowed hard. *You aren't going to tell him anything's wrong. Remember? If he knows what's worrying you it'll only hurt him.* She swallowed again but the lump in her throat stayed exactly where it was.

"Those beans were a mistake, for sure," Jackson said lightly. "You ready to go?

Olly sat up, careful not to look out the window, and pulled on her seatbelt. Her eye caught on something on the dash. "You're kidding me. That's still there?"

Jackson swore and reached over. She slapped his hand away, laughing. "You haven't cleaned your truck in a *year*?"

"I vacuum!"

"You couldn't vacuum up a fruit sticker?"

She picked it off and rolled it between her fingers. "I can't believe you convinced me to eat a whole bucket of... what were they? Nectarines?"

"I don't recall much convincing being required."

"Of course you needed to convince me. Nectarines are *fruit*."

"Delicious fruit." Jackson pulled onto the road. Olly kept her attention on him, and not on anything or anyone outside the truck, but she still couldn't read what his expression meant as the skin around his eyes creased. "You know, you keep saying you give in to your owl too much, but I don't remember things that way. You were always owlish, sure, but you were—are—a woman, too." His cheeks darkened. "I mean, I didn't have to convince you to eat *fruit*."

Olly kept rolling the sticker between her finger and thumb. He was right. He hadn't had to convince her to eat the nectarines, same as she used to be able to go into a building without circling it a half-dozen times first. Once, sure. That was sensible. But over and over until she'd wasted the whole evening?

Her stomach twisted as she looked back on the last twelve months. She'd been so terrified about getting things wrong, and for what?

The worst had already happened.

Jackson being back in her life was the second chance she never thought she'd get. She couldn't let it go to waste.

"We didn't have dessert at Hannah's," she said, putting the rolled-up sticker in her pocket and reaching out to take Jackson's hand. "I think I still have some cookies leftover at home. Want to come over?"

Jackson's gaze heated up. "For dessert?"

"To start with."

She watched him roll the idea around in his mind. "I have a better idea," he said at last. "Let's get that dessert and go for a drive."

*

Olly lived on the edge of town. Not like Meaghan and Caine, off tucked away further along the valley, but on the last street before the rows of houses and streetlights gave way to forest. She used to think it was perfect—a shifter living on the balance point between the wild outdoors and civilization.

Except life wasn't that tidy. If she was going to avoid ever accidentally locking eyes with her real mate, she'd have to get as far away from town as possible.

When are you planning to talk to him about that, again? her owl sniffed.

She was still carefully not answering when she got back into the truck, box of chocolate cookies clutched against her chest. She'd glimpsed her neighbor as she locked her front door, and that had been fine because she knew him already and, therefore, knew he was not her mate, until she remembered he had family to stay for the holiday, and she hadn't met his brother yet—

She shook her head. This was ridiculous. She knew most of the people in town; in fact, she'd known them her whole life. And she couldn't work her tourist job if she was constantly terrified of meeting her mate every time she met someone new. It would be like the hellhounds, but worse.

She was going to have to trust that things would work out for the best. If she and Jackson were going to do this, they had to be strong enough to weather anything.

She'd had enough of running and hiding. She wasn't going to scurry into her own home and hide there like she was under attack.

"Got them. Where to next?" She sounded breathless even to her own ears.

"Back into the wild," Jackson said, and her heart leaped. It was as though he'd read her mind. Out of town, into the woods.

…Okay, maybe she wasn't quite ready to apply her newfound resolve yet.

"Perfect," she said.

"Don't get your hopes up." Classic Jackson.

She looked at him sidelong. "What's the plan? The one I'm not meant to get my hopes up about."

There it was—a thread of secret, prideful pleasure in the corners of his mouth. "You'll see when we get there—"

Her heart jumped unpleasantly. Owlishly fast.

"—and I'm sure you'll pick up all the clues you need along the way."

Tension melted out of her. *Of course Jackson isn't going to spring something on me with no warning.*

He smiled at her in the rear-view mirror and handed her a thermos. "Can you check for me if this is still warm?"

The scent of hot chocolate filled the air as Olly unscrewed the top. Chocolate and cinnamon with a hint of pepper. Memories stirred in the back of her mind.

"You went shopping? This smells like that fancy stuff from Mr. Bell's store." She took a sip. "Yep, definitely is."

She closed her eyes briefly, remembering that afternoon in the sun. This had to be a clue.

Jackson cleared his throat.

"I thought you'd like it more than the instant coffee packets that've been sitting in the glove box since June," he said, turning onto a side-street. Olly kept as good an eye on their route as she could while being careful not to accidentally look at anyone outside the car.

"What happened in June?" she asked absently.

Jackson chuckled. "My Ma came to visit and said if I didn't get myself a proper coffee machine she'd disown me."

They were heading out of town. Olly relaxed. Another clue, and one that told her that her suspicions about the chocolate had been correct.

"At least someone in your family has good taste."

"You haven't asked me why I never threw the old instant packets out."

Olly narrowed her eyes. "And now I don't want to."

"Aw, that's no fun. How am I meant to gross you out saying I just suck on the packets dry if you're not going to ask?"

"Oh, gross! Instant coffee is foul. Normal coffee is bad enough, but instant isn't even… I mean, what is it? Tiny burned, dissolvable crumbs? I don't trust it."

"You trust dissolvable chocolate."

"That's sugar. It's different." Except – she hadn't had hot chocolate all winter. The chocolatey goodness wafting up from the thermos was making her mouth water. How had she forgotten how much she liked it?

Jackson chuckled. "Good to know some things haven't changed. Maybe you should get your hopes up after all."

They drove until the road was pitted with potholes and snow started piling up on the road where the plows had given up trying. The lights of the town were so far away that the stars above blazed in their full glory.

Olly knew exactly where they were. Warmth unfurled inside her and she grazed Jackson's arm with the backs of her knuckles to get his attention.

"It's not going to be as pleasant an evening as last time," she said teasingly.

"No?" Jackson's eyes were laughing. "Why would you say that?"

"There wasn't a foot of snow on the ground, for a start."

"We'll just have to stay off the ground then."

Jackson flashed her a tight, shy smile and jumped out of the truck. His boots crunched in the snow as he walked around the back and pulled the tarp of the truck bed.

Olly watched through the rear window. "Oh, for..." The warmth inside her wriggled happily at what had been hiding under the tarp.

"Ta-dah!" Jackson struck a pose—for about the smallest smidgen of a second imaginable, before he dropped his arms and thrust his hands into his pocket, his wide grin becoming a bashful smile. Olly blinked. Just for a moment, he'd seemed very... not-Jackson.

But that moment was over, and the shy pride beaming from his eyes was all him. Olly slipped out of the passenger seat and went to him. The night air bit at the exposed skin on her cheeks and she buried her chin deeper into coat's fur lining, which did nothing to hide her own delighted smile.

"I can't believe you went to all this trouble!"

Jackson had transformed the skirted truck bed into a picnic station that rivaled the Puppy Express stops. Piles of cushions and blankets turned the hard metal edges of the bed into a cozy nook, and after he swore under his breath and fiddled with something taped to one of the sides, fairy lights started to glitter.

"No fireflies this time of year," Jackson muttered. He helped her up into the truck bed and she let him, even though she could have easily done it herself. The pressure of his hand in hers, the other steadying her at the waist, made her feel solid and grounded.

Olly sank down on one of the cushions. The summer before last—the last summer Jackson had spent in Pine Valley—they'd had a picnic on this part of the mountain. There was meant to be a whole group of them, but what with one thing and another, by mid-afternoon it had only been her and Jackson left. They'd piled everyone's rugs and cushions into one marvelous nest and feasted on the remains of the picnic food until neither of them could move.

They'd almost…

She blinked and gave Jackson a hard, questioning look. He gazed back, his eyes warm.

"We're doing things over, aren't we?" His voice rumbled against her skin, warm and rough. The truck swayed as he climbed up into the bed and sat down next to her. "This is where it all started. I think it needs another go."

"Why? This is when—" Olly felt her cheeks go red, and not because of the cold. "When I first thought I could… I might…"

"I did. Already. For months." Jackson moved closer to her, near enough she could pick out every lash around his dark eyes. "It was the first time I thought you might feel the same way."

Pain slivered through her heart. "We do have to do it over, don't we? Because that's when everything started to go wrong. The hellhounds turned up but none of us knew that yet, just that things kept going wrong, accidents, and I felt so—out of control—and…"

She clapped her hands over her mouth.

Jackson sighed. He turned side-on to her, his back against the truck's cab, and looked out through the trees. "I did wonder—"

"I'm so sorry. Oh, God, I…" Her mouth went dry.

Jackson took her hand. "I was going to say, I did wonder if that was what made you… make the decision you did."

"It's all my fault—"

"And this time it's going to be my fault." Jackson tugged on her hand and she closed the gap between them. She shouldn't have been able to feel any warmth from where her hip pressed against hers, not through half a dozen layers of clothing, so it must have been her imagination that her skin was heating up. "We're doing over. From the start. And if you try to apologize to me again for doing something you thought was right, and *is* right, even if it took us both a year to figure it out, I'll—I'll…" He tipped his head back and glared at her, mock-severe. "I'll make us re-do the first time we met, as well."

"When Lucas got stuck in the stairwell?"

"That's the one."

"You're going to get Lucas shitfaced again and make him climb the stairs?"

"If I have to." Jackson's eyes softened. "Won't be hard to find him, he's probably still sleeping off Jasper's party. Getting him moving, on the other hand…"

Olly wriggled closer to him. "I'd better stop whining then."

Something flashed behind Jackson's eyes, but he kissed her before she could figure out what it was. His lips brushed against hers, cold at first, then shiveringly warm. "Don't stop anything," he murmured. "Just be happy. That's all I want."

That's all I want for you, she told him silently. That flash of *something* on his face had her worried.

"I'll try," she said. "Starting now."

Jackson hid a smile, then caught her eyes and stopped trying to hide it. He tucked his head down and grinned. "No hellhounds to mess us around this time, at least."

"Oh they'll keep messing us around. It's worse when they're trying to be helpful. And the Heartwell kids are going to be big enough to make some real trouble soon."

"That sounds like two problems with one solution. Even two juvenile dragons couldn't give a whole pack of hellhounds the slip."

Olly leaned against him. "Meaghan would appreciate them having something to distract them over the next… oh… eighteen years?"

"Hmm?"

Olly explained about Meaghan's pregnancy and Jackson laughed.

"Twins! I would've thought she'd want all the help she can get."

"I think…" Olly wrinkled her nose. "I think she'll spend half the time yelling at them all to leave her alone, and the other half yelling at them to come back so she can put them to work. And if the twins are shifters… Oh God. Imagine toddlers who can literally climb the walls. Climb *into* the walls."

"They might not be." Jackson's voice was light—which was always suspicious.

"Which would be a *relief*," she insisted. "And you're right. Meaghan's not a shifter and if one parent isn't, their kids might not be either."

"Or both parents." Jackson's voice was barely audible, a rumble in the very back of his throat. He shook his head, frowning, as though he was trying to get rid of a clinging thought. "My father's in town."

Olly unpacked that statement. "Oh. Uh… sorry?"

Jackson snorted. "He's picked the worst possible time, and dragged his poor assistant along with him, too. Delphine Belgrave—you saw her drop me off, remember?" He waited for Olly to nod. "I suppose it makes sense he'd want to surround himself with other mythic shifters."

Olly wound her arms around him and squeezed until the line between his eyebrows smoothed away. "You know, I don't recall talking about hellhounds and child menaces during our summer picnic. I remember eating until I thought I'd explode."

"Because you thought if you stuffed yourself your owl would stop trying to jump out of you to hunt fireflies." His eyes were warm, and the expression in them said: *I see what you're doing. Distracting me from wallowing in a grump. Thank you.*

She kissed him. "We won't have that problem this time. My owl isn't going to try to hunt—wait, what are they?" She prodded the string of fairy lights with the toe of her boot.

She leaned closer. "Are they… Santa Clauses?"

Jackson made a strangled, embarrassed noise. "Got them from Mr. Bell's."

"God, they're… hideous." Laughter bubbled out of her. The tiny glass Santas looked like they'd been repurposed from Halloween decorations. Their bulbous bodies could have been pumpkins in a past life, and their painted faces got creepier the longer she looked at them.

"He said they were normal lights when I bought them."

"And you trusted him?" Everyone knew Mr. Bell valued a sale now over a return customer later.

"I was focusing on these."

He pulled out a bag from under one of the cushions and opened it. More thermoses. Olly's eyes widened.

"The chocolate—"

"It all melted anyway the last time, didn't it?" Jackson placed the thermoses one by one on the bed in front of them.

"Little cups of goo instead of truffles. They were still tasty, thought. And I could tell what they all were anyway."

"So you claimed."

"I could!"

"Well." Jackson kissed her. "This time we can really put it to the test."

He unscrewed one flask and poured an inch of steaming hot chocolate into the cap. Olly watched his eyes. He was quietly pleased with himself, and probably didn't even know he was showing it. It was adorable.

"What do you think this one is?"

Olly breathed in the vapor from the hot chocolate. "You got these all from Mr. Bell's place?"

"Perhaps."

"Ooh, that's not fair…"

She knew all the brands Mr. Bell stocked. This time of year, it was all Christmassy flavors, which wasn't as limited a variety as you might think. She'd already tried the cinnamon and pepper while they were driving, and this was similar, but…

"Nutmeg," she declared.

"Hmmph." Jackson confiscated the cap and opened another flask. "What about this one?"

"Mint. Obviously."

"What sort?"

"There's sorts?"

Jackson gave her a look that gave nothing away except how much fun he was having. She narrowed her eyes at him as she sipped the hot chocolate.

"Peppermint." She took another sip. "Wait! No. Spearmint and … cinnamon again?"

"Bad?"

"Interesting." She tried it again and it stayed… interesting. "How am I doing so far?"

"Hmm."

"That's not an answer!" she complained as he offered her another capful of hot chocolate. All the flavors were mixing together in her palate – sweet and spicy and…

"Jackson, this is just rum."

"Not *just* rum."

"Fine. Rum and that stuff Hannah drinks? Alcohol… cream… stuff. Is there even any chocolate in here? Wait." She drained the cap. "No."

"I'll tell Mr. Bell to keep those ones out of the kids' pick and mix."

"How am I going then?"

"No idea."

"But you said…"

"I forgot to mark the bottles."

Olly stared at him. Laughter bubbled up and escaped. "You forgot—"

"I've got all the labels still. I just don't know which ones they match up to." He fumbled in his pocket, gloved hands clumsy, and Olly laughed and pushed him over.

She clambered on top of him, the same as she'd done the night before. A thrill went through her.

"Why don't you try?" she suggested, and kissed him.

He mumbled something against her lips. She hummed a question back and he repeated: "Irish cream."

"What?"

"Rum and Irish cream."

She fumbled for one of the other thermoses and took a sip. "And this one?"

Another kiss. Long and lingering. Her toes curled inside her boots and her fingers curled around the thermos, aching to touch him instead.

"Peppermint."

"And?"

"You know I'm not as good at this sort of thing as you, Olly."

"I only said it a minute ago!"

"Maybe I need another taste to be sure."

This time she couldn't stop herself. She peeled her gloves off. The cold air bit at her hands and then she thrust them under his hat, curling them into his hair so she could kiss him properly.

"Cinnamon," he said eventually.

"Is it?"

"You tell me! You bought them."

"I'm finding myself somewhat distracted…"

The look in his eyes heated her from the inside out.

"Distracted?" she murmured. "Like last time?"

"We didn't get this far last time." Jackson's lips twitched. "Too much food and too little courage."

Too little courage. She was the one who was being cowardly, now. Not telling him how afraid she was that she was going to ruin this, hurt him, again.

"What about now?" she whispered.

Jackson pulled off his gloves and lifted one hand to caress her cheek. "Now I know I love you. I know there's nowhere I'd rather be than here with you. And I know that if I mess this up for the second time you'll never let me hear the end of it."

Olly smiled and he cocked his head. "You're smiling."

"Never is a long time."

"Not long enough."

"What would be, then?"

Jackson kissed her, his lips warm and soft. "Forever."

He hunted for something in his jacket pocket. The heat rushing through Olly's veins suddenly went very hot and very cold at the same time. "Jackson, what are you—what is—wait, what *is* that?"

He pulled his hand out. Something glittered in it, but not what she'd expected.

"I thought you were going to—" she began.

"It's a ring sizer," he said at the same time.

Olly froze. Her owl turned its head around very, very slowly.

A ring sizer? it asked.

For rings, she explained, uselessly.

What about the ring I found?

We have to give that back, she thought, and then: *Oh, God, I really have to remember not to leave it behind this time—*

Tell me more about the ring sizer, her owl insisted.

Olly's lips twitched into a smile. Warmth bubbled inside her. *It's for my ring,* she told it, and it perked up.

Good!

She licked her lips. "So you were," she began, "this is… you're… how was I meant to see this coming?"

The last words came out as a squeak.

Jackson half-sat up and she stayed on his lap. Even if she wasn't completely sure of what was happening, some part of her—probably owlish—wanted to keep him pinned down until she had a better grip on the situation.

He held the ring sizer between them, holding it awkwardly. "We're doing things over," he said gruffly. "Last night you gave me a ring that didn't fit. I'd better get you one that does."

She felt his eyes on her. It didn't make her itch like other people looking at her did, but it felt… expectant.

She lifted her own eyes to meet his gaze.

"Marry me, Olive Lockey."

One heartbeat. "Yes."

The corners of Jackson's eyes creased. "As fast as that? You don't want to think about it? Examine it from all angles?"

"No!" Olly's breath stuck in her throat. She gestured haphazardly while she waited for it to come unstuck and Jackson's eyebrows went up. Her heart felt so big there was no room for her lungs. At last she gave up and just laughed, and that seemed to free everything up. "Of course I don't need to think about it. I wasn't expecting it but it's perfect. It's exactly what I want."

"I didn't get you a ring. I thought you'd want to choose your own. There's that jeweler in town with the coffee shop opposite, you could scope it out as long as you liked. And you can use this to know what size you need in advance so once you know the style you want, we can swoop in…"

She kissed him to shut him up. It didn't work.

"The way it works is you try on the different ring blanks here, then slip them on the stick and read where it fits to—"

Olly wrestled the sizer off him and thrust it into her pocket, then got back to kissing him.

This time, it worked.

20

JACKSON

CHRISTMAS EVE

Jackson wasn't awake yet. He knew he wasn't awake, because he could feel the warm weight of another body in bed next to him, soft and smooth-skinned. Olly. The woman of his dreams and so this had to be a dream. How many times would he have to pull himself out of this imagined paradise and wake up into the real world—

Wait.

Jackson's body tried to sit up. He forced himself to lie still. Sitting up right now would make him the biggest idiot in the world because this wasn't a dream, Olly was *there*, lying against his side, her breasts pressed against his ribs and one arm lying possessively across his chest. Her hand was palm-down over his heart, the touch of her fingertips feather-light.

The ring sizer was tucked under her fingers against his chest.

His heart thundered in his ears. It wasn't a dream. *None* of it was a dream.

Olly had agreed to marry him, to be with him for as long as they both lived, and sitting up right now and spilling her out of bed would be the worst thing he could possibly do.

They were back at the cottage near the Puppy Express. After their ... *experiences* in the cabin, Jackson hadn't been able to handle the idea of going to his cold, locked-up house, the one he hadn't been to in a year. The house meant nothing to him. The cabin did. And they were rentals for vacationers, right? So he had rented this one. His old house was just a house, but this place ... this felt like *theirs*.

His breath caught as he looked at Olly. And it stayed caught as his eyes roved over her body, soaking in every detail of her. The light hairs on her arms. The way her waist curved down to her hips, and on to her muscular thighs. The thatch of blond hair pressed hard against his leg. *All* of her pressed hard against him, as though even asleep she refused to let him go.

Something welled up inside him, bright and triumphant. His ribs ached with it, as though his body wasn't enough to contain all of this—all of—

A crease formed between Olly's eyebrows. She murmured something sleepy and disgruntled and he let out his breath and remembered to take another one, this time.

Jackson huffed out a soft laugh so sudden it surprised him. "I'm not allowed to stop breathing, huh?" he whispered to her. He placed his hand over hers on his heart. "I should have had you around six months ago."

Shouldn't have left twelve months ago and gotten myself into that trouble in the first place. Jackson sighed. This was apparently as acceptable to the slumbering Olly as his laughter had been, because she didn't so much as flicker an eyelash.

He rubbed his forehead, brushing lightly over the scar. It didn't hurt as much as it had done even a few days ago, he realized. And the tightness in his chest was gone, too, replaced by that triumphant sunrise-feeling. It surged again as he thought about it, as though reacting to his attention, and he forced it down. He was half-worried that if he let the feeling out, he'd end up whooping with joy, or something equally likely to ruin Olly's sleep.

He wanted to lie with her like this forever, safe in this half-awake moment before the real world took hold again.

That moment ended too soon. A certain bodily urgency made itself known; the real world making itself known in the least dignified way possible. Jackson thudded down from his cloud with a groan.

He muttered an apology to Olly and tried to ease her off him. She clung on stubbornly.

"I need to use the bathroom," he murmured, and she let him go with a reluctant groan.

"Come back quickly."

Her voice lit up that cloud-feeling inside him again, but he had other things on his mind now. He grabbed his boxers from the floor and made his way quickly downstairs.

Bathroom first, then breakfast in bed for the woman of his dreams. He'd stocked the fridge and pantry after his shopping trip the day before. He had everything he needed to make Olly a delicious breakfast that even her owl wouldn't disapprove of.

For the first time in his life, everything was going right.

He used the toilet, washed his hands and gave his underarms a test sniff.

New plan: bathroom, shower, *then* breakfast in bed.

He turned on the shower and hunted out a towel as steam started to fill the room. He'd bought toiletries as well, but what the hell had he done with them? Where was the soap?

He ducked to check the cupboard under the vanity and caught a glimpse of himself in the mirror as he straightened. He looked like... well, either a guy who'd just had either the best or the worst night of his life, which was appropriate. His hair had dried in clumps and he teased a long-dead leaf out of it as he checked his scar. Still there, still tender, but it didn't hurt as much anymore.

None of it did.

Jackson took a deep breath.

He might look like shit, but he'd never felt better.

He'd spent his whole life thinking that being the non-shifter son of two shifters meant there was something wrong with him. He'd thought that being a shifter's mate would change that, fix him somehow… but he'd been wrong.

He didn't need to be a shifter to be happy. Or even a shifter's mate. He wasn't broken, or something to be ashamed about.

He was human, and for the first time in his life that didn't feel like a mistake.

The sunrise feeling inside his chest rose up again and this time he let it. Joy spread through him like dawn light, filling his body with light and warmth. He felt as though he was floating on a cloud as the world around him came into focus. Colors brighter, light more intense, smells and sensations tuned to perfection…

He let out a soft burst of laughter. All his life, he'd put up walls around his heart, scared that if he let anyone know how he felt about himself they'd realize he was right. That there was something wrong with him. Now, at last, those walls were coming down. He could be free and open with Olly. His true self. Happy with who he was.

As the last of his defenses faded away, the lightness he'd felt when he woke up felt as though it was filling his whole body.

For the first time in his life, he was content with himself. He was Jackson Gilles, human, and if Olly was happy with him just the way he was then he could be, too.

The bathroom was filling with steam. He swiped the mirror clean to have one last look at himself before he jumped in the shower—

His heart almost stopped.

He looked in the mirror. His reflection looked back. But it couldn't be his reflection, because the face looking back at him didn't have his brown eyes.

He steadied himself against the sink.

His eyes in the mirror were *silver*.

"What the *fuck*," he burst out.

"Jackson? Are you having a shower? Wait for me…"

Olly's voice echoed through the house. And through *him*.

The sunrise feeling inside him soared. Strange energy filled him, from his heart to his fingertips. And further.

Jackson cried out wordlessly as sparks shimmered at the tips of his fingers. His legs gave out beneath him. Maybe this was a dream after all because there was no way in fuck this was happening.

The shimmers surrounded his body, then sank back into it. And his body changed.

He lay gasping on the floor. He tried to get up, but his legs—oh, no. Oh, *shit* no.

Jackson staggered to his feet. All four of them. And they weren't feet, they were hooves.

Steam was filling the bathroom now. He could just make out his reflection in the mirror.

He was a pegasus.

This isn't possible. Jackson's mind rebelled as hooves—*his* hooves—slid on the slippery tiles. People didn't just *become* shifters. Except for hellhounds. But normally, people were either born as shifters, able to communicate telepathically even before they gained their animal forms, or they stayed human. Even if their animal forms came in late, there was always some hint.

A pit opened up inside him, hollow and gnawing. He'd been right all along. He had been broken. Walking around the world half-finished. His true nature had been waiting inside him all this time.

The universe must have it in for him. The moment he finally felt happy with who he was, who he was changed.

"No," he tried to gasp, but it came out as *nhhhhrrrr!* He stepped back and almost slipped, hooves clattering on the tile floor. Both wings whipped out. The towel cupboard went flying.

Joy bubbled up inside him in equal amounts to the horror creeping down his spine. But it wasn't *his* joy.

Hello! a voice echoed inside his head. *Oh, isn't it a wonderful morning to be alive?*

"What," Jackson tried to say. In the mirror, the pegasus' nostrils flared.

I can't talk, he thought. *Of course I can't, horses can't—*

Talk? You're talking now! We're *talking now! Isn't it marvelous?*

The pegasus—he—no, it was definitely the pegasus—*pranced.*

Oh God, Jackson thought-said.

I've been waiting so long for this moment! To really exist! Now we're together, our fates will—ooh, what's that? Is that fog? Why's it so warm?

The pegasus's voice was like an orchestra in full swing. Jackson would have clutched his head, if he had hands. And a normal head.

What are you talking about, our fates? he demanded instead. *What are you—how are you—how am I—*

Andrew. His stomach sank.

This was why Andrew had come. He'd somehow known that Jackson was a shifter, and he'd...

A shifter. No, I can't be…

"Jackson? Are you in there?"

The bathroom door bumped against the pegasus' hindquarters.

Someone's calling for you! his pegasus gasped wondrously. *Who is it? Do you know them?*

Jackson's heart joined his stomach. *She's…*

My dream woman. The best thing ever to happen to me. My… my Olly.

Dread coursed through his veins. *I can't let her see me like this!*

See you? Don't worry, she'll only see me!

That's what I meant!

"Jackson?" The door handle rattled. "Unlock the door! It's freezing out here…"

Jackson groaned. If she was cold, she probably hadn't bothered to get dressed. He could imagine her standing right there on the other side of the door, naked and gorgeous and in love with him.

No. Not *him.* With the man she thought he was. The man *he'd* thought he was, too.

How was he going to explain this to her?

"Are you okay in there?" Olly's voice held a hint of concern. "I can sense something… strange."

Jackson went completely still. To his relief, his pegasus went still, as well. Not one feather so much as trembled.

"It's almost as if… as if…" Olly's voice trailed away. "We are the only ones here, aren't we?"

Who is she? His pegasus wondered. Its nostrils flared. *She smells like…*

I need to talk to her, Jackson told it.

Okay! His pegasus replied, and did nothing.

In human form.

"I think someone might be coming." There was a soft noise like Olly was resting her hand against the door. "It feels like…" A short, negative sound. "I'll just go… check it out."

Listen to her! She's already sensing something's wrong. If she sees me—us—you like this, she'll freak out. I have to explain it to her. In person. He paused. *Human person.*

Jackson felt a strange pressure against his mind. It was like his pegasus's voice, but from outside. He pushed it away without thinking.

Aw… His pegasus shook its mane out and, with a swoosh of feathers, somehow dove *back* inside him.

Jackson gasped and opened his eyes. The first thing he saw were his hands, splayed on the floor. *His* hands. Human hands. Fingers. Thumbs.

"Thank God," he muttered, and jumped to his feet. "Olly—"

He pulled the door open. Olly was halfway down the hallway. In front of her, an open doorway led into the living room. Windows opened out from the living room to the frozen forest beyond, but she wasn't looking at them. Her head was angled up, as though she was trying to glare straight through the building into the sky.

Jackson couldn't help stopping to stare at her. She was as naked as he'd imagined, outlined in the light coming through the doorway like a statue of some ancient, wild goddess. Every line of her body radiated feminine beauty as she lowered her head, still facing away from him.

His pegasus stirred. *Is she—*

CRASH!

21

OLLY

He's here!

Olly's owl screeched with joy. She shook her head, confused. *Who's here?*

As soon as Jackson had vanished into the bathroom, her owl had sensed... *something.* Something that made it sit up and practically start to sing with excitement. Jackson wasn't coming out of the bathroom, and all she could think of was that her owl must have sensed someone outside, since it had never gotten this excited about Jackson before, and they were the only ones in the house. She flung open the door, barely noticing the cold, caught up in her owl's excitement.

It's him! her owl trilled. *Yes, this is the best thing that could have happened! Can't you smell him? Hear him?*

Her senses blazed. She tasted starlight on clouds, the bright ice of midnight air. Fireworks went off inside her brain. Her owl was so overcome it couldn't use words. Wonder and amazement billowed inside her, like clouds parting to let the sun in.

She blinked, and when her eyes cleared they locked onto one thing. Standing on the snow outside, with snow settling around it from its abrupt landing, was a massive, silver-winged pegasus.

It's him? What's him?... No. You can't mean…

Jackson's voice filtered through her owl's rapture. "How the hell did my father find out where I was staying?"

His father?

Jackson's father. Jackson's father the pegasus shifter. Jackson's father the pegasus shifter, whose sudden appearance had made her owl flop around in rapturous happiness.

There was only one thing that could mean.

Oh God. Oh, no no no no no.

Her breath rattled in her lungs. "I've got to—"

She backed away as fast as she could, colliding with Jackson. His strong hands held her up, but she couldn't look at him. She couldn't look out the windows, either.

This was how it was *meant* to work. She knew that, now. Her owl had sensed her mate before she'd even set eyes on him. Which meant he might have sensed her, too, if his animal was anything like as watchful as hers. If it wasn't… maybe she still had a chance to escape her fate.

If she caught his eyes, he'd definitely know. And then it would all be over.

There were several key steps to forming a mate bond. Every shifter who'd gotten past puberty knew about them.

First, you lock eyes with your potential mate. Your animal knows at once who they are and that you're meant to be together. Then, to form the actual, real mate bond… you sleep together.

Olly's throat locked tight, holding back the tears that were burning behind her eyes. Now that she'd felt the true mate connection, she felt like even more of a fool for thinking Jackson was her mate.

Her breath hitched. She could barely force the words out. "I'm sorry, I've got to…"

"I'm the one who's sorry." Jackson's voice was grim. "I didn't know he was going to turn up like this. I know you hate surprises. If you need to take off—"

"Yes," Olly gasped, clinging to the excuse and hating herself for it. She dragged herself out of his grasp and ran up the stairs.

She had to get away.

At the top of the stairs, she shifted so fast her head spun. She'd forgotten to open the window first and attacked it with beak and claws until it opened. The icy morning air whispered across her feathers.

What's the problem? her owl asked, coming down from its dizzy haze. *I thought you'd be happy!*

Happy? Olly flung herself into the air, desperate to get as far away from the cottage as possible. *How could this make me happy?*

She couldn't blame her owl for being so happy. This was natural for it—more natural than doing its best *not* to find her mate, like it had tried to do.

Her owl had found her mate.

And it was Jackson's father.

22

JACKSON

Why did she run away?

Jackson ground his teeth. His pegasus' voice was like… sparkles. *Sad* sparkles. Like puffs of glitter shaped like unhappy faces in his brain. *I told you. She doesn't like surprises.*

But we didn't surprise her!

No, Jackson agreed, his shoulders slumping. *He did.*

…I suppose it is a little bit my fault, then. Somehow, even though it only existed inside his head, his pegasus managed to scuff one hoof. Sadly.

You know who he is? Jackson stalked back into the bathroom, picked up his towel and wrapped it around his waist.

Of course I do! He's my sire. Your… daddy?

Jackson winced. *My father.*

He paused and groaned. Of course his pegasus was the reason Andrew was here. Why else would his father turn up after so long?

Jackson was finally worth paying attention to.

He walked back out into the living room, wishing with each step that the earth would swallow him up. Andrew was still on the front yard, and still in pegasus form. He fluttered his wings as he saw Jackson through the windows.

Kiddo!

Jackson jerked and put a hand to his temple.

That was his fa—Andrew's voice. Inside his head.

"How did you do that?"

The Pegasus trotted up to the window and shrugged. Its wings rippled expressively. *The same way I always do.*

Jackson's head hurt. He ran one hand over his face. He should have seen this coming. Telepathy came part and parcel with being a shifter, and if that's what he was, then…

"Olly," he muttered. "I could talk to her—but I don't know how…"

What was that? These old ears, you know, they just don't work like they used to. Andrew the pegasus flicked his ears.

"I said—" Jackson stilled himself.

He didn't even know how to start.

But he'd heard Andrew's voice in his head. He focused on that.

What had Olly said once? That sometimes being a shifter was like having your whole brain be an open field ready for people to dive-bomb. He didn't want that. He imagined his mind like a room, and Andrew's voice filtering in through a half-open door.

A door he could close, if he wanted to.

He bent his head, the hairs on the back of his neck prickling with self-consciousness and his insides prickling with disgust. Why was he worried about making a fool of himself in front of this asshole?

Better to get it wrong now and figure out how to do it right, than mess up more with Olly.

Yes! his pegasus piped up suddenly. *We can't embarrass ourselves in front of outsiders!*

Olly's not an outsider, Jackson argued. *She's…*

Yoo-hoo? Son? Still alive in there?

Jackson worked his jaw. *This is bullshit. Something's gone wrong here. I'm not a shifter, I'm—*

Something clicked inside his head.

—I'm nothing but human.

The pegasus outside bridled its wings. *Au contraire, son. You're nothing* like *human.*

Somewhere inside him, Jackson's pegasus flicked its mane. Cold pooled on every inch of Jackson's skin. *No. This has to be a—*

You're not drunk, or dreaming. You're a pegasus shifter, son, just like your old dad.

"This doesn't make any sense. If I was a shifter, wouldn't I have known about it before now?"

You do know. Right now. The pegasus shook out its mane. *We pegasus shifters are different to the common sort, son. We may take longer than the average shifter to arise, but when we do, we're more exceptional than any other creature under the sun. Take me, for instance. I was seventeen before my pegasus fledged. Seventeen!* He huffed. *Mid-twenties is taking it a bit far, but…*

"I'm almost thirty."

Really?

Jackson had never seen a pegasus shrug before. Light glittered off a thousand gleaming feathers.

Better late than never. Oh, and don't go shouting that around, will you? I don't need it getting out that I'm pushing fifty.

Right, because God forbid… Jackson stopped.

Telepathy. He was speaking telepathically, and it felt as natural as breathing.

Oh, hell.

How could I stay away? Andrew's silver wings gleamed in the morning sunlight. *You've finally made your debut, son, and I wouldn't miss it for the world. My first fledgling, out in the world at last.*

Of course you wouldn't. Jackson closed his eyes briefly and his mind leaped to Olly—wherever she was. Flying to safety. Without him.

He concentrated. Was that—could he really sense—like a star peeking through the treetops, bright and pure—

Who's flying? Ooh, shall we fly? Yes! I want to try!

Jackson snapped his attention back to the kitchen. "No!" he gasped, the single word garbled as his body started to transform. "Not now!"

He managed to hold on to his human form. He didn't know *how*, but when he clutched at his forehead, it was with human hands, not hooves.

Andrew was still waiting outside, watching him.

He sighed. *You'd better come in,* he called, and went around to open the front door. *But before we talk, I'm going to have a goddamned shower.*

Andrew had shifted back by the time Jackson got out of the shower. He was wearing another suit. He even had a bloody tie on, Jackson noted sourly. With a gold pin.

He looked closer and swore.

Andrew preened. "Great, isn't it? I had them made special. I'll give you the number for the jeweler."

"Horse-head pins aren't really my style."

"It's a *pegasus* head. Now, what about some breakfast? Tell me you've got some coffee in this place."

Jackson was tempted to go and get the old instant coffee packets out of the glove box in his truck, but that would be as much a punishment for himself as for Andrew. He put on a fresh pot of coffee and Andrew followed him into the kitchen.

So, he thought, pulling two mugs from the cupboard. He was a pegasus shifter. He could either deny what he'd seen with his own eyes and experienced with his own body, or he could find out what it meant to be one—from the only other pegasus shifter around.

He knew what Olly would do.

He cleared his throat. "How did you know…"

"That you'd shifted for the first time?" Andrew beamed at him and tapped himself on the chest. "Felt it. Right in here. Been having flashes on and off for the last few months, and then earlier today—whoosh! Never felt anything like it. Guess this is what fatherhood is really like, huh?"

Don't react to that, Jackson told himself. "You said I'm your first fledgling," he went on, and Andrew raised both hands.

"Not for want of trying, don't get me wrong!"

"You're saying I've got half-siblings out there?" Jackson's mind was already running ahead. If his father had other children but none of them had turned out to be pegasus shifters, did that mean they'd all been shifters already? Had he… fledged?… because he'd started off an ordinary human?

Or had his pegasus always been waiting inside him?

Don't ask me, his pegasus said brightly. *I don't remember anything from before this morning!*

"No, no. No other kids. Can you imagine?" Andrew scoffed. "I mean, no lack of *trying*." He winked.

That was his dad, all right, making the same joke until he managed to get a laugh. Jackson refused to play along; he grimaced and rubbed his stubble. "But how can I be a shifter at all?"

Andrew blew out his cheeks. "Straight to the big one, huh?"

"It doesn't make sense. Until this morning, I was human. No telepathy, no enhanced senses, no… pegasus. Or anything else. I don't remember you biting me to turn me into a shifter like what happens with hellhounds, so how is this possible?"

"Well. See, the thing is…" Andrew leaned forward conspiratorially. Then one of his eyes twitched and he rubbed his hands together feverishly.

"Say, you don't have a drink around here by any chance?"

There was the rest of the chocolate cocktail from last night, and he'd bought a six-pack for if Olly wanted to stay in another evening, but—

"No," Jackson said firmly.

"Ah, well. I gotta say this would be easier with a drink in my hand, but… hoo. Okay." Andrew gestured. "Thing is, no one knows how this really works, do they?" He paused, but Jackson stayed silent. "This whole shifter business. Oh, folks talk big about genetics, but they're basically making it up. How can *magic* be explained by something as normal as that? No, kiddo. People like you and me, we're special. *Chosen.* And when it comes to mythic shifters like yours truly, the animal only comes to the *truly* worthy."

Jackson's limbs felt heavy. "You came all this way to tell me I'm unworthy," he said flatly.

Andrew's eyes gleamed. "Not anymore." Something approaching a fond smile appeared on his lips. "I thought my pegasus had it wrong at first. Good things take time and you've stretched that almost to its limits. But here you are. Fashionably late. My first fledgling."

He raised his hand as though he was holding a glass. "And I'm here to teach you what that means."

Andrew looked at him as though he expected Jackson to be pleased. Nothing could be further than the truth. He still didn't know why he was suddenly a shifter. Whatever Andrew said, it wasn't—couldn't be—anything to do with being *worthy*. He couldn't let himself believe that.

But there was something worse than that.

He loved Olly. He'd loved her since long before last Christmas and all the way through the last miserable year and he loved her now.

He couldn't lose her. But if he wasn't careful, he was going to. For the first time he truly understood what Olly had gone through last Christmas. Why she'd looked at him with such horror… and why only last night, she'd been so keen to get out of town without anyone seeing her. Without *her* seeing anyone else.

Because if he was a shifter then somewhere out there was his mate.

He straightened his shoulders. He'd made Olly a promise. All but given her a ring. They were engaged, and he was going to marry her, and no shifter magic was going to change that.

23

OLLY

This is wonderful! Olly's owl wailed as she flew over the tops of the trees, heading for home. *Wonderful!*

No, it's terrible! Olly snapped. *How can this be happening?*

Her owl was beating its wings frantically and almost flew straight into a branch. Olly tried to wrestle control back and almost crashed again.

Get a hold of yourself! she shouted at it.

Something wonderful! her owl wailed. *I mean, something terrible! Oh, no, this is even worse than before! I thought it was Jackson, I thought you'd be happy, this is awful! But it's also…*

A sense-vision appeared in Olly's mind. The heavy beat of huge wings. The crunch of snow beneath hooves. The hiss of sunlight over shimmering feathers and the spark-crackle of awareness: *there he is, mine, wonderful, mine!*

No, she thought. *That can't be—*

We have to get away! Don't we? Yes! Away, and forget all about him, and then you can be happy!

Her owl was frantic. Olly was caught between the impulse to soothe it—which normally made it prickly, but at least distracted it from whatever was freaking it out—and freaking out herself.

There was no denying what had just happened. Her owl had identified her mate.

Wings. Hooves. There was only one shifter in town who matched that description, and if she'd had any doubts, the fact that her owl had exploded with blissful recognition the moment he'd landed outside made it clear.

Meaghan had said there was a pegasus shifter in town. And Jackson had recognized him.

Her mate was Jackson's father. Her *fiancé's* father.

This can't be happening.

It isn't! It's not going to! I won't let— Her owl's voice fractured into a symphony of images and feelings. Too much. Olly didn't have time to filter through them before her owl snatched them back under control and replaced them with a single shriek of determination. *I won't let this ruin your happiness!*

We can think our way out of this, Olly told it, hoping her internal voice sounded more confident than she felt. Not that that would help. Her owl could feel how she felt, every sickening lurch of horror. *We can… somehow… there must be a way around this!*

Yes, her owl agreed, *we just have to never see…*

The sensory cocktail of the pegasus's presence burst into her mind again and her owl wailed.

But he's so wonderful, it cried.

Before Olly could reply, another voice sang out in her head.

Olls? That you? Thank Christmas. We're overrun down here.

Uncle Bob?

No, Santa Claus. Who'd you think? Look, I know you're— His psychic voice crackled like a bad radio reception and Olly thought she heard-felt the echo of a sneeze. *We could really use your help at the Express if you're done love-birding for the day.*

Done love-birding? She swallowed hard. If Bob knew what she was—no. She couldn't tell him. *I'll be there at once.*

No! We have to hide away—think—

Her owl tried to wheel around to fly up to the most remote part of the valley, but Olly caught the turn and pointed her beak towards the Puppy Express.

Shimmer-feather-gleaming-hooves-sky-wing-wind-wonder-*mine*—

Olly and her owl shrieked in unison. Her owl was right. It was wonderful-terrible.

And the wonderful just made it more terrible.

We won't get any information from up there, she told her owl, even as her whole body felt it was shaking apart beneath her owl's feathers. *At least if we're close… maybe we can get enough information to figure out how to fix this.*

Olly had made plenty of bad decisions in her life.

This was one of the worst.

Jackson's cottage was a good mile and a half up the valley from the Puppy Express building, but even with that distance the sparkle-sparkle-yay of her mate's presence was a constant prickle at the edges of her attention. Her *mate*. Jackson's father!

At least it was only recognition. The mate bond hadn't formed. At least, she thought it hadn't. She was *sure* you had to sleep together for that. So, all she had to do was never set eyes on the pegasus shifter again.

Her future father-in-law.

Does the universe hate me? She sized up the next group of customers as they came inside, checking whether they had the appropriate gear for the trail and mentally cross-referencing it against the Puppy Express rental supplies. *I had it all figured out. I knew this was a risk, but… now? And him?*

Jackson's father. Until this Christmas, all she'd known about him was a big fat nothing. An *informative* nothing. He'd left a gap in Jackson's life, even if Jackson didn't like to admit it. And this

Christmas, she'd added to that *nothing* the fact that he'd crash-landed in the middle of Jasper's party, drunk out of his skull! And he was meant to be her *mate?*

At least she didn't need to watch out for other strangers anymore. She could do her shift at the Puppy Express without worrying about some tourist driving up and sending her world upside down. It wasn't like she was going to bump into *another* mate. But that was the thinnest of silver linings.

Silver, just like the pegasus's wings.

Ugh, she and her owl thought in unison, and then her owl added, guiltily: *But so shiny…*

"The universe is an *asshole,*" she muttered darkly.

"Er… excuse me?"

Olly blinked. A woman was standing in front of her. *Yeek!* her owl shrieked as Olly's brain caught up with her eyes. *She snuck up on us!*

No, she didn't, I was just… distracted. Olly pushed down the urge to duck behind the counter.

"We've got a booking…"

The woman looked nervous, and Olly didn't blame her. She was with two teenaged boys who, Olly suspected from long experience, were exactly the wrong age to enjoy a Puppy Express ride. Too old to think it was fun and too young to think it was ironic—or have circled back around to letting themselves have fun without worrying about being cool.

By the harried expression on the woman's face, she was starting to suspect the same thing.

Olly shook her head and reminded herself to smile. The tense expression on the other woman's face eased and she pushed a lock of faded blonde hair off her face.

"Belgrave family?" The name sounded familiar—then again, it had been there on the screen in front of her all morning. She picked up the windproof jackets she'd been partway through sorting before her thoughts got away with her.

"Yes, we're—oh, we don't need those." Mrs. Belgrave paused. "That is, we've already been skating and we were snug as anything—"

"You'd be surprised how chilly it can get when you're sitting on a sled compared to skating around."

"Why don't you give us wetsuits instead?" The voice was belligerent and male; one of the teen boys. She glanced up at him, then gave him a harder look as he kept talking: "Yeah, this guy at the place we're staying won't stop going on about it. Says it's really unsafe and there aren't any fences and he just, like, fell through the ice."

"He keeps complaining about that stupid ring! He told me what it cost, it's not even that much."

The ring! Olly bit back a very customer-service-unfriendly groan. She'd forgotten it *again.* It was back at the cottage… where Andrew was.

She could call Jackson on the shop phone and ask him to bring it over, but then he might bring Andrew with him. She swallowed. *Better not.*

"If it's *really* unsafe, maybe it will be fun after all."

The two teens grinned at each other. Were they twins? Olly wondered. They looked alike, except while the first one was belligerent, the second was just scornful.

"Vance, Anders…" Mrs. Belgrave groaned, but Olly just shrugged.

"Sure, it is unsafe, if you're dumb enough to jump around on ice half an inch thick and be surprised when you fall in the water." There—she had it. A flicker of animal behind the boys' eyes. But what? "Are either of you that dumb?"

"No!"

Olly hid a victorious smile. The teenagers were definitely shifters. Something feline—with a hint of feathers. And now she remembered where she'd heard the name Belgrave before, and the glimpse of the woman who'd given Jackson a ride to the Puppy Express the other day. His father's PA.

Are you Delphine's family? she asked, broadcasting the question to all three of them.

Surprise flickered cat-like in their eyes as the boys crowded in front of their mother.

Oh! Excuse me. I didn't expect… oh, boys, really. Mrs. Belgrave patted them out of the way. "We were meant to meet my daughter Delphine here. Have you seen her? Blonde hair, about your age?"

"She hasn't been in, sorry." Olly glanced at the security cam feed in the corner of her screen.

"Oh…"

Vance-or-Anders jutted his chin out. "If she's not here, why can't we go stalk tourists in the woods instead?"

"Yeah, she's the one who wanted to do this stupid—"

Olly cleared her throat. "Actually, this might be her now," she said as the door swung open.

"Sorry I'm late!"

Delphine hurried in, her cheeks pink with cold. She flashed her mother a warm smile and then groaned theatrically at her brothers, hands on her hips. "Well, look who the cat dragged in. Neither of you managed to fall off the mountain yet? I'm disappointed."

"Mum, she called you a cat!"

"Kids, don't pick fights. Grown-up kids included, Delphy." Mrs. Belgrave fiddled with her purse and added silently: *They're winged lion shifters. And you *are… I mean, I'm assuming you must be a shifter of some sort?*

Olly blinked. She couldn't tell? *Snowy owl,* she explained.

Oh, how lovely.

"I can't believe you all made it here on such short notice!" Delphine said, smiling brightly. Almost too brightly, Olly thought. "You know I have to work all the way through to New Year's, I thought you'd be going back to the UK for the holiday."

"Same," one of her brothers grumbled.

Her mother elbowed him gently. "When you said you had to work for Christmas—well I thought it was such a shame. We hardly get to see you these days! And this place is so... so…"

"Boring."

"Relaxing." Mrs. Belgrave sighed. "It's a nice change from our usual family Christmases. So much quieter."

Vance-or-Anders groaned and she smiled fondly at him.

"Even if poor Delphine's boss dragged her along on his vacation." Mrs. Belgrave clicked her tongue. "Really, darling, I don't know why you put up with it."

"You should *fight* him," Vance-or-Anders declared. *Or we could!*

The other one joined in. *Yeah! We could totally take him. He's just a measly pegasus and we're lions!*

SKY LIONS! Attacking from above!

"You work for Jackson's dad, right?" Olly asked Delphine.

"Oh! Er, yes? I'm his PA." Delphine's eyebrows shot up. She already looked nervous—now she looked dazed, too. "Do you know Jackson?"

"Yeah." Olly tried to sound casual, but her owl was intensely focused on the other woman. "I don't suppose you know what your boss's plans are today? I know he, uh, went to see Jackson this morning."

"His calendar's booked out for the whole day," Delphine said. "Family time."

"Which means we get a chance to see each other too," Mrs. Belgrave added.

So they'll both be together all day. I won't be able to talk to Jackson without seeing his father, too. Olly swallowed hard.

"We'd better get you started on that, then," she said, doing her best to sound chirpy. She handed over the windproof parkas. "We've got you booked in for the Polar Adventure, is that right?"

"I'm going to throw myself in the lake," Vance-or-Anders whispered conspiratorially.

"This one doesn't go past the lake." Just to be on the safe side, she added: "And although the trails are private, we're not completely isolated up here. There are vacation cabins all around the valley, so don't be surprised if some random hikers or skiers pop up out of nowhere."

"Aw!" Both boys turned to their mother. "Come *on*, Mum, what's the point in being in the middle of *nowhere* if we can't even—"

Someone's coming, Olly said telepathically, seeing movement on the security feed.

Both boys fell silent just as the bell above the door rang again. Olly was relieved. Even the terrible fate of not being able to shift on vacation wasn't enough to make them forget to keep the existence of shifters safe from outsiders, it seemed.

She waved to the group that had just arrived. "I'll be with you in a moment! Okay, so, here's the map with all the routes on it. Manu—" She concentrated and called the hellhound shifter in from outside. "—Manu here is going to take you around the tracks today. Hey, Manu!"

The teenagers still looked fidgety, so she sent the whole group a final, secret message: **Manu is a hellhound shifter. Have you ever met one of those before?**

The change in the winged lion shifter teenagers was instant. "Woah," one of them whispered, and the other added: "Cool!" Their mother gave Olly a grateful look, but Delphine didn't react.

That's them sorted, Olly thought. *Hopefully they'll be too distracted trying to impress another super-magical shifter to cause trouble.* She caught Delphine's eye as Manu herded them all out to meet their dog team.

What she found in Delphine's quick glance wasn't what she'd expected. It wasn't what *was* there, as much as what wasn't. Her family might be all winged lion shifters, but there was no animal hiding behind Delphine's eyes.

Huh, she thought. *She isn't a shifter?* She ran over the conversation in her head again. Olly had included her in her telepathic speech, and Delphine hadn't reacted. She'd thought that meant the other woman didn't have anything to say, but maybe she just hadn't heard her at all.

Olly felt sorry for her, and then thought *Well, maybe she's a late bloomer,* and then felt guilty about both thoughts. She'd never heard of any shifters not developing their animals until they were adults, and not being a shifter didn't make anyone any less of a *person.*

It just made them… She didn't want to say a *different* person. She'd been tiny when her owl turned up, but she still remembered how it had felt. It was as though there had been a place inside her waiting for it, which she hadn't noticed until it was there. Things like her watchfulness and how much she liked to cram herself into small places suddenly made sense. She hadn't been half a person before her owl manifested, but once it was there, she was… right.

Until now, her owl chirped, very quietly.

Olly pressed her lips together. *Don't say that!*

But if I wasn't here, you wouldn't have the wrong mate.

If you weren't—Olly's cheeks went hot, then ice cold. *Don't you dare go anywhere.*

It's not like I can go anywhere. I'm not a Heartwell. No-one cursed the Lockey owls. Maybe they should have. I've tried to help you all year and I keep getting it wrong, and now I couldn't even keep away from the mate you don't want. It shrunk down inside her, very small. *You would be a different person without me, you know. Maybe you wouldn't even be the pegasus's mate.*

Olly clenched her fists. *Stop talking like this! Okay, so, yes, Jackson's dad is my fated mate. That doesn't mean I have to bond with him.*

I can go live in one of those hunter's cabins out in the middle of nowhere, and forget all about Jackson's dad. So long as he never comes close enough for you to sense him, we can make this work.

I just have to tell Jackson that his dad is my fated mate.

She gulped. *That's a big 'just'.*

24

JACKSON

"First things first," Andrew said, buffing his hands together. "Let's get you shifted."

They were outside. Jackson's breakfast was sitting uneasily in his gut. In fact, everything was sitting uneasily with him.

For about five minutes that morning, his life had been perfect. How had it gotten so fucked, so fast?

"I've already shifted," he pointed out.

"But by accident, right?" Andrew laughed at the expression on his face. "And you have no idea how it happened, or how to stop it happening in the future. Am I wrong?" He clapped Jackson on the shoulder. "You gotta get these things locked down, kiddo. Make sure you only shift when *you* want to, not when your pegasus sees something shiny, or someone else shifts nearby and you get sucked in."

"Is that what happened to you at the Heartwells' party?"

Andrew lifted his hand off Jackson's shoulder and put on a wounded expression. "Hey, ouch! Can't blame a man for needing a bit of extra courage, can you? It was a big day!" He snapped his fingers. "And it turned out well in the end, didn't it? You hadn't even fledged yet. And I get the feeling you wouldn't have believed me if I'd told you what you really were that night, anyway."

"So you getting wasted out of your mind was—"

"Fate." Andrew spread his hands. "Now let's get started. A Petrakis is always in control of his shifts. *And* his clothes," he added as Jackson reluctantly started to unzip his parka. "Keep it on, kid, we're not hippies here."

Jackson nodded, but still unstrapped his watch and placed it carefully on the windowsill. "How does this work, then?"

His pegasus was quivering with excitement, in its… bit of his mind… where it existed. *I guess that means you want out?*

Flying! I want to try flying!

Flying. Jackson closed his eyes. Oh, God.

Right now!

Jackson's skin started to fizz. He lurched forward suddenly, as though his body had forgotten he was meant to walk on two legs. Which was probably because—oh, God, this was so fucking *weird*—

Uh-uh! Andrew's voice drove into Jackson's head like a bolt of migraine. Out loud, he tsked and waved a finger at Jackson. "I said we're teaching *you* to shift. Your pegasus already knows how. It's way ahead of you."

"It's only existed for a few hours," Jackson grumbled. "How can it know how to shift already?"

"How can a foal know how to walk as soon as it's born? Or a human baby to… well, whatever it is human babies can do? Cry?" Andrew shrugged. "Our pegasuses manifest fully grown, kiddo. It's a mythic thing."

"Really." The more confident Andrew sounded, the more Jackson suspected he was talking out his ass. Especially given he'd seen a mythic toddler transform into a tiny baby dragon just the other day. He flexed his shoulders. The near-shift had left his skin itchy, as though it was still waiting for wings to sprout out of his back. "Okay. How do I do this without my pegasus taking over?"

"Think about what it means to be a pegasus. But for *you*, not it. Your pegasus is part of your essential nature. Some part of you already knows what it means to be what you've become."

I thought you said we weren't hippies. Jackson bit his tongue on the teenagerly response and closed his eyes.

Right. Think pegasus-y thoughts. What the hell did that mean? The only pegasus he knew was his father, and he didn't think that imagining himself drunkenly gate-crashing a Christmas party was going to end well. Or abandoning his infant son. Was that part of his essential pegasus-ness, as well?

Jackson ground his teeth. *Some part of me already knows what I've become?* No part of him knew anything about any of this.

He knew who he was. Or he thought he knew. Jackson Gilles. Not a shifter, but a good man. If that had all been untrue…

He scrubbed his hands across his face. *I'm not a shifter. But that isn't true anymore. So if I'm not not a shifter—*

His mind came up against a mental wall so solid he almost swore out loud.

Inside his head, his pegasus was watching him. He glared at it. At least, he glared, and thought glaring-ness at it.

Fine, he told himself. *I am a shifter. And that means…*

He knew what the wall was. It was another bit of that essential, internal architecture he'd built his sense of self around. Like the one around his heart.

He'd built it himself, carefully, brick by brick, when he realized he was a normal human. He'd put all his dreams about being a shifter behind it, all the things he *wasn't*, so he could focus on what he was.

Strong. Dependable. A force for good in the world. A good son and a good man. Everything his father wasn't.

He took a deep breath and looked past the wall into all the things he hadn't let himself imagine since he was a kid.

A sudden leap of excitement. Sheer, white-hot curiosity: what was it like? To shift? To have an animal's senses alongside your own? To be able to talk to people with your *mind*—to be part of the silent understanding that he'd seen pass between his Ma and other shifters so many times. That instant connection. Community. And…

Not just being part of the community of shifters, but having a whole new relationship with the world. He'd seen the seasons change through human eyes and seen his mother watch them change through her deer's eyes, and never understood the difference. Now he did. His human side was a creature of the earth, snow crunching underfoot and the sky a weight above him. His pegasus…

Smack. There was the wall again.

"All good there, kiddo?"

Jackson turned away and swallowed. Like hell he was going to let his father see him—shit. Shit! What was wrong with him? He'd dealt with this years ago. It hadn't been hard. He'd laid it out straight for himself: he wasn't a shifter. He'd moved on. What was so tough about moving back?

His pegasus shuffled its wings. *His* pegasus. Magic. His magic. He had—he *was*—magic. He could do more than just shift, he could *fly*.

He took a deep breath. Don't think about the rest of it, he told himself. Everything you've missed out on. Don't think about what you put away behind that wall because, shit, that never included *flying*.

Something caught in his mind. Not behind the wall, but above it. He concentrated. If he wanted to get *up there*, he would need…

This time, the shift wasn't a confused explosion. He slipped into his pegasus form like a diver slipping into the water. His skin didn't itch as wings and hair burst through it—his whole body gave a sigh of relief.

As though this was what he was meant to be.

Nicely done! Andrew's voice echoed in his head. *Very slick. Not as, uh…*

Jackson turned around. His pegasus adjusted its wings to keep balance and that was enough to make him remember *shit, four legs, not two* and that was enough to send him skittering groundwards—

Help! he yelped.

His pegasus jumped into action. Jackson felt the change as it took control of his body—its body, really, its *shape*—and fluttered back upright.

Ta-da! it announced.

...Not the classic look, Andrew continued. *But never mind that. Moving on.*

What do you mean, not the classic look? Even telepathy was easier in this form. Not having a human mouth to confuse things probably helped.

His father ignored the question. He'd transformed, too, and his pegasus gleamed in the dappled sunlight breaking through the clouds.

Let's get you in the air. After that, I want to put Delphine back in the picture. See if anything's changed there.

His father's psychic voice was edged with cunning. Jackson frowned—at least, he thought he was frowning. God knew what his pegasus face was doing. *What do you mean, changed?*

I told you, didn't I, there's something about that girl. I knew it the moment I laid eyes on her. Smart, beautiful, great family—she's the one for you, son. And maybe now you've caught up with the rest of us, you'll be the one for her.

That's ridiculous. I've already met her, anyway. There wasn't a spark or whatever is meant to happen.

But that was before you were you. He could feel the grin in Andrew's psychic voice. *You've changed. That might have, too. I told you, I have a good feeling about this. You, Delphine, this dinky little town—it's all connected. How do you think I knew to come up here?*

Jackson's heart sank. Would all this have gone better or worse, if he'd stayed out of Pine Valley?

I wouldn't have Olly if I hadn't come back. Cold rippled down his spine. *But can I keep her, now that I'm a different person? What if Delphine really is my…*

He couldn't even say it. Think it. Think-say it, telepathically or in the privacy of his own head. Not that his own head was particularly private anymore.

Our mate! cried his pegasus, delighted. *Where?*

How do you even know what a mate is?

His pegasus flicked its ears curiously. *How do you?*

I—

His mother had told him about mates first, of course, when he was still figuring out what he was and wasn't. But it was Olly who sprang into his mind. Olly, with her hair so fine it went wispy in the slightest breeze and her eyes that could keep you pinned down even if her mind had wandered off to think about something else.

Ooh, his pegasus said, greatly intrigued, *who's she?* and Jackson slammed a mental door on the image of Olly.

She was—his. Nothing to do with his pegasus.

His stomach sank. But Delphine was. According to his father. And his father might be a drunk and a showman and overall untrustworthy… but unless he wanted to go tell Jasper all about his dirty laundry—which was basically the same thing as telling the entire town—Andrew was the closest thing Jackson had right now to an expert on mythic shifter business. Unfortunately. *Could* a mythic shifter recognize another mythic shifter's mate?

I know what a mate is, his pegasus mused. *The knowledge is… here. Waiting.*

Something flipped open in Jackson's mind and suddenly his pegasus's knowledge was his, as well. It wasn't complicated: just like his pegasus knew that its hooves went on the ground and its wings took it into the air, it knew that finding its mate was the one thing that would make it the happiest.

It's the one thing, isn't it? The one thing. Singular. Perfect. And you wonder why I drink! Andrew's voice held a laughter that rang hollow inside Jackson's head. *This is what it means to be a pegasus, son. We're Zeus's carrier pigeons and what we most want to deliver is ourselves. I'm still searching for my final address, but you… Well. Doesn't every parent want better for their kid than they got themselves?*

Jackson stayed silent. Andrew hesitated a moment, then kept talking, apparently as unwilling to let the insides of their heads stay silent as he was to let the conversation lag in human form.

Delphine's a great girl. Sharp as a whip.

She's not my mate, Da—Andrew, Jackson reminded him. *We've already met.* But then he remembered what Andrew had said earlier. *Wait, what did you mean, I wasn't me then?*

* You hadn't fledged yet.* His father shrugged, his wings shimmering like a waterfall of glitter. *Our shifter animals make us complete. Of course we can't recognize our mates until then. You're not the same man you were the other night. Thank goodness! Can you imagine? Me coming all this way for nothing?* He shook out his wings. *And if she's not right for you, well, there's more fish in the sea, right? You're my heir, kiddo—Jackson. I'm going to do right by you if it's the first right thing I do.*

And that means finding my mate. Each word felt like another weight on his shoulders. He was a different person? He didn't feel any different. He felt like himself, plus an annoying, chirpy pegasus.

He was still in love with Olly. That hadn't changed. *God*, he thought suddenly, *please don't let that change. I don't want to be someone else. I just want to be me. For the first time in my life.*

That's right. Come on, kiddo, no need to sound so glum! The mate bond isn't like marriage. You're not going to be stuck to some old ball and chain. Well, stuck, sure. But I'm told it's a great time. The best. He paused. *I only want the best for you, son. Don't worry. Whoever the girl is who's the one for you, we're going to find her.*

Jackson sighed and his pegasus let out a frustrated huff.

Why is he talking about finding our mate? We've already found her!

Jackson's world stood still.

What did you just say?

We already found her! It pranced with excitement. *That's why we have to learn how to fly, and talk properly, and everything else! So we can impress her!*

But… who?

Her!

His pegasus stretched its senses, pushing Jackson's awareness along with them. He gasped as sensations filled his mind.

An apex predator's sleek strength. Powerful wings. Ability and agility in one creature, wild and free. The queen of the sky.

Jackson shied in surprise, his wings beating the air. He went airborne—just for a second, but long enough for the sensation of no ground beneath his hooves to meet the sudden panic in his heart and send him thudding back to earth.

He'd—*felt* her. A winged shifter who called out to the creature inside him with a siren's song.

Delphine?

He didn't realize he'd spoken out loud—no, not spoken, damn it, and not out loud—until Andrew's chuckle wafted across his mind.

**Easy, kiddo. First things first. You want to win some winged shifter's heart, you better learn how to fly first.*

*Besides, she's off for the afternoon. Her family showed up out of nowhere and she managed to get them a booking at some Santa's sleigh tourist whatever.**

The Puppy Express. It had to be. And that sudden sensation—his new psychic abilities must have brushed up against her presence.

Shit.

It should have been the most wonderful moment of his life. His pegasus was practically vibrating with excitement—but it wasn't flying away on him. What had it said before—it didn't want to embarrass itself?

Maybe he and his pegasus were more alike than he'd thought. He wouldn't be crash-landing through any ceilings with a dramatic announcement. It wanted to make a good impression.

And so did he. Just not on the same woman his pegasus was probably thinking about.

Flying practice, he said, hoping his psychic voice didn't betray his true feelings. **Sounds easy enough.**

Say that again in an hour, kiddo.

This bit of the valley won't do, though. Not this close to the Puppy Express trails. Not if Delphine was there. **There's a place further up the valley, where the clouds hang around all winter long. I know the dragon family who own land up there, they won't mind us visiting. We can take my truck—I'll drive.**

You're in with the local dragon clan? Andrew's voice was sincerely impressed. *Networking! Maybe you take after your old man after all!*

Jackson ground his teeth. Learn to fly, learn to speak with his mind, learn every other goddamned shifter trick his father could think of—that would be easy.

Telling Delphine that he was sorry, but there was no way in hell he was going to be her mate? That would be hard. She seemed like a nice enough person, but… no. There was nothing between them and he didn't care what the sparkly dumbass inside his head thought, magic was no basis for a relationship. Not the sort of relationship he wanted.

Not the sort he'd thought he finally had. God, he should have got her a ring. A real ring, not that nonsense with the sizer. Or he should have taken that ring she dove into the lake for and squeezed it onto his finger, just to have something solid that said he was hers. Forever. Heart and mind and… not soul.

He swallowed.

Telling Olly that his soul belonged to someone else?

That would be worst of all.

25

OLLY

The excruciating nearness of her mate faded mid afternoon. Olly relaxed—just in time for the next crisis to come through the door.

Literally.

"Bob, what the hell are you doing here?"

"Busiest day of the—" He broke off in a coughing fit. *Busiest day of the year,* he continued telepathically, continuing to cough now he didn't need to use his breath to talk with. *Couldn't leave you to deal with it alone.*

I'm not alone. Caine sent the whole pack over for the rest of the week, as apologies for stealing the huskies. Olly glared at him from behind her computer screen. "You look like shit."

"Merry Christmas to you, too, favorite niece."

Olly's uncle Bob had gone gray early in life and cultivated a bushy white beard every year to help with the Puppy Express Santa look. Today his cheeks were ruddy red, but not from jolliness. He looked one decent sneeze away from collapsing.

He did sneeze, explosively, and Olly was around the counter in a flash. "You should be in bed! I thought when I got here and you weren't here that you'd made the sensible choice for once. You had yesterday off. Take today off, too, like a normal person!"

"That's be out of character, wouldn't it? Ah—shit. Do you have a tissue?"

"Behind the front desk." Olly pushed Bob in the right direction, then ran and tucked herself under him shoulder as he started staggering in the wrong direction. "You can't even walk straight! How did you get down here? Please tell me you didn't drive." She thought again. "Please tell me you didn't fly over and then get dressed in the parking lot."

"No, no." Bob waved her concerns aside and almost smacked over a postcard display. "One of Hannah's nephews gave me a ride. Nice guy. Don't worry, I told him you and Jackson were back together and I told him to tell Hannah that, too."

Olly went still. Hannah was infamous for trying to partner off her endless supply of nephews, but—

"What do you mean, Jackson and I are back together?"

Bob shot her a look that shouldn't have been so sharp, given how congested and blotchy he was. Then again, he was an owl shifter. Looks were what they were best at. *I figured, when you didn't come home after you and Jackson got Fleance out of that pickle...*

"We're not—" Olly tried again. "That doesn't mean—and he—he's not my mate," she said at last.

"So?"

"What do you mean, *so?*"

"He's here. And he's making you happy. What more do you want?" He blew his nose. "Not to sound like an asshole about it, Olls, but you hit the goddamn jackpot here. Most shifters are lazy as shit about love. We just hang around waiting for our mate to turn up and think, great, sorted. Forget about mates. You've got someone who likes you just the way you are, and you like him back."

"What if I decide to be with Jackson and then do meet my mate, though?" Olly bit her tongue. Could Bob tell this wasn't just a theoretical question?

Her uncle was quiet for a few minutes. At last he shook his head. "Just because someone's your mate doesn't mean they're the right person for you," he muttered.

Olly stared at him. "But I thought the mate bond—"

"Look, I don't pretend to know how any of this works. Frankly, anyone who does is probably bullshitting you. Where shifters came from, how we can have these creatures in our heads—hell, look at the Heartwells and their curse. How does something like that make sense?" Bob shrugged. "The world's a crazy place. You've found a piece of it that works for you? Don't let it go." He exploded into another sneezing fit, blew his nose, and croaked: "I should have talked to you sooner."

"Well, you've been sick—"

"Before then." It seemed to take him a lot of effort to raise his head again. "All year. I thought maybe you needed time to sort through things yourself, and you've always been quiet, but seeing you these last few days, you're so much more…"

He gestured as though he was searching for the right word. Olly stood frozen in place.

"…Happy."

Olly swallowed. Had it been that obvious?

Bob was still talking. "I'm sorry, Olls. I should've noticed you weren't in a good way."

"I'm a grown up. I can look after myself," Olly replied, and winced at how non-grown-up her words sounded. "Anyway, what did we agree when I moved up here?"

"That I was going to be the cool uncle and not stick my beak in your business," Bob recited in a dull drone. "I think I understand why my beloved sister laughed so much when I told her that."

He sighed so hard it set him coughing again. Olly sat up, watching him warily.

"Are you sure you're okay?"

"Someone needs to keep the hellhounds in line."

Olly glared at him. "*I'm* keeping the hellhounds in line. With Meaghan as my backup threat. Go home!"

"It's the busiest time of the year…"

"And you really feel up to harnessing up the dogs, and dealing with screaming children, and playing nice with the customers when the credit card machine goes down?"

"It's not going to—"

"It's Christmas Eve. Of course the system's going to go down. And if Meaghan so much as blows her nose, all the dogs *and* all your staff are going to run off like their tails are on fire. Do you really feel up to sorting that out?"

"…No. Oh, God."

Olly relented. "Why don't you go sort out the post for tonight?"

"The…" Bob hauled himself upright, something approaching determination in his eyes. "Yes! Through wind and snow and… snot…"

Olly ferried him through to the back room. The Christmas sacks were stacked high, ready for the Christmas Eve delivery. She left Bob to his piles of postcards and dealt with the next two lots of customers, and the next time she poked her head around the door, he was fast asleep.

Good, she thought. *That's one problem dealt with.* Until that evening, at least, when she'd have to convince Bob that no one wanted their Christmas postcards delivered by a snot-nosed Santa. She'd have to corral the hellhounds into doing it. If they all pitched in, they'd get the whole delivery done in no time...

Why are you wasting time thinking about postcards? her owl wailed. *That's not important! We have to—to—*

Olly's hands clenched. Her sense of her mate's presence had faded, but now it washed over her again, like air pushed before a storm front. Her owl shrieked and hit its head under its wings. Olly's chest ached. This should be the happiest day of her life—of her owl's life, too—and instead, her owl was denying itself. For her. So that she could be happy with Jackson, and not her fated mate. Even though she'd spent all year lying to her owl, it still wanted to help her.

She swallowed. *I won't let your sacrifice be for nothing,* she told it. *And when this is all sorted out, we're going to have the biggest plate of liver and kidneys anyone in this town has ever seen.*

Her owl perked up. Olly's mind started whirring. Bob was right: She *didn't* want to let Jackson go. She wanted to go to him right now and...

...Not see his father.

Okay. But it wasn't like they were joined at the hip, right?

She just had to stay out of Andrew's way until she could talk to Jackson. She hated the idea of telling him what had happened… but she couldn't lie to him. Not if they were going to make this work.

Tonight, the hellhounds would deliver the post. Jackson's father would be at his accommodation, and Olly had done her homework on the Pine Valley gossip lines in between looking after customers—she knew exactly where he was staying. Far enough away that he wouldn't be any more of a problem than he already was.

She just needed to wait for Andrew to get out of range, and then talk to Jackson.

Her own phone hadn't survived its encounter with Sweetheart Lake. Olly grabbed one of the work phones that Bob kept stock for situations just like this, and dredged up Jackson's number from her memory.

Was this a good idea? She didn't know. But she didn't have any better ones.

She tapped out a message.

Meet me tonight at Sweetheart Lake? Send.

She put her phone away, fretted, and pulled it out again. Tapped out another message.

There's something I have to tell you.

"What am I thinking?" she muttered to herself, and deleted it without sending. Of all the ways to scare him off… No.

She dithered, tidied a few shelves, sold a husky plushy to a customer, and checked her phone. Nothing. And—what was wrong with her? Jackson wouldn't have the office cellphone number in his contacts.

This is Olly by the way.

And of course just saying 'Tonight' wasn't enough information.

I'll be there around five to pick up the post. There. But—

Five was early. What if Andrew was still with him?

I just want to see you. By yourself.

That wasn't giving too much away, was it? She sent one last message:

I love you.

She didn't wait for a response. And if she sent any more messages she'd look like she'd gone mad. And even if that was true…

Olly pocketed her phone again and, to be sure, zipped the pocket shut.

26

JACKSON

*B*zzt-bzzt.

Jackson's pegasus pranced in mid-air, and almost fell out of it. He dropped a good ten feet before the creature remembered its wings.

What was that? it fluted at him.

He was as confused as it was. *Bzzt-bzzt.*

The sound didn't exist. He was sure of that. It wasn't even in his head, like his pegasus's voice or, he guessed, his own voice, given at the moment he didn't really exist as anything other than a disembodied grumpiness inside the mind of a creature that shouldn't exist at all.

That wasn't a pleasant thought.

You exist! his pegasus cried encouragingly. *I'm sure of it!*

That's reassuring. Jackson frowned, or thought he did. The sound that hadn't been a sound had sounded like…

Let's land, he said.

Okay! His Pegasus landed lightly on the mountainside. They were far from the valley where the small township and all its tourist trails lay—over a ridge and past enough impassable snow and forest that no humans would come across his flying lessons.

What's the matter, son? Wings getting tired?

Jackson shook his head. Possibly. His pegasus flicked its mane, and he decided that would do for an answer.

Right, he thought as his father landed beside him. Shifting, but not just my body. Clothing.

He concentrated.

His human body, he decided, was tucked away in some sort of pocket dimension. All of him was still *there*, ready to exist in the real world again.

And so were his pants.

Human *and* pants, he thought desperately as lights began to twinkle into existence around his pegasus's form. Human and pants, human and pants, human and pants and shirt and boots, for the love of God.

He transformed with his eyes closed. A puff of wind whistled against his face, his neck... and nowhere lower.

He opened his eyes and glanced down warily. Fully clothed. Thank God.

Very smooth. He couldn't tell if Andrew was proud or disappointed. *But change back. We've got to focus on your landing technique.*

"Just a sec." Jackson slid one hand into his jacket pocket and found his phone.

Bzzt-bzzt. Really, what else would it have been? He looked up, wondering if Andrew would be impressed that he'd managed to shift with his phone as well as everything else, but the other pegasus was busy trying to reflect the afternoon sunlight off his wings.

He unlocked his phone. The number wasn't in his contacts… Oh. Of course it wasn't.

His face went stiff as he saw who'd texted him. It was automatic, and his face stayed frozen as he searched for why that was. When the answer came to him, his mouth twisted.

He didn't want his father to know about Olly.

But that wasn't all. He didn't want *himself* to know about Olly. Not this new him. He'd gone with Andrew to find out as much as he could about who he was now before he told Olly what had happened, but the more time he spent with his pegasus, the more he—

Who's Olly?

—felt as though he was walking towards a bottomless pit.

He flicked open her message.

What does it say? his pegasus asked, innocently curious as ever.

He cleared his throat and pocketed his phone. *Just a message*, he replied. He checked the time. If he was going to meet Olly at five, he would have to shake off his father soon. Without crossing paths with Delphine.

His stomach gurgled. "How long have we been out here?" he asked, turning to his father and squinting slightly at the light reflecting off his silvered wings.

Not that long, his father said. He mantled his wings. *We've got a few hours to go, at least. Time to focus on that landing. Come on…*

"A few hours to go until what?" Suspicion prickled on the back of Jackson's neck.

He'd taken up his father's idea of a training day to give himself time and information to figure out what he was going to tell Olly. He could have hit himself. He should have guessed his father had an ulterior motive, too.

Nothing important. His father scuffed his hooves and tossed his head nonchalantly. *It's Christmas Eve. I've made a dinner booking in town. Well, Delphine did.*

Jackson repressed another statue impression at the name of the winged lion shifter.

Wings? his pegasus chirped. *Like—*

Jackson pushed his pegasus back before he said or thought something he would regret.

Not sure where she booked us in, but she said she'll check in after her little family get-together. Now I had some thoughts about that, as well. If a horse with wings could look shamefaced, this was it. *I admit I made a few mistakes with that first meeting, and I told you, I want to do things better. We'll set it up all right. Candles. Music, if I have to strangle every DJ this side of the state to stop them playing that godawful Christmas shit. It'll all go right, you'll see.*

"You're very certain she's the one for me," Jackson muttered.

Well, see, I—ah, the hell with this. There was an explosion of magical lights, and Andrew stood in front of him, his tailored suit at odds with the rugged mountain surroundings. He smoothed his hair back. "I told you, I have a good feeling."

"A good feeling," Jackson repeated as his father patted his pockets in a way that suggested—"You're kidding me. You shifted with a drink in your pocket?"

Andrew unscrewed the top of the flask and shrugged. "What? No laws against it."

"Drinking and flying? I can think of a few."

"Not for shifters, though! And hey, at least I saved it for after our first lesson." He took a swig and shook himself. "Brr. Anyway, dinner. Maybe you want to change first, get into something a bit more suitable…"

Jackson considered arguing, or even saying he didn't feel like being wheeled out in front of Delphine's family like a prize pigeon, but he just shook his head.

"If you're booked in for dinner then we'd better head back," he said.

"What?" Andrew snorted. "Maybe you knock off early on the force, kiddo, but here—"

"Here in the country people eat when the sun goes down, and town closes ten minutes later," Jackson said calmly. He patted his pocket to reassure himself his phone was still there, with Olly's invitation, and concentrated.

Four hooves. Wings. Would that ever feel normal?

Better get moving if you want to eat tonight, he told his father, and let his pegasus leap into the sky.

The world whirled beneath him. Clouds clung to the mountains up here, and to his wings as well as he soared through them. It was—incredible. Magical.

I'm not saying you need to wear a tux. Andrew's voice cut through the magic. *But you must have a suit, right? Something with a jacket. I'll lend you one of my tie pins.*

You'd have to lend me a tie as well, Jackson told him, *if I was going to join you. But I'm not.*

What?

I've got something else to take care of.

To take care of first, you mean. You'll meet us after.

I wouldn't bet on it.

He managed to shake off his father at his vacation house outside of town. By then it was dark enough that he felt safe flying closer to his own cottage. There was no shiver of awareness from his shifter senses—Delphine must have already gone back to town. He shook off his pegasus with a sigh of relief and walked the rest of the way.

A shower and change of clothes was almost enough to make him feel human again—hah—until he automatically reached for Ma's watch, which he'd left on the windowsill.

Something for you to keep safe, she'd said, and laughed. *Something you* can *keep safe. I won't have to worry about you shifting and blowing it into a thousand pieces.*

She didn't have to worry about that now, either. His ribs tightened. What would she say, when she found out what he was? She'd always said there was nothing wrong with him not being a shifter.

He strapped on the watch with the promise to himself that he wouldn't let his mother down. No more thinking he was a mistake.

He paused and looked at himself in the mirror.

"Any of those special pegasus feelings?" he asked his reflection. "Good or bad?"

I'm a little bit hungry, his pegasus replied.

Jackson chuckled despite himself, then shook his head.

I'm heading out to meet… a friend, he said. *Someone who's important to me. But I want to talk to her myself, first. I wonder, can you… make yourself scarce?*

Scarce? A flutter of wings. Jackson winced. He still hadn't gotten a clear look at his pegasus, other than his spindly legs and the occasional burst of feathers, but if it was anything as grand as his father's, hiding probably wasn't in its nature. Glittering, more like.

You know how we sensed… He swallowed. *Our mate? Earlier?*

Oh, yes! His pegasus's joy fluttered in his chest.

Do you think you could make sure nobody could sense you like that?

That sounds hard…

Think of it as another lesson. Something else we'll be able to do to impress… people.

Okay! His pegasus hunkered down, fluffing its wings above its head.

Jackson rubbed his forehead. He was just going to have to trust that this would work. Olly was good at figuring out when someone was a shifter—she could even tell what sort of shifter they were, more often than not. And he'd seen her somehow sense when another shifter was about, before they were in hearing or seeing range.

His stomach twisted. What if she'd sensed him that morning? If that was why she'd left—if she thought he'd been somehow lying to her about being a shifter—

He shook his head. He couldn't do anything about that now. But maybe now, if his pegasus stayed down long enough, he would be able to find Olly and explain everything to her.

And it wasn't just Olly he was worried about. If Delphine sensed his presence…

Jackson swallowed, hard. *Just stay low, okay, buddy?* he pleaded with his pegasus.

Sure!

Sweetheart Lake. He knew how to get there from his cottage, at least. He made his way down one of the trails packed down by weeks of sleigh rides. With his pegasus preoccupied, he was alone with his own thoughts.

Strings of fairy lights hung from the trees either side, marking the track more merrily than the standard orange tags. Which there also were, tacked to the trees—after his time working as Pine Valley's deputy, he checked automatically. Shifters could be laissez faire about the reminders humans needed to find their way in the wilderness.

But of course he shouldn't have worried. Olly wouldn't let things like that fall into disrepair, if only so that her owl could know exactly where her customers were at all times. Health and safety meets predatory anxiety-bird.

Except that hadn't helped when the couple trying to propose had gone off-track. And where had Olly's careful attention to detail been when she threw herself into the lake after they'd already been rescued?

Jackson stopped in the middle of the trail. The night was closing in around him.

Maybe being alone with his own thoughts wasn't such a great thing after all.

Olly never did anything like that. At the time, he'd been too scared she was hurt to really consider what had happened, but the more he thought about it the less it made sense. Olly's need to look at a situation from all angles before coming to a conclusion wasn't one hundred percent reliable, but she'd never put herself at risk like that before.

Except…

Except when she'd put all her faith into him, and found him lacking in every way that counted.

He staggered as though the air had been knocked out of him.

What's wrong? His pegasus leaped up, full of sparkling concern. Jackson ran a shaking hand across his jaw.

Nothing. It's nothing. Everything's fine.

...Okay. His pegasus shook out its mane and Jackson found himself stretching his neck in harmony with it. That was the sort of thing that was meant to feel right as a shifter, he knew, but instead it made his stomach churn.

His pegasus jumped. *I knew it! Everything* isn't *fine.*

It's nothing you need to worry about.

But I could help!

Jackson snorted. *I don't think so.*

Why not? I have to be here for some *reason.* His pegasus shuffled its wings. *I could do lots of things to help. Like fly. Or...* Its voice faded out. *I'm sure there's something else I could do,* it added at last, its voice small and distant inside Jackson's head. *Instead of just make problems.*

You're not—

Yes, I am. Another pause. *You don't want me to be here, do you?*

I don't— Jackson groaned and found a fallen log to sit on. He buried his head in his hands. *I don't know what you're doing here. That's all.*

Another silence, long enough to make the guilt already pooling in his gut start to thicken.

If you don't know why I'm here... am I a mistake?

"Oh, for the love of…" Jackson clutched his forehead. "No, you're not—" *You're not a mistake. Things are just… complicated.*

That was putting it lightly. Complicated was him and Olly and her owl. Adding his pegasus to the mix brought it from complicated to…

There has to be something *I can do right!* The sparkle was back in his pegasus's voice. Even with everything else, that made Jackson feel better. *There must be a reason I'm here. Something important. Something like—*

Jackson's senses stretched. Pressure built up behind his eyes as though his brain was trying to sneeze. He blew out a sharp breath. "What the—"

Sensations flooded his mind.

There! That's what I'm here for! To find her!

Jackson swore and jumped to his feet. *You've got to hide. Now!*

Okay! Fizzing with excitement, his pegasus ducked down inside his mind. Jackson paced around the trail, his mind buzzing.

That was what his pegasus was here for? To find—

He groaned as the sensations and images his pegasus had opened his mind to rose up again. The whisper of moonlight on feathered wings. A feeling he'd never felt before but recognized instantly: the wonder and freedom of flying in open skies, not grating under his father's hectic training but soaring with the woman who was his fated mate.

Delphine was somewhere nearby.

Jackson racked his brain. What had his father said? Delphine's family had arrived suddenly, and he'd given her the day off to spend with them. So that he could train up his son to not be an embarrassment when he orchestrated their mate-recognition meeting. Jackson's stomach churned.

He looked around haphazardly, as though Delphine and a whole pride of winged lion shifters might be about to jump out from behind a tree. There was no one there, of course. His sense of where his mate—oh, God—was had told him she was some distance away.

If I can sense her, she'll be able to sense me.

Jackson's blood chilled. He licked his lips. *Stay hidden, right?* he told his pegasus. *This is the big test. Don't let anyone see or sense you.*

He felt it agree with him and some of the immediate tension lifted from his shoulders. He looked around again, more in control, and frowned.

This is the same track I took when—

The words in his head stopped, but the images didn't. As sudden and unstoppable as when his pegasus had sensed his mate. He was walking on the track he'd taken when he pulled Olly's cold body out of the lake and taken her back to the cottage.

And now he was going to meet her there again. At the place where her owl had almost accidentally killed her. And he was meeting her there to tell her...

Jackson's throat tightened with every step until his breath felt like it was being squeezed between steel plates.

How could he tell Olly that he'd found the woman who was meant to be his mate? That despite everything he felt in his heart, his soul was promised to someone else?

The chill spread from his blood into every crevice of his body. He'd wondered what had made Olly go to war with her owl, tearing herself apart until she'd almost gotten herself killed. It was the same thing that had made her lose herself bit by bit for the last year.

How hadn't he seen the answer?

It was all him. Every bad thing that had happened to her was his fault.

27

OLLY

He will come, won't he?

Olly's stomach lurched. She wasn't quick enough to stop the sudden creeping doubt, and once it had its claws into her it wasn't letting go. She fumbled for her phone. *He never replied to my message.*

Her owl clacked its beak. *He did read it, though. See? There's the little word that says so.* It chittered its beak a bit more, and added: *He'll come. He's very reliable. It's one of his best attributes. One of many.*

In spite of her anxiety, Olly couldn't help smiling. *I like hearing you say nice things about Jackson. It's a nice change from earlier.*

It wasn't all bad, her owl thought back. *Even last year you were very happy about the sex side of things.*

"What?" Olly's cheeks burned.

The sex. You really liked the sex. Even without the mate bond, the sex—

Stop! Olly groaned and closed her eyes. "That's quite enough of that," she told her owl.

Not that there was anyone else to talk to, or anything to distract her from her owl picking over how good in bed Jackson was. The cheerful Christmas lights lit up a whole lot of nothing. She turned back to the mailbox and shoved her phone in her pocket. "He's not going to call anyway," she reasoned to herself.

Her phone started to buzz.

She blinked at it. For one long second, her brain didn't connect the sound of 'Jingle Bells' tinnily echoing around the clearing with the phone in her hand. When she finally connected the dots—with a jerk that almost sent the phone flying—the name that popped up on the phone screen made her freeze again.

Jackson.

Jackson was calling her and it should have been a relief, but instead it felt… wrong.

She fumbled one hand out of its glove and took the call. "Hello?"

"Olly?"

Oh…

It was exactly like that first split-second after she turned around and saw him at the party. Sudden, wonderful, terrible awareness. Her senses sang. It should have put her on edge, but instead, something inside of her relaxed.

Without thinking, she ducked down behind the mailbox, wedging herself into the gap between it and the tree behind it. Her owl ruffled its feathers approvingly. Squeezed tight in with her feet tucked up, nobody would be able to see her from the trail or the clearing.

And she could let all her focus sink into his voice.

"Jackson?" She knew it was him, but her heart still leaped when he made a small sound of affirmation. Inside her boots, her toes curled like her owl holding tight to its favorite branch.

This had to be true love. Didn't it? Just the sound of his voice making everything seem better. Not like the sickening lurch of reality being pulled from under her feet when she thought of—

What *was* that flicker of *something* at the edge of her owl's awareness? And what was Jackson calling her for, anyway?

She felt like she was flying through fog. Any minute, something might loom out of the whiteness and clothesline her. The need for certainty hollowed out the space under her ribs. She needed to know—

Don't ask him if he got your message, her owl said sharply. "Did you get my message?"

She winced as her owl screeched in disgust. *Never show weakness! Now he'll know there's something wrong!*

Olly strained her ears for Jackson's response. "Yes, I—" he began, and broke off with a sharp breath. "Damn it. Did you just feel…?"

The hairs on the back of Olly's neck prickled. "What was that? Is everything okay?"

"It's—"

"Is someone there with you?" Oh God. Her skin crawled as she gathered herself to say the next bit: "How was your day… with your… father? Are you still with him?"

Her insides twisted as though her body wanted to turn itself inside out to get away from what she'd just said. Let alone hear Jackson's answer. But she couldn't *not* say anything. She'd been rude enough flying away earlier like she had a pack of hellhounds after her. The least she could do now was ask after him, especially if…

She swallowed guiltily. Especially because she desperately needed to keep track of where Andrew Petrakis was at every moment in time.

Jackson cleared his throat. "No, I'm by myself. Andrew's headed off to do his own thing for the evening."

Act normal. Act normal! Olly swallowed down a screech. Her owl's understanding of the word *normal* was not what she needed right now. That… sensation of something…

Her owl hunkered down inside her, pulling privacy around it like another set of wings. It left Olly with nothing in her head but herself, but even without her owl's interfering influence she was still trying to figure out what *her* version of normal should be when Jackson started talking again.

"I did get your message. I was—I'm on my way over. But there's something I need to—" His voice became garbled, as though he'd turned away from the phone. She might have been able to hear him with her owl's enhanced senses, but—

No, her owl muttered. *Not right now.*

"I can't hear you," Olly said, twining her fingers anxiously together. "How far away are you?"

"Olly, I need to tell you something." His voice had jagged edges and Olly's breath caught in her throat. She didn't need her owl to tell her something was wrong.

Those words were far too close to *there's something we need to talk about.*

"What?" It wasn't a screech. Or even a gasp. Just a thin flutter of breath. Olly wedged herself behind the mailbox, making herself small, like she always did when she felt this way. As if she could hide from her feelings as easily as from the world around her.

"I…" There was a scrape of static. "I thought this would be easier if I didn't have to look you in the face." Jackson chuckled weakly, and *that* send warning alarms blaring in Olly's brain. "Oh, God." His voice wasn't ragged. It was *hurt*. Tearing into pieces. "You're the one person who could understand."

"So tell me." Olly's heartbeat thundered in her ears. "I can help."

"That's the problem. You'll help, but you shouldn't. All this is my fault. I pushed you too much last year, hoping for something that wasn't true. I pushed you again, coming back here. And now—I can't do that to you again."

She thought she could hear something over the pounding in her ears and the painful scrape of his voice. The crunch of snow? He'd said he was on his way—how close was he?

"If you're talking about us—" Olly couldn't wedge herself any further. She was packed as small as she could make herself, tiny and angry and afraid. "I love you. *That's* true. I don't want anything else."

"But that's not how this works, is it? Magic doesn't care about what we want."

"We'll *make* it work that way."

"I wish—" He swore. Olly could imagine what he was doing: pressing his fingertips against his forehead as though he could force the right words out. He was trying to do the right thing by her, and that only made it worse. *Damn* him! "I wish I could explain."

"Why can't you?" The words tumbled like shards of ice off Olly's tongue. She groaned. If her owl was being its usual busybody self, she never would have let herself say that.

A long pause that clawed at her insides. At last Jackson sighed.

"I don't want to hurt you again." He laughed, but there was no happiness in it. "You deserve better than—" His voice faded out.

"What was that? I swear, Jackson, if you're going to leave me alone out here because you think that makes you a *good man* when *I'm* the one who hurt *you* last year—"

That's not going to help! Her owl tried to make her bite her tongue, but it had crept back too far to wrestle control from her that easily. *Don't remind him of all the reasons he shouldn't stay with you!*

Then help *me!* Olly clenched her fists. *Stop hiding and use your senses! How can I keep him if I don't even know where he is?*

But…

Help me!

Her owl flew up, so close to the surface that pin-prick feathers shivered under Olly's skin. The world around her hummed with secrets her human body was too poorly tuned to pick up.

The creak of frozen trees. The tiny scritch-scritch movements of tiny creatures hiding beneath the snow. The very, very distant yips and excitement of the Puppy Express dogs, and there, at the very edge of her senses—

Nothing.

Olly frowned. *Why can't I sense anything there?*

"You needed certainty and I thought I could give it to you." Jackson's tone was bordering on the voice he used when he found a shifter stuck somewhere they shouldn't be, and Olly bristled. How dare he be staid and sensible at *her?* "Instead I gave you a year of unhappiness. God, Olly, I'd have to be blind not to see how bad things had gotten for you here. I messed up, and you turned into a shadow of what you used to be."

"A *shadow?*" Olly leaned on her owl, willing it to stare into the blind spot that she just *knew* it was keeping from her deliberately. "*I* messed up, and *you* went off and got yourself *shot!*"

"I was doing my job!"

"You never got shot doing your job here!" *Show me!*

"No, I didn't get shot, I just broke both of our hearts!"

Fine! Don't blame me when you see who he's with and get upset again!

He said he wasn't with anyone—

The blind spot opened up. Olly jumped to her feet, so suddenly that she almost knocked the mailbox over. Snow crashed down all around her.

Something *was* there. Her owl had been hiding it. Something wonderful-terrible.

Something that was getting closer.

A pegasus. *And* Jackson.

"Olly, I can't do that to you again. And I can't stand in the way if you—what was that?" Jackson's voice shook and he swore under his breath. "God. I'm sorry, Olly, I've got to go."

Olly stayed silent, concentrating so fiercely her whole body was shaking. This couldn't be possible.

The wonderful-terrible was moving away. And maybe she'd been right in the first place and it *was* his father, and she was about to make a horrible mistake…

Olly started to run.

28

JACKSON

*S**he's there!*

I don't care! Jackson told his pegasus desperately. He turned around, legs suddenly clumsy as he tried to run away from the…

He'd thought he was safe for that night, at least. Delphine was busy with her family and he'd have time to explain to Olly…

But she's so perfect!

You've never even met her. He didn't know why he was trying to reason with it. The moment his pegasus had sensed the other shifter—and *how* it had managed that he had no idea—it had started acting like a cartoon character with hearts coming out of its eyes.

I don't need to. Can't you tell how wonderful she is already?

"I can't believe this is happening," Jackson growled out loud, forgetting he still had his phone clamped against his ear.

The sudden silence on the other end made his blood turn to ice.

"Olly, I—"

"Hm?" She sounded breathless. Or like she was trying not to let her feelings out. He'd gotten this all wrong—and it was about to get worse.

Why are we running away? The bloody thing was confused now. Like a puppy that had turned around and lost sight of its own tail. Jackson ground his teeth.

Because there's no way in hell I'm going to talk to Olly if there's any chance Delphine Belgrave is going to show up.

But why?

Because you won't be able to hide how you feel about her, and I don't want Olly to see that! He was running now. Not towards the cottage—he couldn't bear that. Or back towards the Puppy Express. Off the trail, deeper into the frozen forest. Unfindable.

Except the goddamn fairy-light explosion in his head that had to be Delphine Belgrave was getting closer.

But—

I can't break her heart again, damn you!

He didn't realize he'd spoken telepathically out loud until Olly's voice filled his head.

Jackson?!

Her voice was the morning sun and the warmth of fire at midnight. He stumbled and turned around.

Olly burst through the trees. Her cheeks were red with exertion and her eyes were bright with joy or frustration or some typical combination of the two, perfect for her. All of the breath left Jackson's body in a gasp that was her name.

"Olly…"

Recognition crackled between them. And not only them.

It's her! his pegasus cried, its voice like a choir of angels.

Olly's eyes widened. "You're—"

It's him!

Olly smiled wider than he'd ever seen her smile before. His heart lifted. And then—

"Oh, no," he tried to shout, but couldn't, because his pegasus was taking form in a shower of glimmering lights.

Olly shrieked—or her owl did. She leaped into the air and shifted in one smooth movement, snow-white wings beating the air. His pegasus craned its head, watching her flight.

And she dive-bombed him.

Fly with me! It wasn't Olly's voice. And it wasn't talking to *him.*

His pegasus pranced on the spot. *Marvelous!* it caroled, and cantered itself airborne as the owl swooped around for another attack. *She's so graceful—so powerful!*

What a creature! It had to be Olly's owl. Her animal's voice, in *his* head.

Jackson would have been rocked by the realization that he was hearing Olly's owl, but that would have meant he'd already gotten over the big one. The sudden kick to the brain that made all his dreams come true.

His mind felt like it'd been left behind on the frozen ground as his pegasus and Olly's owl wheeled up above the treetops, into the darkening sky. The owl shrieked with predatory delight and dived at him again. This time, his pegasus was ready. It slipped sideways, turning the dodge into a dance that took them both soaring high in the mountains.

Jackson let it fly. His heart was flying, too, caught up in a wonder he'd never thought possible.

He was a shifter. He was a different person than he'd been the day before, but the important things stayed the same. He was in love with Olly Lockey, and now that his pegasus had fledged, some final piece of the puzzle that was their relationship had fallen into place.

Olly was his mate.

And he was *hers*.

A question brushed up against his mind, a psychic signature that tasted like snow and warmed him like a winter bonfire.

Is it really you, Jackson?

It is, he reassured her, and now he knew why telepathy came to him so easily. It was so he could speak to *her*.

But when—how—since when are you—?

He laughed, inside his head and hers and his pegasus let out a gleeful whinny that should have embarrassed him but didn't. *Since today.*

And you're really—?

Yours.

The word hung between them, bright and pure as the moon in the sky.

Then Olly launched herself towards him.

His pegasus flared its wings and the two of them tumbled wing over hoof over claw through the air. Jackson only knew they'd hit the tree line again when he *hit* the trees. Snow and frozen branches exploded under his wings and he barely had time to think *This is a bad idea* before Olly landed on his neck, sunk her claws in, and shifted.

The force of her shift pulled at him so hard he forgot he had wings. He hit snow so deep the world around him disappeared. He just had time to realize he was human again and his pegasus had made a cave when it landed, driving and packing the snow with its wings, when Olly landed on top of him. Her fingers dug into his chest the same way her claws had and she was beautifully, gloriously naked. The moonlight pouring in from above caressed her skin and filtered through her hair, making the frozen cave feel like a hidden grotto.

He was sprawled on his back with his mate on top of him, naked and shining in the moonlight. Even in his wildest fantasies, he wouldn't have let himself imagine this. "Oh God!" she cried out. "Why are you still dressed? *How* are you still—no." Her eyes shone with wondrous curiosity. "You're my mate."

"And you're mine." There was no doubt in his mind or his heart. Wildest fantasies? He felt as though he was dreaming, but no dream could be this rich with detail. Their breath puffed in clouds of vapor, mingling in the air. Olly smelled like sweat and starlight. Her skin prickled with goosebumps.

Not a dream. He took off his coat and wrapped it around her, and her eyes shone with more than just reflected moonlight.

"This is what I was missing last year? I never imagined it would be like this. So… certain." Olly brushed her fingertips along his jaw and his skin thrilled at her touch. Amazement danced in her eyes. "But why now, and not…"

"I'm a shifter now," Jackson said. His voice caught. "A different person."

"No, you're not," Olly's fingernails pressed into his skin. She pulled her hand away with an annoyed hiss. "Stop it, owl!"

Her eyes flicked sideways as she listened to her owl.

You're not a different person, his pegasus mused. *I mean, I don't think you are? I've only known you for today. But I feel like* me, *and you feel like* you, *and together, we're…*

"My owl…" Olly groaned. "You're telling me this *now?*" she added in an undertone, and shook her head. "It says last time, it really was surprised that the mate bond didn't form, and now it thinks it's because you weren't ready."

"I hadn't *fledged.*" Jackson couldn't keep a hint of bitterness from his voice, but Olly looked delighted.

"Is that what you're calling it? Fledging! Like when I got my first wing feathers." She wriggled her shoulders as though she was remembering what it felt like to have wings, and to fly for the first time. "I'm so relieved."

Jackson was thrown. "What?"

"Because…" She touched his face again. "I already love you. And now you're a shifter, and you're going to be my mate, and everything is *perfect.*"

"Going to be?"

Olly's eyes flashed with unbridled desire. "We've recognized each other as mates. There's still one more step before the mate bond forms for real." For a moment Jackson thought she was going to tear his clothes off right there in the snow cave.

For a moment, he would have let her, and damn the fact they'd both end up with important bits frozen off.

Then Olly laughed with delight as glee overtook the need in her eyes. "How? How are you a shifter? I might as well just ask! I want to know everything about this, right now. I don't want to wait around and try to figure it out on my own. You're too important."

Jackson shook his head. He didn't know what she was talking about, but as for her question… "I don't know."

"How can you not know?"

"Well, how are *you* a shifter?"

She gaped at him. Then she laughed, bright and clear as a bell. "I don't know! But I am, and you are, and this is…" The sharp glee on her face softened. "Maybe fate is on our side after all."

Warmth rose inside him. He grinned sheepishly. "It took its goddamn time."

She laughed again, and kept laughing as he pulled the hood of his coat over her head and tucked it more closely around her. "What are you doing?"

"I don't want you to freeze," he murmured, his voice like sandpaper. She shivered against him. "And if you keep laughing like that with the coat falling open, I'm going to do something stupid that ends up in us both freezing."

She bared her teeth in a cheeky grin. "That'd be a poor way to start out happily ever after, wouldn't it?"

"Happily ever after." He pulled her close and crushed his lips against hers, pouring all his relief and wonder into the kiss. She made a soft, urgent noise that made him wish he'd let his clothes dissolve as he shifted. "I thought my pegasus appearing would take my happy ever after away from me, not make it even better. Now I think your owl didn't recognize me before because my pegasus wasn't here to recognize it back."

Olly's eyes were wide. "Can it really be that simple? That we had to wait for you to fledge? But you didn't have any idea that was even an option—and I've never heard of any shifter than manifests so late. If you hadn't come back, we might never have…"

Her arms tightened around him. "I don't want to even think about that."

I almost didn't come back. If I'd told Jasper to go to hell with his paperwork—

"But I did. And now everything has changed in a way I never thought possible. My world's gone upside down because that was the only way to turn it the right side up." He gazed into her eyes. "You're my mate."

"Not quite yet." Olly wriggled against him, shamelessly teasing. "There's still one thing we need to do about that, remember."

Jackson went hard instantly.

"Exactly how long are you planning to keep me trapped in this snow cave for?" he asked gruffly.

She pinned him with happy eyes. "Do you have somewhere better in mind for me to trap you?"

Jackson's chest swelled. "The cabin's not too far away…"

A shimmer of light and she was in owl form. She flew up onto the mouth of the snow cavern, tested the snow, and folded her wings. *Are you coming?*

He retrieved his coat from where she'd dropped it and slipped into his pegasus's shape, knocking snow around as he leaped lightly into the air.

How do you do that? she wondered. *You sort of fold your clothes away as you shift— No, you can tell me later. Right now…*

29
OLLY

He's so magnificent! her owl crooned. *Those wings—that mane! So grand! So elegant!*

Olly laughed, and must have let Jackson hear her, because she felt the careful brush of his mind against hers. *What's funny?* he asked.

My owl going gooey over your pegasus.

She heard what could only be a mental throat-clearing. *If that's what we're talking about… my guy thinks your owl is pretty incredible, too.*

Magnificent?

Glorious.

Hmm… you're also very elegant.

And you're— He broke off with a groan that dissolved into helpless laughter. *As graceful as the wind, beautiful and white as the moon… with claws.*

The moon with claws. If Olly's owl hadn't been busy flying, it would have preened at that. *I like it.*

They landed on the cottage roof together: she lightly, he stumbling, clumsy on his hooves like a newborn. He laughed at himself and she laughed, too, and then they were both human and clambering down to a window, breaking into their new home after all. Straight into the bedroom.

"You're *still dressed*," she cried out in disgust, tearing at his clothes.

"You're not." His hands found her waist, her breasts, the curve of her hips, getting in the way of her stripping him down. "And freezing."

"Warm me up."

It was a challenge and a wish he couldn't refuse.

He dragged his coat around her and she moaned as the fur lining slithered against her soft skin. He wrapped her tight, teasing, and laughed as she growled and tried to fight her way out.

He caught her complaints in a kiss. "I don't want you to freeze."

"I'm a shifter. We don't *freeze*."

"Your feet must not be shifters, then."

"You—"

He picked her up and carried her, still wrapped in his coat, to the bed. When he put her down she didn't give him even a second to catch his breath. She climbed on top of him, pulling his shirt off so roughly that buttons pinged around the room.

He grumbled at her, a tease that deepened to a moan of appreciation as she kissed him.

"What are you complaining about?" she murmured into his lips.

"I thought one of the benefits of being able to shift with my clothes was keeping them in one piece."

"Not around me." She kissed him again, hard and hot, her hands swiftly undoing or shredding what was left of his clothes.

"I'll remember that."

She ran her hands down his chest and over his abs. Her nails drifted across his ribs, making him gasp, and then she dug her fingertips into his glutes and ground herself against him. His hips bucked and she groaned.

"Do that again!"

He rolled his hips again, driving his cock hard between her thighs. She moaned deep in her throat and opened her legs.

She was slick and wet and ready, and Jackson's gasp as he felt that made her shiver deep inside.

"Olly, wait." There was an echo of gravel in his voice that made her pause.

She met his eyes. Her mind reached out to his, as gentle as a kiss, and felt his hesitation. *I'm not guessing, this time,* she reassured him.

I know.

We're doing this over. The right way, this time.

I know.

Frustration hummed along the edges of her desire. Every beat of her heart was a drum of longing, of *need.*

It's going to be different.

I know. He cupped her face in his hands. "That's why I want to say this first."

She slid down close to him and he wrapped her in his arms. Her heartbeat was a baby bird, fluttering too fast for her chest.

He took one of her hands in his. "I love you," he said.

"I know," she whispered back, feeling as though she was missing something.

"I love you now. Without the mate bond fully formed. I know we're not guessing this time, in fact given how much my pegasus is shouting at me I think our chances of this working out are pretty high, but I want you to know, before everything changes… You would still be the only one I wanted, even without this."

Sunlight filled Olly's veins. "And you'd be the only one I wanted," she replied. "Even if we had to live in the middle of nowhere and never see anyone else ever again, I'd want that, and you, more than anything else in the world. My Jackson." She grinned at him. "*Mine.* With or without the mate bond."

"With or without," he agreed, and kissed her. "Want to get started on 'with'?"

30

JACKSON

"Yes!"

He pulled her on top of him, holding her in his arms and his heart, his *mind*…

Olly gasped. "Did you feel—" she began, and then, her voice carrying with it a warmth that twined around the deepest parts of his soul: *When you touch me, it feels like… I know we can send emotion telepathically but this is more than that, this is…*

…Right, Jackson completed for her. He kissed her and then buried his face in her tumbling hair, unable to stop himself from smiling. Even now, pressed naked against him, his wonderful Olly couldn't stop herself from trying to figure things out.

Hey! I heard that. Felt it. Something. She nuzzled against him.

You're overthinking.

For me, this is just thinking. Her eyes danced. *And I'm thinking…*

She wrapped her legs around him and lowered herself slowly. Jackson groaned, need thrumming through every inch of his body. *You're going to have to do the thinking for both of us in that case.*

She laughed, kissed him, and eased him inside her.

Jackson swore under his breath as he pushed into her. Sex was one thing—a great thing, sure—but this was Olly, *his* Olly, and this was more than just physical. More than it had been last night or last year.

Longing, bright and fierce, sprang into his mind. It thrummed in his head, his veins, across his skin. His and Olly's both.

He met her eyes and they were shining. "I love you," she whispered. "You feel that, right?"

This was what they'd both been searching for all those months ago. A certainty that burned in their hearts and sank deep into their bones.

"God, Olly," he gasped. "I never stopped loving you. And I never will."

Her breath stuttered against his neck as he buried his cock deep inside her. Her back arched and the extra pressure urged him to thrust up. Her breath caught and Jackson felt an echo of it in his own lungs.

Her fingernails scrabbled against his chest. He picked her hands up and kissed them, one by one, then wrapped her arms around his shoulders and rolled on top of her.

"Tell me I'm not dreaming." His voice was so gravelly he was surprised she understood him.

She grinned. Her teeth flashed white in the moonlight streaming in through the bedroom window.

And she ghosted one cold foot along the inside of his calf.

Jackson kissed her to make her stop laughing. It didn't work. He kept kissing her, anyway, tasting her lips, biting her until her gulping laughter turned into gasps, covering her delicate, strong body with his and thrusting into her until she clutched at him and her gasps turned into cries of joy.

His cock tightened and he came with a sensation like fireworks going off behind his eyes. Olly held him close, not letting him go even when both their breathing slowed and their heartbeats fell into a slow, satisfied rhythm.

Her eyes were shut. Her lashes flickered, as though she was hunting for something behind her eyelids, or still lost in the aftershocks of her climax.

Despite everything, despite the mythical creature inside his head and the sheer rapturous glee he'd felt emanate from Olly's mind when she finally had him in her arms… he was afraid.

Somehow, all of this had to be a mistake.

"Stop it," Olly murmured. She cracked open one eye, then the other. "If you're a mistake, you're the best mistake I've ever made."

"How did you know—" He stopped himself and dropped his head, his breath tickling her ear. "Of course you know."

"Of course I do." There was a trace of her owl's smugness in her voice. "And I'm going to keep knowing. And… Oh, God. If I can know what you're feeling, then you're going to start knowing exactly all the weird shit that goes through my head."

"Am I?" He let himself sink down. Olly was warm, soft… his. They lay tangled together in a bed of snow and torn clothing.

Jackson searched inside himself. There was a new warmth inside his chest, a… light, in the same way his pegasus was somehow *there* inside him. He looked at it, the same way he looked at his pegasus.

There was a thread leading out from it. He followed it, as intensely aware of the strangeness of that sensation as he was of how amazing it felt to hold Olly in his arms.

And there she was, in his arms and at the other end of the thread.

She jumped slightly. "Oh!" Feelings flooded along the thread, this strange, magical connection between them—heart-leaping happiness, a shiver of excitement at this *newness*, something new in herself and in him and between them, and had her owl been *talking* to him earlier?

To my pegasus, he told her.

I didn't think that to you!

This was going to take some getting used to.

Olly raised her head until she was staring into his eyes. "Did you just think…?" she asked, and groaned. "Oh, God. *Some* getting used to might be putting it lightly."

"I'm still getting used to having someone else living in my head," Jackson admitted. "Might as well have you in there as well. You'll be better company than the other guy."

She snorted and wriggled closer against him. They were already close as could be, so the result was almost enough to make him forget what they'd been talking about.

"Still in love?" she asked him.

"Still in love," he confirmed gravely. He kissed her forehead and sent a feelings-kiss down the mate bond as he added "Even with all this magic rubbish."

"Christmas magic," she murmured.

"I guess so." He stroked her back, making her wriggle against him some more. "Makes as much sense as anything—what's wrong?"

He'd felt something shiver through the mate bond. Olly groaned. "Christmas magic," she muttered against his chest. "The mail for the Puppy Express. The Heartwells' Christmas party…"

"Wasn't that the other night, at your work?"

"That was their Christmas *Week* party," she groaned. "For the local shifters. Followed by their Christmas *Eve* party, for local shifters who don't have their own family things on, then the Christmas Day party, which is just for the Heartwells." She huffed out a breath. "Bob and I always get an invite to the Christmas Eve party. I really should go… and I need to check with the hellhounds about the mail…"

"Bob can't deal with both of those?"

"The last time I saw him, he was sleeping in the back office with a tissue stuffed up each nostril." She sighed. "But I don't want to get out of bed…"

Jackson frowned as a thought struck him, and Olly nudged him. "What?"

"I don't want to get out of bed either, but… You still want to give those tourists that ring back, don't you?"

31

OLLY

They drove to the Puppy Express because even if Jackson had magical keep-his-clothes-on shifter powers, Olly still didn't. She'd borrowed some of his clothes at the cottage to replace those she'd burst out of when she shifted in the woods, but given how little he'd packed for the trip, that wasn't a strategy that would survive more than a couple of shifts.

Plus, this time she had the engagement ring with her. Shifting now and losing it in a flurry of feathers would ruin all of her plans.

"The lights are still on," she said as Jackson parked his truck in front of the Puppy Express. *Bob? You still around?*

There was no reply. She raised her eyebrows at Jackson. "You want to try?"

"I think having a bad cold is hard enough without a strange shifter yelling at him."

"You're not a *stranger*." She hung onto his arm as they headed for the front door. "And he told me I should snap you up without you being my mate, anyway."

"He did?"

"Earlier today." She huffed out a frustrated breath. "Wish he could have told me a year ago, but from what I'm picking up, everyone's been tiptoeing around me since I got hit by the hellfire."

"Yeah, they should have told you to get over your trauma, get your head out of your ass and get on with life."

"Hey!" She elbowed him.

"I should have been here to tell you." His voice was gravelly. She wound her arm around his, delight leaping in her heart as he automatically leaned closer to her.

"But you would have needed someone to tell you to get *your* head out of your ass first, and I'm the only one who's allowed to do that, and I wasn't in any shape for it." She tipped her head back and looked at him from under lowered lashes. "Maybe we needed all of that shit to happen to get us to this point, though."

She reached out to him along the strange, shining mate bond that stretched between them, and he smiled.

"Except for you getting shot," she added with a growl, and tweaked the bond.

"Ow! Hey!"

He chased her inside and kissed her.

"I hope you don't think that's going to make me apologize," she told him. "You're just giving me a good reason to do it again."

He gave her a look that made her want to go back to the cottage right that instant.

Tease, she hissed at him, and headed for the back office. "Hey, Bob, are you… still asleep. Cool."

Her uncle was right where she'd left him, comfortably nestled in his desk chair. He stirred as she crossed his light.

"Gotta… postcards," he murmured.

"Uh-huh." She smiled at him fondly. *Don't worry. We'll look after it.*

Zzz.

Jackson nudged her mind. *No sign of the hellhounds. I'll check the dogs have been fed.* He as back a moment later. *No sign of the dogs, either.*

Those thieving hellhounds! Olly's owl hissed. *All that talk about punishing wrongdoers. Stealing is wrong! Why don't they punish themselves?*

Olly had a pretty good idea of where the dogs were, and why, but she called the Guinnesses anyway. Meaghan answered.

"Sorry, babe," she said when she knew who she was talking to. "Yeah, they're all here. And they're not moving." She sighed. "I don't think even Caine will be able to convince any of the boys to go back to work tonight, either."

Olly wished her a merry Christmas and hung up with a sigh. "Well, I did the whole delivery last year," she said. "It only took literally *until* Christmas Day…"

"Last year, you didn't have a pegasus."

Aaaaaaah! Olly's owl screamed.

"This is amazing!" she whooped out loud as Jackson's pegasus soared into the air.

It's unnatural! her owl insisted. *What if we fall off?*

Then I'll shift and you can take care of it! Olly felt her fingers start to harden into claws. *Not yet! I want to enjoy this.*

Are you okay up there? Jackson asked. *I'm getting mixed signals.*

Olly snorted. *I'm fine. My owl's not a fan of flying without being the one* doing *the flying.*

It doesn't trust my dashing, elegant pegasus?

Of course I do! her owl huffed, and Jackson laughed.

Where to first? he asked.

Olly fastened the fingers of one hand into his mane, and reached into the sack on her lap with the other. *Holly Lane. You remember where that is?*

Delivering postcards by pegasus was even better than delivering them by dogsled, and miles better than flying around as an owl with cards stuffed in her beak. Jackson landed on snow-covered roofs one by one, hooves clattering festively, she would drop the postcards on the front step or through an open window, and they'd both be flying off into the night by the time the doors or windows were flung open with cries of "Santa's here!"

We might be delivering the post, but I think we're messing up a lot of parents' present plans tonight, Jackson said ruefully.

Olly giggled. *They knew what they were getting into when they put the cards in the postbox.*

What about that couple? They must be coming up.

Olly picked up the last two cards. The couple must have written them for each other and posted them before their little dip in the lake. She had tied the two cards together with a ribbon, and threaded the ring through it. *They're our last stop. At the hotel."

Jackson landed lightly on the hotel roof. He was getting better at landings, Olly's owl noted with prim smugness. Probably because he was showing off for her.

The couple was staying on the top floor, which made it easy for Olly to climb down onto their veranda and carefully place the cards and ring where they could see them from inside. She caught a glimpse of the couple inside, and a murmur of conversation. As she climbed back out of sight, she tapped the window.

The veranda door opened. "Is someone there?" It was the woman. She looked around, eyes confused—then glanced down. Her mouth dropped open. "Oh my God! Rick! You'll never guess…"

"I'm glad we could help them," Olly told Jackson as she climbed onto his back. He rustled his wings. "If they hadn't lost their ring, how would my owl have ever made its grand romantic gesture?"

That's what it's calling getting you stuck under the ice?

Her owl whispered something to Olly, and she laughed. *My owl says, it was just making an opportunity for you to make a grand romantic gesture.*

Jackson grumbled. Even his pegasus made a grumpy noise. *Grand romantic pah.*

Yeah, I wasn't even conscious to appreciate it.

You— He grumbled again. *Now who's teasing?*

Olly shook out her hair as though she was a pegasus. *Stop complaining. That was the last delivery—let's head to the party.*

32

JACKSON

Jackson wasn't sure what to expect. He'd been to the Heartwells' parties before: barbeques in summer, apple bobbing at Halloween, flower festivals in the spring and, of course, their Christmas parties.

He knew them. But they didn't know this new him.

A huge bonfire was burning in the courtyard behind the main, castle-like building, with clusters of humans and various creatures gathered around. He spotted Cole's parents, Opal and Hank: Opal was in her dragon form, her tail poking the fire, while Hank was being chased by a pack of kids armed with snowballs and two small dragons armed with…

I guess Jasper's not worried about them setting their own property on fire, he remarked to Olly. *How are we going to do this?*

We could land out back and let the Heartwells know we're here, or—

Right in the middle of the party!

Wait, no—

Jackson's pegasus didn't listen. It saw a gap in front of the bonfire, and swooped down to land in it.

A rumble of surprise filled the courtyard. Jackson knew that if he'd had human cheeks right then, they would have been burning, but his pegasus thrilled at the attention.

Hello, everyone! it trilled. *Wait—they can't hear me! Quick, say hello!*

"That isn't the same pegasus that crashed the last party, was it?"

"Who's that on its back?"

"It can't be—Olly?"

Thanks, Jackson. Olly sent a psychic prod with the words. *You know how I love being the center of attention.*

Sorry. Sorry. *Want me to steal the show?*

She chuckled. *Go for it.*

She slid off his pegasus's back. Jackson spread his wings and concentrated.

Human with pants, human with pants…

He shifted in an explosion of shimmering lights. The moment he was human, Olly took his hand and squeezed it.

"Getting it over with all at once, huh? Maybe that's not such a bad idea," she muttered.

Jackson waved weakly to the nearest shifters: a couple of the Holborn nephews, Suki from the grocery store, and that sheep he still didn't recognize. "Hey, everyone."

"Alright, Mr. Petrakis, once was bad enough, but this is—" Jasper Heartwell pushed to the front of the crowd and stopped when he saw them both. His mouth dropped open. "Jackson? Olly?"

"Hi, Jasper." Jackson ran one hand through his hair and looked down at Olly. She smiled back, her eyes shining. "We've got some news for everyone."

"I'll bet." Jasper folded his arms, grinning. "Go on then. Let's hear it."

Jackson took a deep breath. He settled his most serious expression on his face and directed it at the dragon shifter. "You know that cottage by Sweetheart Lake? I'd like to buy it."

Olly gave him a hard nudge.

"Oh right, and come to think of it, Olly and I are mates after all."

Her face lit up as everyone around them cheered. Under the cover of their friends' delight, Olly leaned in close and murmured, "The cottage, huh?"

"It feels like our place already. Doesn't it? I bet Jasper will let me do a straight-across swap for the house I already own, since he owns both. And that other house never meant anything to me anyway. I walked away without a second thought. The cottage, though…"

"Lots of good memories," she murmured, lacing her arms around his neck.

"The best."

Everyone was legitimately happy for them. Confused as all hell, because no one had heard of people spontaneously becoming shifters as late in life as Jackson, but happy.

"How did it happen?" Caine asked. "I mean, I'm guessing you didn't get bitten by another pegasus shifter…"

Jackson shook his head. "Apparently pegasus shifters take longer to manifest."

"Well, I'm glad you caught up with yourself at last," Meaghan joked. "Though—huh. What would happen if you were already *going* to be a pegasus shifter, but you got bitten by a hellhound, and then…"

Caine steered her gently away. "I think he probably has enough to worry about without thinking about that, love."

She wrinkled her nose at him and let herself be steered to a comfortable chair.

Jackson grinned. Enough to worry about? He had nothing to worry about. Even Olly didn't hate all the attention they were getting. He checked in with her through the mate bond as another old friend came up, squealed drunkenly, and wrapped them both in a massive hug.

I'm all good, she replied. *My owl actually likes showing you off.*

That made his pegasus so pleased he was surprised he didn't grow wings.

"Jackson?"

He spun around. "Ma?"

Louisa Gilles pulled him into a bone-crushing hug. "I just got here. I told you I was coming, didn't I?"

"You did, but…" He stepped back and pulled Olly forward. Their fingers twined together and no power in the world could help the stupid grin that spread across his face. *Things have changed a bit since we talked.*

Louisa's eyes widened. *You can use telepathy? You—you're not telling me your father was right about something, for once in his life?*

That depends what he actually told you he wanted to see me about.

Louisa folded her arms. "Last week, your father called me up saying you were about to 'fledge', whatever that means, and he'd found a mate for you."

"Well," Olly said, "he was right about Jackson turning out as a shifter, and right about him finding a mate… he was just wrong about them, too."

"Now, you can't be anyone except the Olly Lockey I've heard so much about." Louisa hugged her. "Does this mean…? But I thought, last year?"

Jackson and Olly exchanged a look. "It's a long story," they said in unison.

"I only spoke to you two days ago, Jackson! How long can the story be?" Louisa looped her arm into his. "I've been driving all day, darling. Why don't we get some of that mulled wine from the nice dragon in the kitchen and you can tell me all about it?"

They found a quiet nook in the corner of the courtyard where they could sit with mugs of steaming mulled wine and talk with a bit of privacy. Louisa's eyes flicked between Olly and Jackson as they took turns telling parts of the story.

"…But I still don't understand why this happened now. At first I thought it had something to do with being shot." Jackson rubbed his scar. "The whole near-death experience thing. But if that's the case, why wouldn't my pegasus turn up then? Why would it wait six months?"

Louisa pursed her lips. "Your father did say he had one of his *feelings*," she said. "But frankly, I've never trusted those."

"He did get here right in time for me to shift for the first time," Jackson said morosely. "Maybe he's right about that, then. He says shifters' animals only find them when they become worthy."

Olly's eyes narrowed. "Bullshit."

"He—"

"Bullshit! Worthy? He's saying you weren't worthy last year? Or before that? You—you… argh!"

She pressed her forehead against his. Love and frustration and a ferocious protectiveness that burned hotter than Jackson could have imagined possible flooded out of her. For him.

"That's ridiculous," she growled. "I'm not going to accept that."

"Neither am I," his mother added. "What a load of nonsense. *Worthy*. Really. Where is he now, by the way?"

"At dinner with his PA and her family." He grimaced. "His PA's the one he thought was my mate."

"And he was wrong about that," Olly interjected. "There has to be something that made you shift for the first time today, though. Something that changed. It can't be that we…" She went red.

Louisa laughed, and Jackson went red, as well. "Oh, you two! Don't worry, I don't need to hear any of *those* details."

Jackson groaned and buried his head in his hands as Olly giggled.

"Well, it can't be *that*, can it, otherwise your pegasus would have turned up last year." She slipped her hand into his. "So what was new about this morning? Why did you fledge now?"

"I don't know."

"You think you might, though." Olly tipped her head back and peered at him through her lashes. "I know that tone."

Jackson looked down. "I'd asked you to marry me."

Louisa gasped. "You left that out in your story!"

"You said you just wanted the highlights—"

"That *is* a highlight, my favorite, idiotest son." Louisa tutted fondly. "Go on."

"That's not all," Olly said, correctly, her eyes fixed on him.

"I think—" Jackson looked away, embarrassed, and she poked him until he was looking at her again. "This morning, I was the happiest I'd ever been. Everything felt right in the world. *I* felt right in the world. I…" He cleared his throat. "All my life, I've kept some things locked inside me, so deep I forgot they were even there. How much I wished I were a shifter. All the dreams I had about being a deer like Ma, or a pegasus like my father. I walled them up inside me, until this morning, when I just… let go. Of wanting them, and wanting to not want them. I was… content. And as soon as that happened—bang."

"Bang?"

"And whoosh. And glitter."

"And pegasus?"

He nodded. "I thought the universe was playing a dirty trick. Instead, it was giving me everything I ever wanted."

"You needed to see there wasn't anything wrong with you before you could be your full self." Louisa sighed sadly. "Oh, Jackson, sweetheart." She pulled him into a hug. "You always kept yourself to yourself so well, I thought you had put that all behind you years ago."

"I thought so, too." *And now I'm here!* his pegasus announced happily. Jackson watched Olly's lips twitch in a barely hidden laugh.

"I was confused, too," she admitted out loud. "About what I wanted, and what my owl wanted. If I'd just talked to myself instead of denying what I felt, my owl and I might have figured out that you weren't wrong for me, you were just…" She frowned. "Still brewing? Or proofing? The oven was still preheating?"

"He's more like a beer waiting to get carbonated," Louisa suggested with a sparkle in her eye.

Whee! his pegasus trilled, its voice like bubbles against Jackson's brain.

"Everything turned out," Jackson said, reaching for Olly's hand and twining his fingers around hers. "Maybe my pegasus isn't the only part of me that's slow off the mark, but I wouldn't change a thing about this now."

"Not getting shot?" his mother interjected.

Jackson tightened his grip on Olly's fingers. "Well—"

"If we're redoing this, I want to not jump in the lake this time," Olly muttered, her eyes dancing.

"No more re-does!" Jackson stood up, pulling Olly with him, and wrapped her in a bearhug that transformed into a passionate kiss in record time. "We made it work, Olly," he whispered when they finally pulled apart.

"We did the wrong thing and it couldn't have turned out better," she whispered back.

Come on, everyone! It's time for carols!" Cole bounded up, shouting happily and burping out little puffs of smoke. *Come onnn! Everyone has to sing!*

Laughing, Jackson let himself be dragged back to the group around the bonfire. Olly tucked herself against his side as everyone raised their voices in song. Not everyone knew all the words and hardly anyone was in tune—and some people were still dragons, but Jackson's heart felt so full it was about to burst.

Silent night, holy night…

The night was anything but silent. But it was perfect.

He was home.

The carol finished with a ragged cheer. Someone started to drunkenly sing 'Auld Lang Syne' and was drowned out by a burst of Jingle Bells. Olly tugged on Jackson's arm and when he turned to her, dragged him down for a kiss.

"Merry Christmas," she whispered to him, and the shining mate bond between them glowed brighter than the bonfire. "My mate."

EPILOGUE
OLLY

1 MONTH LATER

"D o you see it?"

"It hasn't moved."

"And you're sure it's—"

"Yes." Olly reinforced the word with a wave of telepathic yes-ness. Her owl rustled its wings contentedly. "I've been watching it all month. It's the one."

"In that case." Jackson finished his coffee, stood up and ostentatiously brushed himself off. Olly stifled a giggle. That new flair for the dramatic was his pegasus's influence, she was sure.

He held out his hand. "Shall we?"

She put her hand in his. "Let's."

The bell above the jewelry store door rang as they walked through. Olly had been scoping out the place for the last month. Not the anxious, wary scoping out that she'd been stuck in for the last year, but a thrilling spying-stalking that she'd enjoyed as much as her owl had.

She'd spotted the ring one week in, inspected it carefully from the café across the street for another week, sent Meaghan in with the ring size the next and now, she was sure.

"Good afternoon!" The shopkeeper, an alligator shifter called Lori, smiled perkily at them both. "How can I help you? Whatever it is you're after, we've got a lovely range of—"

"That one." Olly pointed.

The ring had a white gold band, with a single circular-cut diamond and smaller chips not arranged neatly around it, but scattered across the band. It looked even better close up than it did through the binoculars Jackson had bought her for her spying.

"Ooh, good choice. But, it would be a *teeny* bit hard to resize, so let's just check…" Lori slipped the ring out from the display and held it out to Olly.

Jackson took it and turned it over in his fingers. "You're right," he murmured. "It is perfect. A beautiful moon for your claw."

She snorted at him.

"Oh, er, that's, real romantic." Lori sounded like she was trying very hard to stay perky.

"Shall we see if it fits?"

"It will." Olly held out her hand and he slowly slid the ring onto her finger. "See?" she said, staring into his eyes. "It's perfect."

He stared back, his gaze heavy with love. "And all it took was a month of sitting around and staring at it." He pulled her close and kissed her. *Now let's go spy out some venues.*

I had an idea about that. Olly sent images down the mate bond. Jackson almost choked.

"Sweetheart Lake?"

"What's a bigger romantic gesture than a wedding?" she challenged him, and couldn't help diving in for another kiss.

"Alright," he grumbled. The words reverberated deliciously against her lips. "If that's what my mate wants."

"Don't worry. I'll tell my owl to ignore any shiny things under the surface." She tucked her hands into his back pockets so he couldn't get away. "And there won't be any ice. A summer wedding."

And marriage. And married life. And watching Meaghan and Caine's pack grow, and the Heartwell kids get bigger, and… who knows?

Olly didn't bother to hide a smile as Jackson felt the shape of her thoughts. His cheeks darkened with happiness.

One day, Pine Valley would be where their kids grew up, too.

MORE PARANORMAL ROMANCE BY ZOE CHANT

A Mate for Christmas

A Mate for the Christmas Dragon
Christmas Hellhound
Christmas Pegasus
The Hellhound's UnChristmas Miracle
Christmas Griffin

A Gift for the Christmas Dragon (novella)

Shifter Suspense

Claimed by the Panther
Saved by the Billionaire Lion Shifter
Stealing the Snow Leopard's Heart
Craving the Kraken
Falling for the Shadow Dragon
Seducing the Soul-Eater

Hideaway Cove

The Griffin's Mate
The Sea Wolf's Mate
The Lightning Dragon's Mate
The Duskfire Dragon's Mate
The Kelpie's Mate

Standalone books not in series

Her Purr-fect Christmas Mate
Trusting the Tiger
Bear With Me

MONSTER ROMANCE BY MARIE CARDNO

The Monster Girlfriend series

How to Get a Girlfriend (When You're a Terrifying Monster)
How to Get a Date with the Evil Queen
How to Get the Girl (And Not Destroy the World)